Bedlan
at a Devor

CW00435089

OCTOBER HOUSE BOOKS

Illustration © John Gillo
The Old Fish Quay
www.johngillo-gallery.co.uk

ISBN: 9781794025905

They say be careful what you ask for. And the one thing life has taught me is to be specific with wishes. As a child I'd undertaken French lessons with an au pair who lived in a house with a kitchen bigger than the ground floor of my home. This huge place had an indoor swimming pool and tennis courts and – best of all – ten bedrooms. Imagine that!

I could spend one night in each and still have room for my future two children and husband. So, my younger self dreamed of a ten-bedroomed house and, like many of my other simpler wishes, it came true. But with an unexpected twist.

Chapter 1

OUR GUESTHOUSE STOOD BEFORE US, an impressive double-fronted Edwardian building, set over three floors with elegant sash windows framing the door. Perhaps a little more dilapidated than I recalled from our two fleeting viewings, as I couldn't remember the porch missing a few tiles or the snaking crack in the wall by the corner quoins. On the last trip I'd learned the term for the lovely stones that jutted from the corner of the property when I'd questioned the owner about the choice of colour. He'd beamed as he told me he'd painted it in honour of his favourite team, Norwich City.

"That's nice," I'd said and turned back to further examine the green quoins and window ledges that clashed with the canary yellow of the render. Looking on the positive side: at least he wasn't a Watford fan.

The front door opened and the soon-to-be ex-owners of Flotsam Guesthouse stepped out. Jim's stomach bulged over his trousers, while his shirt poked through his open flies. Behind us, our daughter, Emily, sniggered.

"So, from now on you get the pleasure of early mornings and late nights." Jim's belly shook when he laughed. "We'll think of you when we're having a lie-in."

"I'm sure you will." My husband, Jason, took the lead as we trooped in behind them. He and Emily had to bend their heads when they stepped through into the lounge, whereas I could walk anywhere in the guesthouse and not have to worry about its many low doorways.

"While Maureen gets your wife up-to-date with the bookings, you'll want to check the water, electric and a few other bits."

Jim led Jason from the room, leaving Emily and I with Maureen

3

who showed us the booking system and told us a bit about their guests. As she twittered on – her Midlands accent at odds with Jim's Norfolk burr – a weight settled. How would we ever get to grips with everything after an hour's talk? We'd been left under no illusion about follow-up contact if we had questions or issues in the future. We'd offered too little for the property to expect an after-care service.

After a hurried check of the guesthouse rooms, a grinning Jim and Maureen scarpered from our lives with a cheerful ta-ra.

"Did you remember what Maureen said to do if the shower stopped working in room five?" I asked Jason.

"No idea," he said. "Jim was too busy telling me which appliances shouldn't be turned on at the same time if we didn't want to trip the electric."

With our first guests arriving in two days, we didn't have long to find out the answers to these questions or why Maureen had smirked when she'd pointed to their names on the diary system. But before we could start to worry about the days ahead, we had a van to unload and rooms to prepare. It would be a long day.

♦

The worktop shuddered as Jason's fist slammed down. Too tired to react, I rubbed sore hands over eyes that begged for sleep while Emily hovered nearby biting her lip. As the day had progressed, we'd watched Jason morph from his usually calm self to a ranting madman.

"So, he switched the cooker for this broken pile of junk? As if we don't already have enough to do."

The picture on the estate agent's details showed a different cooker to the one now sitting in the middle of the kitchen after Jason had spent the best part of an hour trying to bring it back to

4

life.

"And you've got to mend that shower" Emily angled away from my 'zip it' stare. She may have turned twenty the week before, but she hadn't lost the teenage gift of knowing exactly which buttons to press. "And the wardrobe door in room four and the drawers in room five. And, that's not all…"

"Thank you," I said, meaning anything but.

"You haven't told him about that iron burn under the rug either."

As Jason slumped against the counter, head in his hands, I gave him a hug. He rewarded me with a weary smile and a gentle kiss. He smelled of sweat and grime. We all did. Everything we touched in the kitchen had a strange stickiness and when we'd run knives along the edges of the worktops, grease had curled away like butter. In the rest of the guesthouse dust settled into thick layers on everything above head height or behind the drawers and wardrobes. Dozens of filthy cloths now littered the floor of the utility room and our old toothbrushes lay bruised and blackened in the bin, thanks to the thick mildew that coated the underframe and corners of each shower cubicle. Like so many things, the mastic was beyond help and would need to be dug out and replaced.

With just the three of us lugging all our belongings into the house, we'd had more than a few stressful moments throughout the day and regurgitating all the sickening issues wasn't going to help.

"Have you wondered why that woman, Maureen, grinned when she pointed at the guests' names in the book?" Emily said, continuing her mission to bump up our stress levels. "I've been thinking how odd it was. Like she knew something we didn't."

I'd spent most of the day wondering about that, but tiredness clogged my thoughts. It could wait until tomorrow. "Let's go to bed," I said.

For once, Emily allowed me to usher her upstairs, with Jason following behind, sighing as he snapped off the light in the kitchen.

Flotsam Guesthouse certainly lived up to its name.

♦

After blistering hard work – literally, thanks to an ill-fitting pair of new trainers – and a dash of luck that the new cooker arrived on time, we were ready to open. We made a final check on the guest rooms being used during the next few days. At first glance they looked lovely, with pristine bedding and plump towels but, like the black canvas of a night sky which becomes dotted with stars the longer you gaze at it, when observed the room offered a different picture. The skirting boards were scuffed and chipboard peeked through the melamine on the wardrobes and drawer sets. As we earned enough over the coming months we could replace these with proper wooden ones, along with the curtains, voiles, kettles, cups, cushions, pillows, quilts and so on. The thought of our bank balance never being above zero for years made me shudder, especially when it came to replacing the more expensive stuff. We'd scrubbed stains from the carpets but there was little to be done about worn areas or the iron burn Emily had discovered. Throughout the guesthouse the woodchip wallpaper needed a new coat of paint too. Or, better, stripping it and replastering, but a decision on that would have to wait until the season ended.

We'd been desperate to live in Torringham, with its stunning harbour and breathtaking coastline. But, with money being tight, the only way we could do so was if we bought a place in need of work and Flotsam Guesthouse certainly fitted the bill. For now, we would have to live with what we had and cross our fingers that nothing else went wrong.

I wandered through to the lounge to recheck the guest registration forms and amounts. We had three guests arriving today: Dougal Marriner and a Mr and Mrs Jones. I grimaced when

6

writing the registration form for Dougal, especially with the figure of £35 per night, half the rate of the other couple. What on earth had Maureen been thinking to charge him so little for room four, especially as the only area of saving for a single occupant was for one breakfast and a set of towels. All the rooms were ensuite with double beds, but this was one of the mid-range rooms that also had a small dressing table and a seating area, although the chairs were obviously salvaged from the old breakfast room stock.

Opposite me Jason slumped on the sofa, head back, arms outstretched. He let out a gentle snore. Even in sleep his face seemed drawn with grey smudges beneath his eyes. So much for our new start being easier than our previous roles: ones we'd been so desperate to leave we'd leapt into the frying pan of our dreams without much thought. A glimmer of doubt flickered. Had we done the right thing? While my job at a children's respite centre had become more stressful and Jason's job in sales meant we saw little of each other, there were downsides to our new start. We'd been unable to convince Lucy, his daughter, to join us – I had mixed feelings about that – and we'd dragged Emily, our youngest, miles from her friends. For what? I gazed at the packing boxes and our cramped lounge. Would all our stuff fit in this small space? We'd given up a lovely family home for a living area comprising two bedrooms and a lounge.

As the doorbell rang, Jason woke with a start, bleary eyes gazing round in incomprehension, while I packed my doubts and fears where they belonged, in the deepest corner of my mind. We had to do this. We had no choice.

"Come on," I said. "It must be our guests."

A young couple stood on the doorstep. Hands shaken, luggage handed over, we took them to their room. They didn't seem to notice the tired furniture or the clashing curtains.

"Ooh, your duvet set is gorgeous." The woman brushed her

hand over the cover. "And it's a fab-sized room."

I heaved a sigh of relief. Our first-ever guests would be just great.

♦

Two people stood at the door. Both wore glasses and hats – his a flat cap and hers a pink rimless thing not seen since the sixties – and matching shocked expressions.

"Y-you're not Maureen," the man stuttered.

"Katie." I held out my hand but let it fall to my side when neither stepped forward.

The woman looked past me into the hallway. "Where's Maureen?"

"They've moved. We're the new owners."

They looked at each other and then back at me. "I don't know if I like this," the woman said.

Two cases sat on the drive, obscured from view behind one of the ornamental pots for our bay trees. Had these people turned up hoping for a room? At that moment Jason came through from the kitchen, wearing a cheery smile. He held out his hand.

"This is Jason, my husband."

As the man glared at him, Jason's hand slid to his side but he maintained his pleasant smile. "And you are?"

The man stiffened. "Mr and Mrs Marriner, of course."

"There's two of you?" When they exchanged perplexed looks, I added. "Maureen said it was just yourself."

"Well, I doubt that very much. Maureen knows we always come together."

"Come in," said Jason. "We'll sort this out inside."

"What is there to sort out?" Mr Marriner spat the last two words but, as Jason picked up the cases, he allowed himself and his wife to be ushered through to the day room, where they were offered a chair. They sat as if ready to spring for freedom.

"You've got our room?" Mr Marriner said.

"Yes, but we were told you were a single occupant. Not that it's a problem. Katie can put extra bits in the room while we chat but it won't be at the rate you were quoted."

"Oh, but it will." Mr Marriner's tone sharpened to steel.

His wife unclipped her handbag and drew out a sheet of paper, which he snatched from her grasp.

"See here." He stabbed the letter. "Maureen said we get room five for £35 a night including breakfast for the two of us."

"Room five? But that's one of the biggest rooms."

"That's our room." Arms folded he leaned back into the chair.

My heart sank. I'd just put Mr and Mrs Jones into that room not an hour ago. Surely, I hadn't misread the booking system?

"Give me a minute." I rushed off to the lounge, leaving a confused Jason holding the fort.

The booking system showed I'd been right. One person – Dougal Marriner – in room four for five nights and the other couple – Mr and Mrs Jones – in room five for two nights. I took the laptop through to the day room to prove my case, where it was immediately waved away as nonsense.

"So, you're saying we're not in our room," Mr Marriner said. "We're not having that. We want our room or else!"

I'd had enough. "You're telling me that Maureen has always charged you just £35 a night for both of you to stay in room five? I'll go back and check."

Mrs Marriner's cheeks reddened and she feigned an interest in her handbag, while Mr Marriner's eyes darted to the sheet. "It says it all here," he said but his voice trembled.

"I bet it does."

Jason placed his hand on my shoulder. "All we can do is put you in room four, our next largest room on the first floor, and move you to room five in a couple of days."

What was he playing at? Not only was he agreeing to the ridiculously low fee but a move mid-stay to the larger room meant extra costs on laundering the bedding. At this rate we'd be paying for guests to stay. These people blooming well knew that the double occupancy fee in the letter was either a typo or a deliberate error. I willed them to look at me, but both averted their eyes.

"We're not happy but it will have to do," Mr Marriner said, echoing my very sentiments.

As we led the way to their room, with the couple huffing behind us, it hit me that we no longer had the luxury of leaving work for the safety and privacy of home. Running a guesthouse meant Mr and Mrs Marriner would be living with us for the next five days. The thought filled me with dread.

Chapter 2

TWO WOMEN STOOD ON THE DOORSTEP. A mismatched pair in every aspect of dress and demeanour. The black woman was tall with a welcoming smile, her braided hair pulled back by a colourful silk ribbon that shimmied in the breeze. Her companion, who was at least a foot shorter with a pasty complexion and spikey blonde-tipped hair, held out a small foil-covered dish.

"Shona." She pushed the dish into my hands. "We would have come earlier but we thought we'd give you a few days to settle in."

"I'm Kim. We're from Jetsam Cottage B&B next door." Well-manicured maroon nails glinted in the sunlight as she extended her hand. They matched her shoes and the pattern in her hair ribbon too. I tucked the dish into the crook of my arm to free up a hand and greet her.

"Come in," I said, hoping they wouldn't. We had too much to do.

They followed me through to our small lounge, waiting while I shunted boxes around to clear a channel to the sofa. What would they make of our living area with its too-big leather sofa that almost blocked the back door? We'd had a nightmare trying to get it through the door, hindered by a century old frame built for smaller statures and a period when furniture encouraged people to sit upright rather than slump down. Even our armchair looked like a mini sofa – each armrest alone could fit a person's backside when needed. When we came to change our sofas, it would be leaving in the hands of professional removers or – more likely – in bits.

From upstairs came the sound of banging as Jason fought with an unruly door, assisted by a fed-up Emily. My job today was to ensure at least two more of the guest rooms were as clean as possible for our next arrivals tomorrow. We'd come prepared with

11

new bedding, sheets and towels, after we'd spotted the threadbare state of some of the linen during our viewings. Unfortunately, our pristine white bedding didn't fit with the seventies-style orange curtains which we vowed would be replaced within a week. Our wish list was fast becoming the size of an Argos catalogue.

"How are you settling in?" Kim asked.

"We've had a few surprises."

"I bet!" said Shona. "We wondered who'd take this place on."

"Shona!" Kim shot her a look. "It wasn't quite like that."

"It's not like we thought you were mugs." Shona said, her Essex twang becoming more pronounced. "I mean, you can see it'll be a lot of work."

"It already has been." I relayed the story of the Marriners' arrival.

"Not that old basket-case Dougal Marriner! We knew Maureen wasn't happy about the price you paid but..." Shona stuttered to a halt under the heat of Kim's angry gaze. Then she shrugged. "It's not like it's a secret or anything. She told everyone who'd listen. Be grateful if booking Dougal in for so little is the worst she did."

During our few meetings and phone calls, Jim and Maureen had often fired barbed comments about how we'd paid too little for this place. But they'd chosen to accept our offer. I sighed. What if giving Dougal a low rate wasn't the worst of it? Surely, she wouldn't be spiteful enough to mess up the bookings.

"We didn't come here to scare you," Kim said. "I'm sure it's just a one-off."

♦

Jason ducked under the doorframe as he wandered into the lounge. His sand-coloured hair was dusted with grit, which speckled his shoulders too. He smeared his hands down his face – the incarnation of 'The Scream' – before crumpling onto the sofa.

"Still at it?"

"I'm having to phone almost every guest to check their rooms and rates. What was she playing at? Spiteful old bag."

He shook his head. "One day down, four to go. It won't be long before the Marriners become a distant memory."

"It can't come soon enough. At least he won't be asking for three pieces of bacon again."

The sofa creaked as Jason sat beside me. The knees of his jeans were coated in grime where he'd been working on a leak in the utility area, but his hands had been scrubbed clean. Drawing me into a tight cuddle, he kissed the top of my head, my nose and finally my lips, rewarded by a smile and kiss in return. We'd promised ourselves we'd be a team, there to support each other and work in harmony, to make Flotsam Guesthouse a success. Right now, with my earlier doubts sealed away, I knew we could. I pushed the paperwork aside, giving myself a few minutes off to bask in the warmth of his body.

"Let's put this down to experience," he said. "How about we see if Emily fancies a walk to the beach?"

With breakfast and the rooms ticked off and no one checking in until tomorrow, I'd set the afternoon aside to deal with the booking issues Maureen had created, starting by phoning guests on the pretext of introducing ourselves as new owners. It proved a useful exercise. Most of the bookings were correct but, for the inaccurate ones, Maureen had chosen people similar in personality to Mr and Mrs Marriner. I'd refused to back down when they argued that they had the booking amount in writing, so we had to take them. For a start, Maureen had agreed the rates and, also, our standard rates were cheaper than many places. The moaners and chancers were welcome to find somewhere else. We didn't need more guests like Dougal sodding Marriner.

Apart from a few unanswered calls, I'd reached September in the bookings so there was no urgency. My mind had become a quagmire of bookings, rates and queries, while our lounge was becoming an oppressive cell. We'd moved here for the change of scenery and lifestyle; not these four walls. Jason didn't need to persuade me to escape.

♦

The harbour was my favourite part of Torringham. Small sailing boats floated at high tide or rested lop-sided on the pebbly bottom when the tide ebbed, while an assortment of colourful cottages lined either side of the bowl hillside, rising in higgledy tiers. Shops, restaurants and pubs clustered the roadside and lanes where tourists jostled for space on summer days. A working town with a thriving fishing industry, the air near the trawlers was as likely to smell of brine as of oil but Torringham was an honest, industrious town. One where even in winter there was always a good pint or meal to be found. We'd stayed in another B&B when we first viewed Flotsam Guesthouse on a crisp January day and the owner had proudly told us that Torringham wasn't filled with second homers who flocked back to London in the winter, unlike many seaside towns further down the coast. After viewing a few B&Bs in the morning, we'd joined other hardy visitors to trek along the wild coastal path before heading to a warm pub that night for a steaming pie and mash by a log fire. That day clinched the deal. No matter how much work needed doing to Flotsam Guesthouse, it was the one for us.

Today the sun warmed our faces and gulls wheeled in a sky the blue of postcards and summer dreams. We caught the odd whiff of fish and chips as we strolled along the front with Emily in the lead, eager to reach the beach where a promised ice cream awaited. That and a chance to beat Jason at stone skimming. She'd inherited his competitive streak. From my seat on a jutting rock I watched them, with their jaws clenched and the same determined look on their faces as they competed for the most bounces. Although they were similar in height, Emily had my darker colouring. Her brown eyes sparkled in delight as she leapt up and down, fists pumping the air. She'd obviously beaten Jason and he wouldn't be allowed to forget it.

Dogs bounded around me, scattering a fountain of droplets as they shook themselves. I laughed until my sides ached when one of the dogs took to chasing madly after the pebbles launched by Jason and Emily.

In the bay, trawler boats thrust towards the open sea, while yachts lazed waiting for the breeze to pick up. One hardy soul swam nearby, his bare arms plunging into the water, his mouth a black chasm with each upturn of his head. I shivered and leaned back to catch more rays.

"They're not allowed." A familiar voice cut through the air, followed by his wife's tut of agreement. "Not on the beach."

Closing my eyes, I groaned and hoped they wouldn't spot me.

"Eeuww!" It sounded like Mrs Marriner. "No! No!"

"Get your dog under control!" came Mr Marriner's booming voice.

I squinted through a half-closed eye to see Mrs Marriner twirling round, squawking, her handbag held aloft as a terrier jumped up and down, bouncing away from Mr Marriner's ham-fisted attempts to catch it.

A man lumbered along the beach, panting and shouting, "Robbie, get 'ere!"

By the water's edge, Jason and Emily kept their backs to the commotion as they shifted like crabs to the safety of the other side of the beach, leaving me statue-like on the rock, unable to move for fear of being spotted.

"That thing shouldn't be here!" Mr Marriner shouted.

Apart from the occasional 'I said I was sorry,' the dog owner didn't get to say much as Mr Marriner launched into a loud rant about dogs on beaches and all the ills of society and what on earth was the world coming to when people couldn't read as it clearly stated 'no dogs on the beach from May to September'.

"It's April," the dog owner said.

"What?"

"I said," although the dog owner shouted it. "It's April. A-P-R-I-L." And with that he scooped up his dog and stomped back the way he'd come.

♦

The next morning, Mr and Mrs Marriner walked into the breakfast room three minutes before the end of service, her thick heels clopping over the laminate flooring. They didn't even glance at me when giving their tea order or when it was brought out. Lips pursed, they stared at the menu before announcing they would have the same as yesterday. While there was no mention of the three bits of bacon Mr Marriner had requested the previous day, a churning undercurrent told me something was up.

Stupidly, I asked, "Is there anything you need?"

Mr Marriner turned around, his gaze level with my chest. Flushing, he spun back to the menu.

"We're not happy," Mrs Marriner said.

On the neighbouring table, Mr and Mrs Jones' cutlery hovered motionless over their plates. I could feel them stretching to hear what was being said.

"I'm sorry about that. Is there something wrong with the tea?"

"Not just the tea. Everything." Mr Marriner took a deep breath as if readying himself for a lengthy tirade.

"How about we sort your breakfasts and we can talk in private afterwards." I shot into the kitchen.

Jason didn't need to ask me what was wrong. He'd heard. Handing him the order slip, I pressed my finger to my lips and shook my head, warning him not to say anything. The silence rolled in ominous waves from the breakfast room, until we heard the screech of a chair being pushed back. It could have been a guest going to get more juice or simply wanting more leg space, but something told me to check. Both Mr and Mrs Marriner were striding from the room.

"We're leaving," Mr Marriner said. "This is the worst stay we have ever had and we won't be paying for it either."

Stranded between trying to maintain a friendly façade with Mr and Mrs Jones in full view and feeling a compulsion to strangle Mr Marriner, Jason saved me when he stomped out of the kitchen in his new checkered trousers. He'd forgotten to take off the 'Smokin' Hot Chef' apron Emily had bought from an online company that printed words and images to order. Beneath the words was a large picture of Jason sucking a sausage as if it were a cigar.

"I'm in the middle of cooking your breakfast. What is the issue?"

"Our room, of course."

Jason's jaw tightened but he maintained his calm composure, while I stewed by the breakfast room door. I could deal with Dougal Marriner all right, but – my fists squeezed into tight balls of anger – maybe it was best to leave this one to Jason.

"But you accepted your stay on the agreement that we would move you when the room became free. Yet, on the day you're moving, you choose to leave."

"Well, we're not happy." As Mr Marriner's bottom lip jutted, I could picture him as a schoolboy, stamping his foot.

"Neither are we," Jason said. "We're sad to see you go but we hope you find somewhere more suitable, although that may be difficult. Can I get your bags?"

"They're in the car," Mrs Marriner said.

"And we won't be paying," Mr Marriner added.

"But you will," Jason dropped his voice. "We're not green enough to let you play another silly game."

"Game? You think we had fun here?" Mr Marriner spluttered.

Jason straightened so he towered over the couple. "We've acted honourably throughout. Pay up or your car won't be leaving our drive until the police arrive."

My wonderful husband looked them straight in the eye without wavering, easily winning the 'who blinks first competition'. With his face a magnificent shade of burgundy, Mr Marriner stuffed notes into Jason's hand. Seeing the colour of his money gave me as much pleasure as seeing the colour of his face. A moment to be savoured. And one only bettered by the slam of the front door and the knowledge that they wouldn't be returning.

Back in the safety of the kitchen we heaved sighs of relief and Jason gave me a much-needed cuddle, cut short by the ring of the doorbell. Shooting worried glances at each other, we headed to the door. Had they left something behind? Or had they found another thing to complain about? The shape through the frosted glass appeared shorter than either of the Marriners.

As Jason opened the door, a woman barked, "Your car?"

Shocked by her confrontational tone, I stepped to his side. Outside, a black car had parked over the path, leaving a small gap between it and the two cars on our driveway: ours and our guests. It had rained overnight and droplets clung to the car bonnets, while a rectangle of dry brick showed where the Marriner's car had sat. Thank goodness their car hadn't been obstructed too.

Without waiting for a response, the woman jabbed her finger at us. "You expect me to push my son into the road, do you?"

Unable to see anyone with her, we followed as she strode off. She pointed to a young boy who sat strapped into a wheelchair abandoned in the middle of a pathway, unable to fit through the space left by the Audi. My heart leapt into my throat. The boy's pale face, wide eyes and contorted wrists, reminded me of little George, from my old job at Hartfield children's respite centre. Even though many of the children had challenging issues, in all the years I'd worked there we'd lost just a few, but each loss reopened an old wound until, with George's death, the scar no longer healed. His wide, toothy smile and huge blue eyes haunted me. Life had been unfair to my chirpy chap who'd been taken by pneumonia days before his tenth birthday. When Jason had asked for the third time about starting afresh, I'd jumped at the chance, handing in my notice and putting the house on the market without a thought to the reality of a two-hundred-mile move.

The lad rewarded my wave with a smile as wide as George's.

"Well?" The woman moved in front of the wheelchair as if to protect her son from us.

When Jason went to answer, I butted in, careful to moderate my voice and not escalate her upset into a row. "We're sorry but that car's got nothing to do with us. We can see why you're cross. I used to work at…"

"Liars too, I see." She grabbed the wheelchair handles and pushed it off the edge of the kerb. As it jolted onto the tarmac road, she turned back. "This is a small town and you'll come unstuck if you try treating us like you did Mo and Jim."

As she marched away, Jason squeezed my shoulder. "Don't worry about it." He waited for me to move but when I didn't, he added, "We best get back to our guests."

He wandered inside shaking his head, leaving me to stand in silence. He might say not to worry but he knew I would. His gentle embrace showed he understood how much this would have upset me.

I longed to run after the woman and tell her we'd never want to cause her further difficulty. Parents of children with disabilities faced so many challenges without more being added. Our respite centre had been a lifeline to them, offering a few days of rest and time to spend with their other children, away from the worries of hoists, feeding tubes, medication and trying to navigate everyday obstructions such as this car.

But I couldn't get over what the woman had said. She'd been right to ask us to move the car but why wouldn't she listen when we'd explained it wasn't ours, and why the snide parting shot? My stomach lurched. What on earth had Jim and Maureen told everyone? Did people whisper and point when we walked through the streets of Torringham? Would word get around, so we struggled for business? The woman and the young boy had reached the bottom of the road where it curved towards the shops. A few more steps and they disappeared from sight.

On the other side of the road, a man came out of the cottages banging the door behind him. I tracked his steps until he reached the Audi.

"You shouldn't block the path like that."

He glared at me. "It was only a minute. What harm has it done?" He looked up and down the empty street as if to prove his point and clambered into the car, muttering, "Daft bat."

No point responding. When the sun dipped behind a cloud casting a gloom in the air, I pulled my arms around myself and, head down, went back indoors. Voices filtered from the breakfast room as Jason chatted and laughed with the young couple, no doubt recounting our adventures with the Marriners. But I couldn't join him. My mind reeled. Had we made a huge mistake? Before moving here, we'd known our seaside idyll wouldn't be all sun and sea with every day a joy. But I hadn't expected it to be like this.

One of my many flaws was reading too much into a situation. But, even so, less than a week into our supposed fresh start I couldn't shake the feeling that the edges of our dream were smouldering ready to burst into flame. If we didn't take care, we could be tossed from the frying pan in which we found ourselves. And I knew where that would lead.

Chapter 3

BREAKFAST DONE AND ROOMS CLEANED, I flopped on to the settee, unable to believe that we had the rest of the day ahead without a single guest checking in or an email to write. We'd been in Torringham for just six weeks but already Emily had stopped working at the guesthouse after finding a better job as a hotel receptionist in nearby Berrinton. Who could blame her? She needed to get out and make friends, but it meant our workload had increased. At least I had a few minutes to myself this afternoon before starting on the ironing, unlike poor Jason who had been co-opted into helping Mike at Seaview with a macerator. Apparently, having one here made us experts, but more likely Mike wanted someone else to deal with his toilet issues.

Kicking off my shoes, I shuffled round to get more comfortable and plumped the cushions behind my head. Remote control in hand, I'd started ploughing through the afternoon TV listings when my phone buzzed. Shona, from Jetsam Cottage next door. 'You won't believe this…' her message began. I laid down the phone, not wishing to be drawn into one of the many sagas she'd told me about. Soon curiosity nibbled at me but as I typed in my password, the doorbell rang.

Our six weeks here had taught me that guesthouse owners are hostages to the door. It could be a guest locked out or some other crisis, although this time the caller was almost certainly blonde and spikey, in more ways than her hair style.

The front door hadn't even opened fully when Shona barged through. When she flung her hands in the air, I knew this would be the start of a long story.

"Can you believe it!" Usually she toned down her Essex accent but this was Romford at its finest. "What sort of people steal duvets and pillows? I told Kim we should say no to those workmen as they sounded dodgy, especially when they turned up in that van, but she wanted to fill that flaming room. It's the John Lewis set too, you know, the one we got in the sale."

She paused, giving me a chance to speak. "The workmen took your new John Lewis set?"

It had been the highlight of the week on the B&Bers' WhatsApp group. How Shona and Kim had managed to buy a £250 duvet set for £36 and then used it in one of their budget rooms. Us B&Bers had interesting conversations.

"And the duvet and pillows. Actually, they left one pillow but still. It's our favourite set. We know how to get them back."

An ominous feeling settled. "Do you?"

"They're working on a house in Berrinton. One of them was chatting to Kim and told us they are doing a few building jobs in the area. Yesterday and today is Berrinton, tomorrow is Plymouth and so on." She took a deep breath. "Can you take us to Berrinton? We'd go but our car's in for its brakes."

"What are you planning to do?"

She ran her hand through her peroxide-tipped hair as if thinking, even though she would have mapped it out before coming around. "We're going to ask for them back." Then she gave me her sweetest smile. "Very nicely, of course."

♦

Scaffolding lined the frontage of the house, while beside a skip brimming with rubble sat the sky-blue hippy van I'd seen on Shona and Kim's drive the day before. We'd found the right place. I leaned against my car as Shona stood on tiptoes to peer into the van. She signalled to Kim who wandered over and turned to me with pursed lips before marching to the door. They'd found their bedding.

While an incongruous couple in height and mannerisms, they both had the same stubborn streak and were more than capable of standing their ground, which balanced out any guilt I felt for standing as far back as possible.

They rapped the knocker and pressed the bell, but no one answered. When Shona cupped her hands against the bay window to gaze inside, I went over. There was no sound of drilling or banging, just the waft of fresh paint.

"They're out." She glanced at her watch. Two o'clock. Sighing, she propped herself against one of the scaffolding poles. "We've got a three thirty check-in. If only we could get the keys to the van."

Kim grabbed her arm and pointed to the bay window. "Look!"

The window appeared shut but then I spotted the slight gap. Maybe the builders had found it open when they left for lunch but, rather than go back inside, they'd pushed it to. Just like we'd done at the guesthouse the other day when we spotted the open breakfast room window as we left to pick up the fruit and veg order. Stupid, but if someone had broken in they wouldn't have been leaving with anything but packets of cereal as we kept the internal door locked.

Kim tucked her fingers under the window and pulled it open. Ignoring our outcry, she stepped onto the window ledge and hauled herself up, curling her long leg over the edge. Then she gave us a grin and a thumbs up and, in one fluid movement, ducked inside.

"Flippin' heck!" Shona darted down the pathway. She looked both ways, before shooting back to rap on the door.

"Is someone coming?" I asked.

She shook her head. "Not yet." She swiped her hand through her hedgehog hair. "But what if someone's inside? Why on earth did I let her go?"

Tapping a finger on her chin, she surveyed the building. "Here, give us a leg up."

Through the bay window I could make out paint pots and dust sheets but nothing beyond the open door. While we hadn't heard anything, silence wasn't always golden. For all we knew Kim could have come across someone who'd stayed behind for a snooze. A dozen movie scenes reeled through my mind: a man leaping from behind to cover a woman's mouth, an intruder walking through a door to be smashed on the back of the head by a hammer or, more likely, the police being called. Kim shouldn't have gone in there. We had to get her out.

In for a penny, in for a pound. Against my better judgement I clasped my hands to help Shona up, grunting in discomfort, not just from her weight but the red Devon mud which caked her boot and squelched in my palm.

My fingers throbbed as though they would snap in two. "Hurry up!"

She hefted herself clear, leaving me to examine my aching, muddy hands. A 'psst' brought my attention back to find her dangling over the lip of the window frame, her legs outside, her body inside. Even when she stretched as far as she could, her arms didn't reach the window sill below. She wriggled forward, more of her inside than out, but the sill was a good two foot away. If she fell she'd make a right racket and probably break her neck too. I grabbed her legs.

"Let go!" she hissed.

Just then the front door rattled open and Kim stepped out, clutching something gold and black to her chest. She gazed at us in surprise.

"Shona, what are you doing?"

Kim shoved the items in her pockets and we both took a leg to drag Shona out, each tug matched by a groan of pain.

Back at the car, Kim threw what was clearly a wallet and gold watch onto the back seat. She hadn't gone in with them, so they must be stolen.

"You're not taking them, are you?"

"Don't worry, it'll all become clear. Have you got a pen and paper?"

While I reached into the glove box, she scanned the road. As she scribbled a note on the bonnet of my car, Shona stood with her top pulled up examining her wounds – a series of red-rimmed vertical scratches on her abdomen.

"What are you writing?"

"A ransom note," Kim told me.

As she pinned the note beneath the hippy van's windscreen wipers, she treated us to her fabulous throaty laugh.

♦

I'd become a boomerang. With every bang of a car door or raised voice, I leapt up and raced to the breakfast room window to check whether the men had arrived next door for the exchange of goods. Jason hadn't arrived back yet, but it might be best if he wasn't there when the men came. If anything went wrong, no doubt Jason would end up in the middle of it. It was all very well Kim writing the note to say she'd found the items in the guesthouse and had come to switch them for an undamaged duvet set but what if she'd taken someone else's belongings? Someone who had never set foot in Jetsam Cottage.

As I bundled another load of towels into the washing machine the distant church bells chimed. Four o'clock. Most workmen finished around now. But Kim said these had to pack up ready to move onto Plymouth, which meant they wouldn't be here for another half hour to forty-five minutes at least. Back in the lounge I folded a heap of dry towels into piles. I'd kept the sound on the TV low, even though it meant straining to hear it above the churning machines in the utility room.

Above it all echoed the unmistakable sound of raised voices. With a thudding heart I raced outside to find several of our guests on the driveway watching the commotion next door. Two men stood on the doorstep to Jetsam Cottage, while behind them sat a van, but not the hippy van.

"You just can't come and take stuff. It's stealing." The older man shouted.

People with necks that red usually had severe sunburn, but it was more likely anger in his case. The way he shook his fist at Shona suggested he was heading towards a heart attack.

"Where's our flaming duvet? Your guys took it." Shona bellowed back, while Kim stood beside her, arms folded, a serene smile in place. If the row had escalated to this level so quickly, I dreaded to think what could happen next.

Hesitantly, I made my way round to Jetsam Cottage, my shoes crunching on their gravel drive.

Shona spotted me. "You tell 'em, Katie."

What could I say? If these men had nothing to do with the stolen duvet, we'd be in dire trouble for taking their belongings, no matter how much Kim and Shona argued otherwise.

Pointing at me, the lad hollered, "It's no good bringing her into it. You've already said you've got my dad's stuff."

The older man swung round, mouth open as if he held an invisible loudspeaker ready to blast me out. A strange expression crossed his face, while a vague feeling of familiarity nibbled at me. Had we come across each other in a local shop or something?

Our eyes met. Oh my goodness! His were the same deep blue of someone I'd loved very much.

"Katie?" He scratched his head. "It looks like you, but w-what are you doing here?"

His gentleness contrasted with the buzz of anger in the air. I waded through my memories, until the past swam into place. Uncle Bert! He'd left Derbyshire for a new life after his wife died years ago. They'd been childless so he must have remarried. Tears pricked my eyes. It *was* him! After all these years. The last time I'd seen him had been – oh! – at my poor mum's funeral.

"It is, isn't it!" His rough hands grasped my arms. For the first time in years I gazed into my mum's – Bert's – eyes. He smiled proudly.

"My, you look just like your mum. Well, I never! Callum, come here and meet your cousin."

I stood shamefaced as he paraded me before Callum. We'd stolen his wallet and watch. What must he think of us?

"Can Bert have his things back?" I asked Shona. Without saying a word she disappeared, coming back out to gently place the items in his outstretched palms. She made no mention of the duvet, although she must have been burning to ask.

"I'm sorry about your things but those workmen took my friends' expensive bedding," I said. "It's no excuse, I know."

Bert turned to Shona and Kim. "I know those lads' boss. You'll get your stuff back, I'll make sure of that. Just don't be taking mine again."

We needed to get away before Shona got a chance to open her plus-size mouth. "Fancy a cuppa," I said to Uncle Bert and Callum. "And a catch up. I'm just next door."

As the three of us walked back to Flotsam Guesthouse, past the guests still planted on our drive, Jason came around the corner surprised to see so many people outside. His t-shirt bore unthinkable stains.

"Did you get my message about stopping on to help Mike with his roof too," he said.

"I've been a tad busy. This is my Uncle Bert, by the way, and Callum, his son."

Confused, Jason glanced from Bert to myself, but he shook both their hands. While ushering Bert and Callum into the guesthouse, I spotted one of the guests – a quiet, gentle man midway through his four-day stay – take Jason aside, so I directed my visitors towards the lounge and rushed back.

"As I said, I just thought you should know," the guest said.

"Is this right?" Jason said to me. He looked worried rather than cross. "Those men caused a scene next door."

"Yes, but no, but yes," I stuttered. "It was a misunderstanding. Look, I'll explain later."

I turned to our guest. "It wasn't his fault. Believe me, he's a lovely man."

The guest's expression said otherwise, while Jason's puzzled look told me I had a lot of explaining to do. That wouldn't be an easy conversation, especially as I'd been the get-away driver, but it wouldn't be right to leave Uncle Bert's reputation stained by my actions. Strange how something so wonderful as meeting Mum's brother had started with the theft of a duvet set. We'd been lucky this time but, lesson learned, there wouldn't be any more ill-considered trips with Shona and Kim. Although it would be difficult, I had to learn to say 'no'.

Chapter 4

WE HAD A DAY OFF! Thanks to Jason spotting the gap in the calendar and closing it out a few weeks before. As he pointed out, there wasn't another free period until the beginning of October, so we had to make the most of it. Somehow, Emily had wangled a day off from her hotel receptionist job, so the three of us agreed to head to Exeter to buy towels for the guesthouse and possibly a few bits to update my summer wardrobe.

During the winter months, when we'd been scouting for guesthouses, we'd stayed overnight in Exeter as I'd wanted to see the bustling Christmas market by the Cathedral. My tummy had rumbled as a variety of food smells wafted in the air and I'd succumbed to a homemade gingerbread man, laughing at Emily's indignation as I bit off his head. As the crisp light of afternoon transformed into a purple and apricot dusk, we'd wandered beneath the twinkling Christmas lights until, footsore and weighed down with shopping bags which bit into our fingers and bumped against our shins, we voted to go back to the B&B. That's when we'd found ourselves in a small café down a side street, where we tucked into the best hot chocolate ever.

Sadly, I doubted we'd find the café again. This time we took a torturous route in, bumper-to-bumper with cars as we headed over the River Exe and along a never-ending road which curved around the shopping area, rather than leading directly to it. Finally, we arrived at a roundabout with a sign giving a choice of car parks and Jason swung the car to the left. He smiled victoriously at me, until Emily chirped from the back seat.

"Next time can we just use the sat-nav?"

She had a point. Exeter had once been Isca, a Roman city, so surely there must be some straight roads, yet somehow Jason had managed to miss them all. Even the car park was one of those where you turned the steering wheel to the left and just kept going until finally we reached the roof and found a free space. Skin tight from an hour in a stuffy car, I stepped out thankful for the light breeze. The lift spilled us into a back street which led to the shopping precinct. Jason took the lead, his hand warm in mine, while Emily sauntered alongside us, gazing through shop windows and, no doubt, planning her shopping spree.

We'd agree the first stop would be Cathedral Green where we'd get some lunch and meander back through the shops. In contrast to winter and the hustle of the Christmas market, the Cathedral stood sedate in the centre of a lawn intersected by paths and dotted with office workers, visitors and students. A couple lazed on the squat wall which enclosed the Green. Behind it sat brick and stone Regency buildings, another smaller church and a lovely black and white building, where we relaxed under the shade of an umbrella, drinking coffee and watching the world go by.

Suddenly, Emily yelped and jumped up, splashing her coffee over the table. "I don't believe it!"

She shot off, leaving myself and Jason shrugging in bemusement as she sprinted across the lawn, waving madly. On reaching a group of young people, she dropped to her knees and stayed there for the next twenty minutes. With her friends' backs to us, I watched her laugh and shake the hair from her face with carefree flicks. More relaxed than we'd seen her for a while.

"She looks cheerful."

Jason squeezed my knee. "Friends from work, perhaps?"

My chair scraped as I shuffled round closer to Jason. It also meant I could spy on her without cricking my neck. Until now, Emily had come in from work morose and uncommunicative but if she was making friends it could only be a good thing. Jason rested his arm on my shoulders and we basked in the warmth of each other, enjoying our daughter's happiness.

When she returned, her eyes sparkled and she wore a glow we'd not seen since she'd been in a relationship the previous year. Sadly, that hadn't ended well.

"Friends?" Jason blithely tossed the remark, but his expectant look told me he too longed for her to tell us about her lovely work colleagues and her plans for an evening out with them.

In silence, she watched her friends walk off in the opposite direction before she plumped herself back down in the chair. As she swung one leg over the other, her foot knocked the table, spilling my coffee into the huge saucer.

"Oops. Sorry." She untangled her feet, planting both soles on the ground. "That was Belle and Adam from work. Do you remember them? They're on a day's training course with only an hour for lunch. How random that I bumped into them."

Jason's frown mirrored my own. The names were familiar but I couldn't place them among the few colleagues she'd mentioned. Sifting through memories, my optimism dissipated. They were from her old job, the one she'd left to move to Torringham. I'd never met Belle or Adam but they'd featured in her Facebook photos. Smiling young people out on the town, clutching Prosecco or gin concoctions. Emily's favourite tipples. Not that she got much chance to go out partying now, unless a trip to the pub with Jason and I counted.

"A long way to come for the day," Jason said.

"Adam's such an idiot. He ticked the Exeter box on the form instead of Coventry and couldn't change it. Belle's not impressed as they left at five this morning." Grinning, she bounced the chair round to face me. "It's so lovely to see them again. We had the most amazing catch-up."

Smiling, I squeezed her arm. It was wonderful to see her bubbling in delight but I wished she had local friends to get

32

enthusiastic about. It was tough being a young person in a new town, too old for college, too young for interest groups other than sports and Emily could never be classed as a sporty type. More than once, I'd wondered how I could help her develop a social life, but it wasn't in my gift to do so. We'd encouraged both her and Lucy, her step-sister, to come down but Lucy, being that bit older, had been unconvinced by our tales of a wonderful life in Devon. Emily had reluctantly agreed to come, more worried about being left behind than eager for a new start. Although Lucy and I had our challenges, at least if she'd joined us, they could have gone out together.

We decided to stay for lunch, enjoying the view and the gentle hubbub, while Emily chatted about her friends and reminisced about the daft things they'd done at work, the hilarious parties and strange boyfriends. Jason and I didn't manage to get a word in, but we didn't mind. Emily said more in an hour than she seemed to have done since we'd moved down and it was a joy to hear.

Like flicking through a family photo album, her stories created different memories for each of us and I remembered with a pang the lovely friends we'd left behind. Seeing them each day on Facebook made me forget that two hundred miles stretched between us, especially when we'd been so busy at the guesthouse. But, unlike Emily, we had the luxury of open-hearted friends here such as Shona and Kim, who took an interest in Emily too. But the day couldn't come soon enough when she'd arrive home babbling in excitement about her new friends.

When we left, we linked arms and the three of us strode together – in size order, with me at one end and Jason at the other – until we were forced apart by the mass of shoppers in the High Street. Later, like Christmas, we stumbled back to the car, tripping over heavy shopping bags. Sadly, this time mine and Jason's were filled with towels for the guesthouse rather than presents but Emily had done well with a bargain pair of trainers and a gorgeous summer cocktail dress. My heart ached as she'd held it aloft, wistfully debating the wisdom of spending money on something she'd never get to wear unless she took a trip back home.

Home. I didn't correct her.

"Or a nice meal out with us?" But I'd thrown crumbs in comparison to a night out with young, fun-loving friends.

As we got back into the car, Emily sighed. "If only we hadn't moved. I mean it's pretty down here, but I do miss everyone."

♦

A few nights later, there was a tap on the bedroom door and a hissed "Mum!". Emily's voice! Something serious must have happened for her to knock at midnight. Half-asleep, I switched on the bedside lamp and stumbled out of bed. Beside me, Jason jerked upright, blinking.

"Hold on!" I whispered. Buzzing with anxiety, I pulled the door open and blinked at the brightness of the landing light.

Barefoot in her pyjamas, Emily stood wide-eyed with alarm. Jason stepped beside me, his hand resting on my shoulder.

I kept my voice low, conscious that guests would be sleeping. "Is everything okay?"

Emily swung round, as if something had tapped her back. "Can't you hear it?"

Nothing, except for faint snoring from a nearby room. But then a thud reverberated through the ceiling, followed by another.

"I think someone's having sex on the stairs," Emily said in a voice too loud for comfort. "They've been bumping up and down for ages."

Surely not? Especially when there was a cosy bed for them. But that was most likely my boring, married view of life. When the ceiling shuddered again – as if something had been dropped from a height – it became doubtful that it was a close encounter of that kind. Even so, when Jason followed me out, I found myself gesturing for him to go back. The last thing anyone needed was an audience, no matter what they were doing.

Nerves mounting, I crept up the stairs to the second floor. The couple couldn't be seen as they were hidden behind a painted board which had been put up years ago to cover the spindles. Why? I had no idea. The sixties had been a harsh time for this house, with many of the original features removed, covered in woodchip or clad in hardboard.

About halfway up the second flight there was a small landing area where the stairs split in two, one section going to the rooms at the front of the house, the other to the rear. As I clutched the newel post to pull myself around the corner, something large flew across my path, landing with a thump on the opposite side of the stairway. I leapt back, finding myself balancing on the lip of a stair. My heart thudded. Thank goodness for my tight grip on the post. It was a long way back down.

As her friend cackled, the woman spun round grinning. Daphne! Which meant the one hidden from view must be her sister, Gloria. In the half-light from the landing below, Daphne appeared to be wearing a pink winceyette nightie, not too dissimilar to the floral garment favoured by my nan in the seventies. Not that I could talk. My comfy pyjamas had been bought at M&S the previous decade, while the ones Jason had bought in the hope of banishing these to the bin lay unloved at the back of the drawer. Like old shoes these fit like air. Although, viewing my pyjamas through the eyes of a stranger, I could see Jason had a point, particularly as the cotton frills had become straggles and there was a hole – thankfully small – over my bust.

"Now your..." Daphne pointed at her sister, but as her eyes

locked with mine her smile faded. She sat down on the step, clutching her nightie round her knees like a young girl, rather than the sixty-year-old she must be. Then, as if she'd had a secret conversation with herself, she chuckled and spoke in a voice thick with alcohol. "We've been flying. From there." She pointed to where Gloria must be sitting. "To here."

Popping my head around the corner, I found Gloria curled over, head in hands, shoulders shaking. A hiccoughed giggle escaped from her huddled form. She looked so funny and the thought of two older women finding so much amusement in jumping across the landing, tickled me. But the sensible B&B landlady came to the fore and I scratched my nose to mask my smile. Behind Gloria the two guest rooms remained in darkness, without the telling strips of light shining beneath the doors. How the other guests had slept through the noise, goodness knows. But we might have done so if Emily hadn't woken us.

"Do you think it's time for bed?" I whispered.

Without saying a word, they scurried back to their bedroom but, as the door closed, one of them snorted with laughter, shushed loudly by the other. I didn't envy their hangovers the next day.

♦

Biting her lip, Gloria hesitated by the breakfast room door. After handing two full Englishes to a young couple, I waved her in. Not meeting anyone's eyes she dashed across the room to take a seat at a table in the farthest corner, where she picked up the menu and sat huddled behind it. When I went over, she kept her head down, showing her crown which appeared to have been licked by a herd of cows facing in different directions.

Wide eyed, she whispered in her gentle Welsh lilt, "I'm so sorry about last night." She nodded towards the other guests. "Did we upset them?"

"They haven't said a word. Where's Daphne?"

"She won't come down. But I needed toast. And black coffee."

My hangover prediction the previous night had come to pass. "She's staying in the room?"

"Says she's not coming out all day. She's mortified."

"There's no need. No one here minds." But Gloria's expression told me there was no persuading her.

All the other guests were eating or were chatting while they finished their coffee. With no one left to serve, I shot upstairs, but paused on reaching Daphne's door. Would she thank me for barging in and dragging her downstairs? Better that than sitting alone too scared to face the other guests who, even if they'd heard the noise, had no idea who'd made it.

I rapped on the door. No answer but the sound of the TV filtered from the room. The second knock hurt my knuckles, but it worked as Daphne called out, "Is that you, Gloria? The door's on the catch."

"It's me."

Not waiting for a response, I pushed the door ajar, to be met by the scent of new carpet which we'd had fitted the previous week. Thankfully, Gloria and Daphne had told me they loved the smell.

In a pose reminiscent of the previous night, Daphne sat on her bed, arms around her knees, pillows plumped behind her, but this morning her nightie sat folded at the foot of the bed, substituted for a pair of jeans and a stripy top. Beside her, a novel lay spread-eagled on the bed, its bowed spine lined and worn. Stephen King. I wouldn't have boxed Daphne as a horror fan but the adage about not judging books most definitely applied to guests.

As I wandered over, her cheeks reddened and she dug pink-varnished toes into the duvet. She jabbed the remote control towards the TV to lower the volume.

37

"I'm sorry about last night."

"Gloria says you won't come down."

"I can't, I just can't."

She shook her head and folded her arms like a stubborn child but her reluctance stemmed from embarrassment rather than obstinacy. With little time to spare as the other guests might want refills or their plates cleared away, I went for every angle.

"No one has mentioned last night. They wouldn't have an idea who it was anyhow and Gloria's down there, sitting alone and I know she'd love you to join her. Even if you just want toast and coffee. Please." When she didn't move, I added, "I've got to go back but it would be lovely if you'd come with me. We'll walk in together."

Her teeth nipped the edge of her lip. "As long as you're sure no one will mind."

She shuffled across the duvet and eased her feet into a pair of sandals tucked beside the bedside table. Taking a deep breath, she stood up.

"We'll be good tonight. No more wine."

I smiled. "You're on holiday. Wine is allowed."

"Okay." She chuckled. "Just maybe not a whole bottle."

Chapter 5

CURTAINS DRAWN, EMILY LAY IN the darkened room, her tresses draped across the pillow like a fairytale princess. Except, this one had lost her lustre. I threw the curtains open to let the beautiful May sunshine flood the room, but she groaned and dragged the duvet over her, pinning it down, so only the top of her head and fingers could be seen. If I could see her face we could have a chat, but it was difficult talking to an unresponsive wall of bedding.

Dust speckles floated through shafts of light, meandering down to join what seemed like a month's worth of their friends. I smeared my finger across her bedside table, rewarded with a telltale grey streak while its counterpart strip gleamed bright against the dusty oak top. Even Emily's ipad lay buried under a heap of receipts and a crumpled pay slip. I fought back the gnawing anxiety. She wasn't talking to her friends either. It wasn't healthy to be spending her day off stuck inside alone. Not when a warm sun and a blue sky beckoned.

"You need to get up." I patted the hump I assumed to be her leg. It sprang from my touch, shifting to the other side of the bed.

"Go away! What's the point?"

"We're going for a walk. To the beach. We haven't got any check-ins today."

She turned away, twisting the duvet around her like a wrung towel. One that needed to be unwrapped with care. I hesitated, swallowing words that might wind her up further, instead plumping for the safer option of food.

"I'll shout you an ice cream. Salted caramel."

Defeated by the wall of silence, I sighed and headed back downstairs, entering the lounge to be blasted by an excited commentator and Jason bouncing up-and-down on the settee.

"Yes!" He punched his fist in the air. "Two-one to England with minutes to go!"

"Emily won't get out of bed."

He took his eyes from the screen to utter, "Again?" His gaze slid back to the figures tracking a ball of air across the pitch.

It had been Jason's idea to go for a walk. I'd wanted to catch up on the ironing but he'd pointed out that a day without any arrivals was a luxury and we should be making the most of it. Also, we could entice Emily out by dangling a trip to the beach in front of her. She'd love that, he'd said.

I'd failed to sell it to her but he might do better than me. After all, he'd been the salesman in his previous job. It helped that she idolised him too.

"Can you speak to her?"

"Okay." But he didn't budge.

The seconds ticked on screen. I willed them to whizz faster. As a whistle blew and cheers rang out, Jason slapped his knees and got to his feet. "Right. I'll go and see her."

He disappeared, leaving me to cross my fingers in hope. I hated seeing the changes in Emily over the past weeks as she'd morphed from our bubbly girl to a listless, monosyllabic being. The more we pressed her to go out, the more she wedged herself within a world that had condensed to little more than her job and bedroom. When asked how work had been, she snarled. When we suggested a night at the cinema, she shook her head. Food worked, if taken to her room.

I loved her so much. I wanted – needed – her to be happy in our new life and look forward with us. But she clung to the past like her first day at school, when she'd clasped my legs and tearfully begged to be taken home. Except Torringham was our chosen home. If only it could be hers.

After what seemed like an age – probably more like ten minutes

– I jumped up, determined to join them, but promptly thumped back down. Jason needed space. Three would be a crowd. I opened the laptop to check our emails, my eyes fluttering over the words, unable to absorb them as I strained to hear the slightest noise that would suggest success or failure.

When the door creaked open and Jason stooped beneath the frame, my heart sank. He was alone. But he broke into a smile.

"She's joining us. On condition that we don't nag her about life or mention the 'w' word."

Puzzled, I stared at him.

"Work. To say she hates her job is an understatement."

"How did you get her to agree?"

"I pointed out the obvious. She's young without a mortgage to worry about. She can do almost anything, so why is she staying somewhere she hates so much?"

"A new job would be…" Interrupted by the door clicking open, I smiled at Emily. A pair of dark sunglasses nestled beneath her fringe, masking her eyes. She didn't return my smile.

♦

Over the next few days the tense atmosphere began to uncoil, until a week later Emily offered to help unload the dishwasher. When one of her favourite songs came on, she turned the radio up a notch and started to sing, drawing a dessert spoon from the basket to use as a microphone. At the chorus, she pointed to me, indicating I should join in. I leaned towards her spoon and howled (I can't sing!) 'whoooo-whoooo, yeah'.

I'd grabbed my own spoon, preparing for the chorus rerun, when Jason raced into the kitchen flapping his arms and hissing, "Keep it down! A guest has just asked if we've got a dog."

As he retreated outside, Emily's spoon clattered onto the

worktop. "That's the problem with this place."

Deprived of our backing vocals, the radio moved on to playing a dreary number, while we filled the dishwasher in silence. As Emily poured the dregs from the mugs, I upended them onto the rack, moving onto the glasses. Our mini production line soon had the job done and as the dishwasher clicked shut, I grinned at Emily.

"Thank you."

"I don't know how you do it," she said.

"What?"

"This! It's not a home is it?" She gazed around the kitchen, her eyes alighting on the food safety signage, the temperature charts on the board, the fire extinguisher and blanket in the corner. Ignoring its correct placement on the other side of the kitchen, she hooked the tea towel over the oven handle. "I think Dad's right."

Before I could respond, she picked up her mobile which vibrated on the side. "How spooky is that? It's Lucy." She headed out of the room. "Luce! You wouldn't believe it."

Puzzled, I rewound the conversation. What had Jason said? I headed outside to accost Jason on the driveway, where he knelt clearing the moss and weeds from between the block paving slabs. After the guests left tomorrow, the driveway would be clear for a few hours, giving him space to paint white lines for the parking bays.

"Have you been speaking to Emily?"

"A dozen times a day. Sometimes more."

I jabbed his thigh with the toe of my shoe. "Be serious. She said you're right about something, so what have you being talking about?"

"I've no idea but I'm sure she's right about me being right."

I shook my head. Sometimes his humour annoyed me. This was one of those times.

"Okay, when you spoke to Emily did you mention anything

about Lucy?"

His dirt-encrusted fingernails scratched his chin. "Like I told you the other day, I just said she'd be much happier if she changed her job. Why? Is Lucy thinking of moving here too?"

A jolt of surprise shook me. That would make sense. It would be good for Emily and Jason to have Lucy around, but what would it mean for me? Lucy was lovely but...

I swallowed, unable to clarify my feelings.

Frowning, Jason scrutinised my face, so I flashed him a perfect smile. "That would be nice."

He sighed and stabbed his trowel into a dandelion. "Could you sound any less enthusiastic?"

♦

Later that afternoon, I tapped on Emily's door to be welcomed with a grunt. She lay on the bed, her ipad held above her glowing face. Stepping over a pair of shoes scattered across the floor, my agitation got the better of me and I turned back to place them neatly beside a box scrawled 'Emily's bedroom' in thick marker pen. The words had been enclosed with squiggles and a band of crosses. Kisses perhaps? But whatever was inside couldn't be important as the packing tape hadn't been removed.

"Have you got time to chat?"

Sighing, she placed her ipad on the bedside table, next to an unopened box of butterfly string lights I'd bought to decorate her room. As I took a seat at the end of her bed, she plumped up the pillows and shuffled upright.

"How is Lucy?"

"Okay."

"That's good." I hesitated. If I wanted to find out what she'd meant earlier, beating around the bush wasn't going to draw it out.

"You mentioned what your dad said. And about Lucy."

Her eyes darted to meet mine but she flushed and looked away. "I- I was going to tell you later." She picked at a thread on the duvet. "When Dad talked about doing something to be happy rather than just sitting around moaning, I spoke to Lucy."

Jason's guess had been correct. Lucy would be moving here. I quelled the instinctive burst of anxiety. From a young age, Lucy had reminded me of a porcupine, firing quills out when threatened or angry. Being the interloper meant I was often the target of her barbs. But that didn't excuse me for not trying harder, especially being her step-mum and the adult in the relationship. Instead I'd allowed myself to be a prickly hedgehog, who curled into a ball of defence while Jason dealt with her. So, our relationship had never matured and while Lucy had become a gorgeous and independent woman, I couldn't tell her that. What had started as a safety fence had been built into an impenetrable barrier between us. I wished I knew how to knock it down.

"When is she coming?"

Emily's head jerked up. "You know! How?"

"You just said." I faltered. "Didn't you?"

The small shake of her head answered me. We sat in silence, each uncertain of our next move until she took a deep breath. "Please listen and don't say anything until I've finished. You know I met my friends from work? Well, I've been chatting to them. It hasn't worked out with the new person who took over my role, so they asked me back and offered me a promotion too. I'll take on part of the office manager's work. It's more money."

She missed her friends. I understood how she felt. Like her I found myself awkward in new company. Thank goodness for our ready-made network of welcoming B&Bers or, like her, I might be focusing on opportunities afforded by the past.

She gazed at me expectantly. She wanted to be told to go ahead and not to worry about us here. And I would. Once my crashing emotions had subsided. We'd chosen to move, towing her with us after asking her to give it a chance. But would she be any better back 'home'? While Lucy lived near Normansby and her mother, Jason's ex, would be on hand for emergencies, we had no other family to offer Emily. No doting grandparents or aunts and uncles, except for the accidental rediscovery of Uncle Bert. But he lived in Devon.

I swallowed. "You're going back. Where will you stay?"

"Lucy's offered me a room."

"What about her flatmate. Where will you sleep?"

"Don't worry, Mum." Emily's smile wavered. "He's gone. I'm moving in next week."

I jerked back in shock. The date was set! This would be happening. But my fear began to ebb. My relationship with Lucy may be strained but she was sensible and loved her sister. I'd miss Emily – more than words could say – but, no matter how much it would hurt to see her go, I wouldn't try to stop her.

"How will you move all your things?"

Two packing boxes sat by the wall. One had become a table of sorts, piled with a mound of books, some littering the floor, while various garments were strewn over the one with the crosses/kisses. Emily crawled across the bed to grab her jacket from where it had been slung over the corner of the box. As she dragged it off, a couple of tops slid to the floor, most likely to stay there until she moved out. She reached into the pocket and handed me a letter.

"Look it's all there. The pay rise and all. They're even offering to put towards my travel expenses back. But I don't need much more than Lucy's petrol money. She's coming down next weekend to fetch me."

The letter was dated from last week. Just a few days after Jason spoke to her. She'd worked fast.

She misread the look on my face, adding, "Don't worry. She can stay in my room. I know you're full."

"So, between you it's all sorted." I didn't mean to sound crabby. After all, Jason had all but told her to go. Not that he knew that his suggestion to change her job had been taken a stage further. "Have you told your dad?"

"Not yet," she said. "I was sort-of hoping you'd do that."

Chapter 6

SHONA AND KIM'S B&B FEATURED a Buddha statue on the front page of its website. I'd wondered why until I walked into their hallway to find it the centrepiece of their reception table draped by trails of ivy that sat in a pot on the shelf above. When Shona told me she had enough to do and was buggered if she was adding another plant to her list, I'd been surprised to learn the ivy was fake. Later, I'd rubbed the leaves to check, rewarded by an imperceptible smear of dust and the definite feel of plastic.

As usual, Jason snuck a few of the humbugs from the bowl in front of Buddha. I gave him a look rarely used since Emily and Lucy had grown too old to be reprimanded but he smiled sweetly at me and sauntered through to the lounge.

"How is it going?" Kim said.

A tray sat on the coffee table heaped with mugs, a jug and teapot and a plate of chocolate biscuits. After Kim had phoned to invite us round, she must have shot through to the kitchen to get everything ready, knowing that when I said we'd be two minutes I meant it, especially as we had to get to the butchers before it closed.

Not for the first time, I dropped onto the settee only to find my knees higher than my backside as the cushion ended up embedded in the springs below. Jason's two previous offers to mend the broken supports had been waved aside by Shona and Kim.

"We're getting that sorted," Shona said as I extracted myself from the dip to plug the gap with a couple of small cushions. "We've got a bit of plywood."

Kim handed me a mug of tea. "Is it this weekend Lucy is leaving?"

Shona slurped her tea and grimaced. As she reached across for the sugar pot, she said, "We'll have to do something nice for her. Maybe a small party."

I took a hurried sip to stop myself blurting my feelings. I dreaded the coming weekend. Unlike a Uni student, there was no promise of a return after each term or a homecoming at the end. The chances of Emily moving back to Torringham in the future were practically zero. From now on, our relationship would be the occasional break when either of us could get away or via Skype. Worse, if she met someone I could end up being a virtual grandparent too. *Stop it!* Was I really worrying about grandchildren when Emily was just twenty? I needed a change of subject.

"I found two pairs of tights tied to the bed frame this morning."

"That's nothing." Shona strolled over to the cabinet, coming back with a cerise-coloured thing in a see-through bag. As she laid it on the coffee table, she burst into an uncontrollable fit of giggles while Kim buried her face in her hands. Jason and I shrugged at each other in confusion, but we had no choice than to wait until they were both in a state to talk.

"Kim's aunt left it behind this morning. She's like nearly seventy odd and goes to church and – you won't believe this bit – she asked for twin beds for her and her new boyfriend."

"Is it an asthma inhaler?" Jason said.

"An asthma inhaler!" Shona screeched, now bent over double with laughter. "What are you like?"

Even I could tell the pink curvy thing wasn't an inhaler although it did have some similarity: both had white bits that jutted out, although this one had a smaller and rounder tip. Shona's reaction gave me an inkling what it might be, although I couldn't for the life of me work out what it did.

Kim broke through Shona's cackling. "Going to church doesn't stop her having fun. I mean this is the twenty-first century."

"But your auntie of all people!" Shona clutched her chest and fell back into the sofa. "Oh my days. I'll never be able to face her again without laughing."

"Well pity me," Kim said. "I'll never be able to look at my mum the same way again either."

"They're identical twins," Shona said. "Hey, Kim. When your mum comes down, we'll have to check her drawers." Then she squealed. "Drawers! Geddit?"

It was annoying being on the outside of a joke, not quite getting it but not wishing to look stupid by admitting it either. I guessed it was a sex toy but nothing like your typical vibrator. I'd seen enough of them from the Ann Summers parties that were all the rage a few decades ago. Thankfully, Jason butted in.

"So, come on, what is it?"

"It's an expensive little sucker." Shona laughed. "Gives the best-ever orgasm apparently. Hope it didn't disappoint Auntie as we know she likes the best of everything."

"It's a clitoral stimulator," Kim said, an edge of primness to her voice. "And if Shona doesn't stop going on, I'll empty her drawers out and see how she likes it. You should see some of the things she has."

"I'm not ashamed," Shona said. "Unlike your auntie, I am what it says on the tin."

"Beans? Full of hot air?" Kim turned to us. "Now about Emily. I like Shona's idea for a party."

♦

We left their B&B, wishing I hadn't mentioned our need to pick up the butcher's order before it closed at five.

"You'll be going past the post office," Shona had said. "Do us a favour. If I package it up can you take it for us?"

The weather forecasters had promised a beautiful spring day and their predictions were proved right as the late afternoon sun warmed our faces and the gentle breeze blew away the cobwebs of a day spent indoors, albeit in two places. We slalomed past clumps of tourists, who meandered through the street weighed down by towels and buckets after a day at the beach, oblivious to our need to make it to the post office and butchers before they closed. A group nestled by the windows of the knick-knack shop, some obscuring the entrance to the butchers so, at first heart-stopping glance, it looked as though he'd closed early for the day. Thankfully, the butchers seemed to be the only empty place in Torringham so we were in and out within minutes. Our luck didn't last. As we took our places at the back of a post office queue that stretched into the main aisle of the grocery store, we cursed Shona.

"I hope we get to the front before closing time," Jason said.

"I hope they don't ask what's inside this," I said.

"You worry too much. Why would they?"

I glanced at the name on the package. Hilda Martin. Strange how names could be used to label people. Hilda: twin-set, pearls, sensible shoes. Certainly not a clitoral-stimulator type. Now, if she'd been called Candice that might be different. What about Katie? Did that fit more with Hilda or did I sit in the Candice camp? Maybe it was more of an age thing? No one would think it odd if a twenty-year-old Hilda went into Ann Summers, although I couldn't imagine there were many young Hildas out there. But, why shouldn't older people enjoy themselves? While Jason and I weren't exactly young at fifty, I could imagine Emily's expression if she found a sex toy in our room. Eeuww.

"Why are you grinning?" Jason asked.

"I'm not." I looked away, finding myself facing a row of tinned beans.

We reached the counter with minutes to spare before closing time. The woman sighed as she glanced at the clock on the wall. I felt for her. She looked like it had been a long day but I wouldn't be the one to tell her that. After I'd weighed the package as she requested, I slid it into the tray.

"What's inside this?" the woman asked.

"Eh?" I turned to Jason but he'd slipped away to sit by the information stand, from where he gave me a little wave.

"I need to know what's inside it," the woman repeated. "You can't post it otherwise."

I sent a silent plea of help to Jason, who smirked from the corner. There'd be no aid from him. My face burned as I wondered what I should call the pink sucking thing other than a sex toy. Behind me someone sniggered.

"Does it contain batteries?" she asked.

I couldn't believe how my cheeks could be this hot and not burst into flame. "Um, I don't know."

"If it contains batteries, you'll have to open the package and take them out."

No way would I be touching that thing. "I remember now." I gave her an enlightened look. "It's got a separate charging unit just like a shaver."

The woman settled back into her chair, satisfied by my response, even if she didn't believe it. When Jason cupped his hands and mouthed 'liar' at me, I showed him my clenched fist, making sure it was hidden from the woman's view. The stragglers in the queue didn't bother to mask their beaming smiles. They'd be feasting out on this story for days to come. When she handed me my change, I stomped out of the shop not waiting for Jason, but I hadn't got far before I felt his Cheshire cat grin hovering over my shoulder.

I jerked to a halt outside the book store and jabbed his chest. "Coward! I can't believe you left me to it."

"I'm not stupid," he said. "Everyone knows they have to ask what's inside a parcel. Why do you think Shona was so keen for you to take it?"

"I'm going to kill her," I said. "Next time she can shove her sex toys where…"

The man gazing through the book store window swung round, shooting me an odd look.

"Hello, Mr Anderson," I said to our guest. "Are you and Mrs Anderson having a nice day?"

Chapter 7

LUCY PULLED UP IN A NEW FIAT, white with black go-faster stripes down the sides. The fan whirred noisily and dead flies littered the bonnet. Maybe the stripes had worked as the trip had taken just over four hours, a record for Lucy, who'd been given the nickname 'Driving Miss Daisy' by Emily after she barely reached fifty going down Telegraph Hill.

Jason and I waited on the driveway while she staged a sit-in, pulling down the sun visor, leaning across to the glove compartment and generally faffing about. Emily had the right idea. She'd gone for a shower, saying she'd be down when Lucy got settled.

"I guess they haven't discussed the amount of luggage there is to take back," Jason said.

"Obviously not. I have a feeling Emily's in for a shock when she realises she can only take half her junk."

"Less than that." Jason nodded towards Lucy. From her Tardis boot she dragged a suitcase that could fit a month's worth of clothes and still have space.

"Are you moving in?" he called.

"Very funny, Dad." She hefted the case onto the driveway. "Give me a hand."

"This one or this one?" He held out one hand and then the other which she slapped away, laughing.

"You're so silly!"

I hung back, giving them space. They were so easy together. After a few minutes I went over but, like a teacher walking into a raucous classroom, my entrance killed the laughter and my buried unease resurfaced.

"Lucy. How lovely to see you!" I even managed to sound like a school teacher.

Both Jason and I had short-lived first marriages – mine childless – so she'd been just seven when we first met. My memory of that encounter remains hazy – I'd been so nervous – but I'd never forgotten her huge yellow Alice band covering her zigzag parting and her uneven pigtails, which had a strange boss-eyed look when viewed from behind. No doubt the fact she wore the same hairstyle for the next few years aided my recollection.

"She's very independent and won't let anyone touch her hair," Jason had confided later.

But at the time she'd clung to her dad's leg and smiled shyly, showing the huge gravestone teeth all children seem to have at that age. Sadly, Lucy and I hadn't outgrown the awkward stage. No matter how much I tried, I didn't feel like a mum to her.

She air-kissed my cheeks. "How are you doing?"

"I'm good, thanks. You're looking well." She did too. She'd had a tint put on her dark hair so it burnished auburn in the sunlight. Like Jason's, her eyes were steel grey but they glinted with warmth when she smiled. Even after a stifling journey in the car the tang of fresh perfume wafted around her, which might explain what she was doing in the glove compartment. I handed her the pass. "Here, let your dad take your case while you park. We've put you in room seven. It's a lovely room."

She glanced across to Jason, who pointed across the road to the small public car park. "We've got someone else coming onto the drive. You're just over there. Put the pass on your dashboard."

While he dragged her case into the guesthouse, I headed over the road, where I loitered by Lucy's car while she did goodness-knows-what in her glove compartment. When she got out, she seemed surprised to find me there.

"Sorry, I'd have been quicker if I'd realised you were waiting."

I bit back the urge to laugh and say, 'Oh yeah!' as I would have done with Emily. Instead, my tongue stuck to the roof of my mouth fearful of saying something that would crack our eggshell relationship. While Lucy may have taken it as a joke, I couldn't risk offending her. I'd forgotten how stilted we were together. It wasn't her. She was a lovely woman. I simply didn't know what to talk about and, when I did speak, my size fives would land me in it.

Oh no! I'd done it again. I shuddered. Only days ago, she'd posted a newspaper article on Facebook which revealed that when people say, 'you're looking well', it really means, 'you're looking a bit plumper than usual'. Within moments of her arriving today, I'd told her that. But she was looking well. My face burned. I felt for the step-mothers in fairy tales. Maybe they weren't all that bad and just had foot-in-mouth disease like me.

In silence we reached the front door of the guesthouse. As I turned the key in the lock, I said, "You're not looking well fat, you're looking well lovely."

She smiled, probably thinking I'd gone mad. And she'd be right. My awkwardness had shifted up a gear, with no reverse. The stairs creaked and to my relief Jason padded down.

"I'll put the kettle on," I said. It gave me something to do and gave them a chance to talk in peace too.

◆

When Shona and Kim had mentioned the possibility of doing a little goodbye party for Emily – just before they sent me off to the post office with that sex toy – I hadn't thought they'd go through with it. But, true to their word, she and Kim had arranged a gathering that mainly comprised fellow B&Bers but also one or two of Emily's bemused ex-colleagues.

"Aren't you worried about upsetting your guests?" I'd asked but she'd shrugged.

"We've got regulars in. They can always join us."

As the night moved on, I learned two things. First, never to be alone with Raymond, the owner of Waves B&B, and his octopus hands. I'd wriggled free to take refuge by Jason in the kitchen where he stood discussing cars with Mike, but there was only so much talk about horse power I could take. Even dancing with Raymond started to seem the more attractive option.

Second, that Emily was a loving drunk. Throughout the evening, she'd come – when I'd escaped from Raymond – to give me a cuddle. She clung to me now, her breath ripe with the smell of vodka and hot against my neck.

"I love you, Mum. I'm going to miss you soooo much."

"Me too, darling," I said for the umpteenth time. But each no less heartfelt. I'd miss her grumpiness, especially in the morning; her laughter and dry sense of humour; her singing in the shower, although not having her screeching her latest favourite song would be a blessing when guests were in the room above. I'd miss her. Full stop.

Shona waved us over to join her and Lucy in the *Cha-Cha Slide* with some of the other B&Bers. Strange how the girls loved joining in with the corny songs and dances. They were great at them too, while I couldn't help but mess up the moves, either facing the wrong way or banging into someone as I slid to the right instead of the left. When Raymond crept back into the group and slowly angled his way towards me, I took my cue to disappear for a breather, first asking Shona to make sure he didn't pester Emily or Lucy.

The night air cooled my flushed cheeks. I hid in the shadows by the house, rather than within the cone of light from the street lamp, in case Raymond appeared. Above, the moon peaked from a patch of glowing cloud, brightening the inky sky. I sat fascinated – helped by the half bottle of Malbec I'd polished off – as a cloud slowly drifted away, revealing the moon's grinning face. I smiled back.

Behind me the front door opened and a chanted 'Hey Macarena' flooded into the night, muted again as the door banged shut. Lucy tottered out, unsteady on her feet. Not hearing me call 'Hi', she slumped against the wall on the other side of the driveway where she rifled through her bag.

"Where have I put them," she muttered.

I heard a chink, followed by an angry curse. She'd hate it if she thought I was spying on her, so I spoke louder this time. "Hi."

"Katie?" She jerked upright, but she didn't spot me. Her tone was deep, blurred by drink. "I've dropped my lighter."

Lighter? I didn't know she smoked. Beneath the street lamp, I spotted a glimmer of metal on the gravel drive and handed the lighter to her. She flicked it into life, the flame reflecting in her shining eyes. As she took a deep lug, I gazed at the burning tip. Why would a woman in her mid-twenties start smoking? Wasn't that a teenager thing? And Lucy had always been so sensible too.

"When did you start smoking?"

She swung round to face me but lost her balance and staggered back into a wheelie bin, thankfully full enough to withstand her weight. Clutching the wall, she pulled herself upright, her head following her body, which gave her an odd arched movement, as if she was lifting herself out of the crab position. A childhood favourite of hers. She jabbed her cigarette at me, keeping one hand planted on the wall.

"Are you judging me?" Her pitch had risen. "You have no idea why I smoke. Look at yourself first. You only gave up a few years back."

"I'm not judging you." I wished I didn't sound so prissy. And what did she mean by 'look at yourself first'? I didn't dare ask, certain it related to more than my ex-smoking habit.

She took a drag of her cigarette, drawing so hard her cheeks hollowed, the shadows lending her an almost skeletal appearance. Lovely but stubborn Lucy. I wished I could hug her but instead I stood there, desperately thinking of something to break the silence that engulfed us. She took another lug and threw the cigarette down, grinding it into the gravel.

"Are you going back in?" I couldn't think what else to say. This was one of the few times I wished I still smoked. I could have asked Lucy for a conspiratorial cigarette.

She couldn't have heard as she lurched off, not stopping even when her heel buckled to one side on the stones. Then I remembered! I could ask about her boyfriend. But the click of the front door told me I'd left it too late.

The faint strains of *Oops Upside Your Head* filtered out. Not one of my favourite songs but something to guarantee a laugh at a party. I'd go back inside and dance with Emily and Lucy. Everyone would be sitting in a row, swaying forwards and backwards, patting the floor on each side.

As I headed to the front door, it opened and Jason stepped out. He didn't smile.

"What are you playing at upsetting Lucy?"

"I didn't."

"I rarely see her. It wouldn't have hurt for you to make an effort to be nice, especially with everything she's going through."

"Eh?"

But before I could question him, he disappeared inside. What on earth had Lucy said? Confused, I reeled our conversation back, but I couldn't see how I'd upset her enough to cause Jason to be angry. And what did he mean about Lucy? I had no idea she'd been having problems. But why would I? I'd chosen to stand on the touchline of her life, so I couldn't expect to be handed the ball.

Someone had turned the music up. The thumping beat vibrated, interspersed by occasional shouts and the sound of laughter. I couldn't face going inside. Not now. People would wonder why I'd left but better that than causing more upset.

With Emily, I'd try to talk through any issues even if I had to tread carefully. I should treat Lucy the same. I'd speak to her tomorrow, once we'd all sobered up. Jason and I had two girls. It was high time I stepped up to the plate for both of them.

Chapter 8

JASON APPEARED FIVE MINUTES BEFORE breakfast started. After spending much of the night stewing over his unwarranted outburst the previous evening, I'd half-hoped he wouldn't come down, although how I'd cook and serve breakfast for eight guests, I didn't know. It doesn't sound a lot, but breakfast is never a simple affair. There's the cold buffet, a range of hot options which are ordered on the morning to be cooked fresh, and as much toast and tea or coffee as people want. A full English involves pretty much every pan, especially when guests ask to change their eggs to poached or scrambled. So, when Jason staggered into the kitchen, I'd reached the conclusion that I'd rather see him than not.

That is, until he said, "It would have been nice for you to say goodbye."

"You had a pop at me for no reason."

"What? Being mean to Lucy?"

"I wasn't."

His harrumph in disbelief rankled me more than it should have done and I found myself ratcheting up the ante, refusing to speak to him, although from the point I opened the breakfast room door and the guests started to troop in, it was outward smiles. But hidden from view we stung each other with hissed barbs and the occasional bit of sign language in case guests heard us. Childish, I know, but sometimes sticking two fingers up at someone can be quite cathartic.

Neither Lucy or Emily had made it out of bed by the time we finished cleaning at one o'clock, so I took out the ironing board and started on the duvet covers until I heard the floorboards creaking in Lucy's room above. I gave myself a few minutes to finish the duvet while I worked up my courage. I had to do this. I'd promised I would speak to Lucy and there was no time like the present.

It took an age for her to come to the door.

"Hold on," she shouted on my first knock. I started to wonder if she'd forgotten me and was just about to knock again when the door clicked open. She peered through the gap.

"Yes?" she said, her tone cool.

"Can I come in?"

She hesitated but finally opened the door, flinging herself onto the bed like a sullen teenager. She'd thrown on a pair of jogging bottoms and a baggy t-shirt, the hem of which she wrung between her fingers. Her bare toes dug into the bedding. Nervous, like me.

I had to take care, unless I wanted a replay of the previous evening. I cleared my throat.

"I'm sorry about last night."

"Why?"

"I didn't mean to sound patronising or anything."

"Why would that be any different to usual?"

She locked eyes with mine, daring me to respond. Get it wrong and the bell would ring for round two. I sat down beside her – not too close – giving myself a moment to think. My hands nestled in my lap. They'd started to show signs of ageing and in daylight looked more like paper mâché than baby soft skin. With age came wrinkles, but it didn't always bring wisdom. I should know what to say. I should be kind and loving and perceptive.

But instead I found myself saying, "Oh for goodness' sake! Do you really think I'm going to say well done for smoking? I may only be your step-mum but I've known you since you were knee-high to a grasshopper. I really, really care about you. More than you know. And I do want to make things better between us. Like they should be."

We both fell silent. She drew up her legs and sat picking her toes, while my gaze dropped back to my hands. To my wedding ring. She'd been one of our bridesmaids. We'd had a job getting her to wear the pink, flouncy dress but coerced her with the promise of chocolate cake. She and Emily – then just a tot – had worn flowery pink bands but, as soon as the ceremony ended, Lucy had switched back to her favourite yellow Alice band. She kept the dress on though, enjoying the attention. It had been a wonderful day. I remember looking at her, Jason and Emily, and feeling hopeful for the future.

"I was just thinking about when your dad and I got married."

"Oh yeah."

"It was such a lovely time."

"For you," she said.

"How do you mean? Please tell me. I won't do my usual trick and go all school teachery on you." I hoped I'd said the right thing.

She resumed inspecting her feet, while I sat listening to the strange click-click of fingernail jabbing toenail and tried not to shudder.

"Funny enough I was just talking to Emily about it last night. The drink made me talk too much. If I don't tell you, no doubt she will. You know what she's like." She smiled and, for a moment, the shadows lifted from her face. "Not that it's a big deal. I feel a bit stupid talking about it to be honest."

"I'd really like to know."

She bit her lower lip and her eyes met mine. This time without a hint of challenge. "I was saying how it all fell apart after Dad got married. Not that your marriage had much to do with Pete leaving Mum."

I'd forgotten about that. Her mum had left Jason for Pete but a few months after our marriage, Pete ran off with another woman. Every time Jason went over to pick up Lucy, she would recount stories of eating cold beans on toast or opening her school lunch box to find a bag of crisps, a chocolate bar and a bottle of pop. It took Marie, her mum, months before she got herself back on track.

"Mum told me off for telling you, so I kept quiet after that." Lucy ripped away the jagged edge of her toenail and flicked it to the floor. "But, as I told Emily, she really fell apart. That's when she discovered gin. And then she went through an uncle's stage." She mimicked apostrophes with her fingers. "While I… well, I just wanted my dad home. I asked and asked but it never happened. Emily and you won."

Glancing at me, she blushed. "Sorry."

I shrugged and rested my hand on her shoulder. No need to apologise. Of course, a child would want their dad back home. I wouldn't hold that against her.

I vaguely remembered Jason mentioning more than once that he'd gone to pick up Lucy to find the house smelling like a distillery. Marie would say she'd had friends over the night before and they'd had a glass or two of wine while watching a film. As Jason only saw Lucy at weekends, we'd assumed Marie's nights were limited to those times, but obviously not.

"Anyhow, the past has happened, and mum is fine now but…" Hugging her legs, she fell silent.

I shifted over to cuddle her. At first, she resisted but then she sank into me. No wonder she'd been so reluctant to talk as a child. We'd let distance grow into a habit but, unlike me, she hadn't had a choice. I should have tried harder to be a loving parent rather than accepting the status quo.

"That was a lot for a young girl to keep hidden. You poor thing."

Should I mention what Jason had told me? It felt right. "Your dad said you were having a tough time at the moment."

Letting out a small laugh, she said, "He knows about the break-up with Josh but that's not the half of it. Look—" She shifted away to the edge of the bed. "I've said enough."

Josh, her boyfriend? I had no idea they'd broken up. She'd kept that off Facebook. Was our relationship so poor that I only knew things about her she was willing to tell the world? I knew the answer to that one and it didn't reflect well on me. Strange that Jason hadn't mentioned it though. Maybe he only found out last night? That would explain why he'd been so sensitive when he thought I'd had a go at Lucy.

I let my hand fall onto hers. "If I can help, I will."

She seemed to move beyond me, into a world of her own. I waited, not speaking, not moving, her hand hot beneath mine, until she whispered, "It's too late for that."

We jumped as someone rapped the door. "Can I come in?" Not waiting for an answer, the door opened and Jason popped his head inside.

"Dad!" Lucy jumped up. "I could have been undressed or something."

"What with Katie in here?" Jason kept his smile, even when his eyes met mine. "Kim and Shona called. As we haven't got any check-ins, I said we could all go for a walk. Emily's packed and ready. What time do you both need to get away?"

"Not until late afternoon," Lucy said. "Give me fifteen minutes to get sorted. It'll be nice to stretch my legs."

Masking my frustration, I left her to get changed. It would be great for us all to get out before the girls left but a group walk gave me little chance to be alone with Lucy. I needed to find out what she'd meant by 'too late'.

♦

The consensus was to head to Shadwell Point. Once away from the crowded harbourside and beach, we entered Shadwell Wood where we passed occasional walkers, some with dogs or children but all offering cheerful 'hellos'. Shona had planted herself between Lucy and Emily, while Kim walked with Jason, leaving me at the rear to admire the views while watching for opportunities to draw Lucy aside. Panting, we climbed wooden steps cut into the red earth. Here and there, tree roots clambered over rocks, unable to break through the hard ground, while the branches formed a canopy of green, shading us from the sun. As we reached the plateau I caught glimpses of the sparkling blue sea below. I stopped to admire the view, not realising I'd dropped so far behind until I heard laughter and sounds of 'Well caught' as Emily and Lucy saved Shona from a nasty fall. I hurried to catch up, meeting them at the edge of the woods, where they gazed out over the vast expanse of sea, dotted by trawlers and yachts and the hulk of a distant tanker.

"This makes me sad to be leaving," Emily said.

I squeezed her arm. "You can come back whenever you have a free weekend. Or for longer."

We set off with Jason falling beside Lucy, Shona with Kim, while Emily and I acted as the rear guard. We chatted about her going back to her old job and how she looked forward to catching up with her friends, until she said, "It'll be nice for me to spend more time with Lucy too."

"Especially after everything she's been through."

She peered at me over the rim of her sunglasses. "She told you about Josh?"

I couldn't lie to my daughter. "She just told me things couldn't be undone."

Frowning, she shifted her sunglasses back up her nose. For a moment I thought we'd reached the end of the conversation, until she added an ominous, "She's not wrong there. But it's not my place to say anything." She pointed towards the archway ahead of us. "I fancy an ice cream. Race you to it!"

To the sound of laughter – hers, not mine – she sprinted off, catching Lucy by the arm and dragging her ahead. I had to give her full marks for a deft change of subject. Most likely, she'd gone to warn Lucy that I'd asked about her, as they'd slowed to a walking pace thirty or so yards ahead of the group. I mulled over what I knew. Not only had Lucy split up with her boyfriend but there was more to it. Was he stalking her or causing other problems? I had no choice but to speak with Lucy again, especially as Emily would be moving in with her.

Arms linked, Lucy and Emily strolled beneath the huge stone arch of the fortifications built to protect England from the threat of invasion several centuries before. The first time we'd come here, we'd been stunned to find ourselves standing before what appeared to be a castle façade. Back then, Emily and Jason had dashed off to explore the cannons that nosed from the parapets but now she passed by with barely a glance, engrossed in conversation. I followed the others tip-toeing across the cattle grid, rather than taking ten steps more to the safer option through the gate. As I crossed beneath the archway, Kim waited for me.

"Shona's joined the girls for ice cream."

As we left the protective barrier of the wall and moved towards the open headland the wind buffeted us. Kim pulled a hairband from her pocket and twisted her braids into a bun to stop them whipping her face.

"You came prepared."

She laughed and rubbed her goose-pimpled arms. "Not enough to remember to bring a jacket. I'd forgotten what it can be like up here."

With Jason and the others queuing for ice creams, we strolled towards the headland. On either side of us, the land dropped away, one side a sheer drop protected by a stone wall, while the other sloped down to the sea, peppered by a jumble of squat trees and bushes hunched by the wind. We meandered along the brow of the slope, preferring the landscape of jagged headlands and rocky outcrops to the urban view of Torringham and the distant Berrinton which shimmered across the bay.

She nodded in the direction of the girls. "You left early last night. Are you stressed about them going?"

"Sorry for not saying goodbye."

She shrugged. "But you're okay. You're very quiet."

"To be honest, I'm a bit worried about Lucy. I need to speak with her before she leaves but I don't think they'll give me the chance."

Lucy and Emily came towards us, arms linked, ice creams in their free hands.

"Glued aren't they? But not for long."

I smiled at her. Many people would be curious to know the issue, but not lovely Kim, who'd put aside any inquisitiveness she felt to help me.

"Hey Shona!" She waved her over. "Go and chat to the girls," she told me. "We'll soon have them unstuck."

I headed over to Lucy and Emily. "It's lovely up here, isn't it?"

Wary looks passed between them but they joined in with my inane chatter about the weather and the view. When they finished their ice creams Shona broke between them, insisting on becoming the centre link in their chain, joined by Kim a moment later.

"Come on, Katie! Don't be boring!" She pulled me between herself and Lucy.

Our chain wandered on with Jason, tagging beside us, until I felt Kim's grip loosen. Lucy jerked round as the group broke apart and stretched out her hand in the hope of relinking.

"I wanted to ask you…"

She tried to yank her arm from mine.

"I know about Josh. It's more than just splitting up."

Her eyes widened. "Emily told you? Great!"

"No, but I want to hear it from the horse's mouth. Does your dad know?"

Her face paled and she flashed a glance at Jason. "Don't tell him. Please!"

She took my silence as agreement. Her mouth parted as she searched for words but seemed unable to find them. This wasn't fair. I shouldn't force her to tell me something that upset her so much. But, if this Josh was harassing her or worse, we had to help her and keep Emily safe too.

Her eyes glistened. "As you know Josh left me." I nodded. "It was because I was pregnant and he didn't want it."

A tear snaked from the corner of her eye which she dabbed with the heel of her palm. Behind us Kim stood with Jason, pointing out to sea, making sure he faced away from us.

My attention turned back to Lucy, pregnant and alone. I put my arm round her.

"When he left he said – well he sort-of said – that he'd come back if I got rid. So, I did."

She buried her face into my chest. I could feel her jerking sobs. "Don't tell anyone. They'll think I'm terrible. I didn't want to kill it."

Oh my! Poor, poor Lucy. As my surroundings blurred, I pulled her tight. Tears burned my cheeks. There was no going back on this, but we could help her move forward.

"No one will think badly of you," I said. "Not me, not your dad. No one."

She shot from my arms. "I don't want him to know."

"You need to speak to someone."

"Mum knows. And Emily." She hesitated. "And now you."

Marie knew. This morning I'd found out about Marie's drunkenness and how Lucy had kept it hidden. Now, I learned that Lucy's relationship with Marie had grown strong enough for her to trust and confide in her mum. I was glad for them. It also made me less worried about Emily. She wouldn't be there to support Lucy alone.

"I'm so sorry this has happened to you but, believe me, you've done nothing other than try to keep someone you loved."

"And I lost them both."

I gave her another cuddle, holding strong against a sudden squall. The others had reached the headland and Emily was frantically signalling for us to come over.

"Hurry up!" Her voice carried in the air.

"I won't say anything to your dad for now. But you told him about splitting up, so please trust him enough to tell him the rest. He loves you very much."

Lucy swiped her arm across her face and sniffed. Only her reddened eyes gave any idea of her swirling emotions. If anyone asked, we'd blame the wind.

As we neared the others, Emily raced over and tugged Lucy towards the edge. I wished they wouldn't stand so close, especially with it being so blustery, but I fought back my anxiety.

"Look! Down there. Dolphins!" Emily pointed.

A grey body arced from the white-tipped waves, followed by three companions. I'd seen the resident seals down by the harbour, cormorants galore and too many gulls to count, but not dolphins, although some of our guests had been lucky enough to spot them. After the shock of learning about Lucy, I couldn't appreciate them. My mind was in turmoil. Torringham was amazing. Where else could a short walk involve a quaint harbour, a modern marina, lush woodland, rocky landscapes, huge fortifications on one of the most stunning headlands in England. But our children would soon be miles away. And when they needed us, we'd be tied to a business we couldn't leave.

Jason's hiss broke into my thoughts. "Have you been upsetting Lucy again?"

"What? No!"

He shook his finger at me. "It's not Lucy's fault Emily is leaving."

"For goodness' sake, Dad!" Lucy butted in. "Leave her alone. She's been nice to me and it wasn't her fault last night either. It was me being a moody cow. You need to stop jumping to conclusions."

And with that advice, she stomped off, leaving Jason open-mouthed, while I just shrugged and followed her.

Chapter 9

THE CAR RUMBLED OFF DOWN THE ROAD, the occupants obscured from view by a mound of cases and other jumble stashed in the back, only Lucy's hand visible as she waved goodbye. I prayed she would remember Jason's words about driving carefully, especially with all the added weight. Kim gave me a hug and I returned it with a weak smile. I dared not speak as a huge ball of hurt had lodged itself in my throat. Emily had gone! Not only that but we wouldn't be able to see her until the end of the summer season, months away. I hoped she would keep her word about coming to visit soon.

"A bit like watching a child going off to Uni," Kim said.

"Except Uni students go back home after a few years." Shona echoed my earlier thoughts. "Though that's not always good. Ten years later and Mum still can't get rid of my brother."

When the car disappeared out of view, Kim turned to us. "Shona's got a friend with a boat. Why don't the two of you join us on it. Name an afternoon next week when you haven't got check-ins."

Jason frowned. "It's a no for me. Once our guest goes we've got to close room six as the shower sounds like it's about to blow up. I might as well retile at the same time, so that's another week of my life gone."

"If nothing goes wrong," I said.

Over one hundred years of bodgers and make-doers at Flotsam made every job a nightmare. Mending a leak and plumbing a new shower sounded easy but beneath the floorboards there'd be a century of grit and dust strewn amongst a maze of lead pipes – some cut off mid-length just to create confusion – that jostled for space with newer copper and plastic pipework. With all the bends and pipes going off in different directions, some terminating in inexplicable places, our plumbing could have been based on London's tube map.

"You could go." Jason said.

"Won't you need me?"

"I can call on Mike. Anyhow, you keep saying you could do with a break. Just wear a life jacket."

We stepped aside as a woman in a mobility scooter trundled past. She gave us a cheery wave. Along each side she'd strung posters that flapped like bunting. 'Four Bugs' were performing live at The Boar. Jason shook his head.

"And Emily thought it was too boring here. She doesn't know what she's missing."

♦

I couldn't find a day without any arrivals for more than a fortnight, but we decided the following Wednesday would be fine as the couple checking-in had advised they wouldn't be arriving until seven o'clock that evening. Thanks to the delivery of shower panels arriving late, Jason was running behind with the work on the ensuite. He needed to get a move on. In four days we had guests booked for the room and, with a full house, nowhere else to put them.

"Don't worry. I'll be back in time to deal with the check-in," I said.

"I hope so. Give me a hand with these before you disappear."

Once I'd helped carry the shower panels into the room, I hurried across to Jetsam Cottage to find Shona coming out. She used her key to shut the door, so it didn't bang.

"Kim can't come. We've got washing machine problems, so she's got to wait for the engineer."

"We can go another day."

"Don't be daft." She hooked her arm into mine and all but dragged me down the road. "Two pm already. We haven't much time."

"Sorry. The rooms took ages."

She shrugged. "You think this is tough. Wait until July and August. Nothing like constant twelve-hour days. One hundred-and-forty days last year between days off. Can you believe it? You'll be dead on your feet by October."

If Shona and Kim had been exhausted after a season with just five rooms, what would we be like with the two of us running eight with all the maintenance on top?

She saw my face and chuckled. "Let's not talk work. Today is meant to be about cheering you up."

♦

Shona pointed to a small white and blue boat moored on the pontoon. It had an outboard motor, which I was pleased about. I didn't relish the thought of rowing; something I hadn't done since college when, after a few too many down the Students' Union bar, we'd decided it would be great fun to hire a boat. It wasn't. I got landed with the oars, while my friends sat back to enjoy the scenery. They didn't get to see much as I kept going in circles, which my drink-filled mates – and just about every onlooker – found hilarious.

Now, stepping gingerly into the wobbling boat, I clutched the side to keep my balance. A pair of oars lay in the bottom while stashed beneath the seat sat two small lifejackets. I put mine on.

"Stay in the middle and hold this tight." Shona handed me a length of rope. Once she'd got in, she unlooped the rope from the mooring post and dropped it into the boat. "All set!"

She positioned herself at the rear, beside the outboard motor, and pulled the string. Nothing. Gritting her teeth with effort, she tugged the cord again. The engine belted out choking fumes and spluttered into silence.

"I hate this flippin' motor. I can never get it started."

Two men leaned against the sea wall, facing our way, although with their sunglasses and baseball caps it was difficult to tell whether they watched us. One flicked a cigarette end into the water and a gull wheeled by to investigate. As a flushed Shona swore and yanked the motor, one of the men pointed in our direction. His laughter echoed around. Unable to face the indignity of abandoning our boat trip before it started, or worse, having to row, I willed the motor into life. Thankfully, when Shona tried again, it fired into action. She grinned victoriously.

As she eased the boat from the mooring, I thought to give the men a little wave, but Shona beat me to it by jabbing her middle finger at them. "Twats."

I grimaced, wishing she'd shown a little more restraint.

"I know," she shouted. "But sometimes it has to be done."

Only the clatter of metal from men working on moored trawlers rose above the outboard motor. It drowned the sound of the gulls, the slap of waves and our voices. We didn't speak as Shona manoeuvred the little boat between the anchored yachts in the outer harbour before heading out into the bay. Although the breeze buffeted us, it couldn't fend off the warm sun and it wasn't long before I took off my cardigan and stretched out my pale arms. It would be good to catch a few rays.

The colourful harbour with its Balamory cottages now shimmered in the distance. The landscape became a green vista; trees dotting the sloped grassland before it turned to barren rocks splashed by waves. Two fishermen stood at the edge, a dog curled on a grassy knoll behind them. Shona curved the boat round their lines.

I shuffled closer to Shona, making sure to keep in the centre of the small boat, and shouted over the din of the engine.

"It's a shame we can't get out more often. It's so lovely here."

"You took a lot on with that place."

The noise of the boat swallowed my sigh. "A bit more than I'd imagined. If we're not cooking breakfasts, we're cleaning, then there's the washing and ironing, the setting up, the check-ins, the admin, the maintenance work. I thought we'd be doing more of this, but I couldn't have been more wrong."

I don't know if she heard everything but she caught the gist.

"Do you regret it?"

I shrugged. What would I say? Emily had gone. Jason and I didn't talk as much as we used to. Although Shona was becoming a good friend, I felt disloyal speaking about Jason behind his back. But it didn't stop me thinking about how our relationship had changed. Living and working together meant we didn't have proper conversations any more. We'd been closer in our old jobs, even though we'd seen little of each other during the week. Then there was his recent behaviour when Lucy came to stay. No matter how distant Lucy and I had been before, I'd never been anything but considerate to her. But he'd acted as if he had to protect her from me. Thank goodness she'd put him right.

"Kim and I had a tough time at first." Shona's holler threw me from my thoughts. "It will get better."

"That's good." I did the thumbs-up in case sign language helped.

"Give it a few years. You'll be knackered, you may even have worked yourself to death, but you'll have a good business."

I smiled. We'd chosen to buy a B&B with eight letting rooms as we needed the income, but we'd also had to buy one that required renovation as anything in good condition was outside our budget. Put simply, we should have waited a few more years to get onto a sounder financial footing before stepping into the world of the self-employed.

"Look!" Shona pointed towards a small cove. "Can you spot the seal?"

I had to shield my eyes to see. Sure enough, a black head protruded from the glittering water. What a shame Emily wasn't here to see it. Both she and Lucy would have loved being so close to a wild seal. As Shona edged the boat closer, I thought it would swim away but it just floated there, soaking in the sun's rays, with a smile on its face. She cut the engine and silence flooded us.

"It's grinning!" I found myself shouting.

Shona chuckled. "I'll get a picture."

She patted the pockets of her jeans, then rifled through her jacket. "Oh great! I've flipping gone and left my phone behind."

I pulled mine out. "I'll get some pics and send them to you."

The seal didn't care that we bobbed beside it. Twice it lowered its head and turned glistening charcoal eyes upon us but then it would lazily lift its nose back to the sky to become an oily rock jutting from the sea.

I could have stayed all day, but it didn't feel right encroaching on its space. After a hat-trick of attempts to start the motor, we chugged onwards again. I watched the seal with its wonderful upturned mouth and secretive smile until it disappeared from view. Tracing the contour of the land, we travelled past thick woodland that swept down the hillside to almost touch the sea but for a strip of barren outcrops. Through the clear water I could see the sea bed and more than once I found myself holding my breath as the boat appeared to almost skim the rocks below. In the hour or so since we'd left, the tide had ebbed further, revealing lime green algae and dark fronds of seaweed blanketing the boulders at the water's edge.

Shona half-closed her eyes and lifted her head towards the sun, the spikey tips of her hair softened by the breeze. My chin rested on my arms as I leant against the edge to stare into the depths, rewarded by the sight of dozens of tiny fish darting below.

We moved onwards, past another cove, and another, the countryside transforming into a rolling pasture which swept down to a sandy beach, lined by colourful beach huts. Above the sound of the engine came excited squeals from children racing into the water.

"They're mad," Shona shouted. Her first words in ages.

I glanced at my mobile phone, shocked to see it was gone five. We'd meandered along the coastline to get here, but even a direct return journey would be at least an hour with our lawnmower speed.

"We need to get back." I gestured towards Torringham, finding sign language a useful addition with the racket of the outboard motor. "I promised Jason I'd be there for the seven o' clock check in."

Her face fell. "I wouldn't have come out this far if I'd realised. Are you okay if we go via Penfold Cove, the one we just passed? I promised Kim I'd get a photo of the old lime kiln. She's got this idea about wanting to paint it for our hallway."

"I didn't know she could paint."

Shona shrugged. "A woman of many talents, my Kim. How come Jason can't do the check-in?"

She turned to face the shoreline, her mouth set in a thin line. Her earlier silence seemed to have brewed a strange moodiness. Or maybe she was getting tired. After all, we'd been out for a while. The sun's warmth had dimmed and goose-bumps prickled my arms. Shivering in anticipation of the cooling dusk, I hitched my cardigan over my shoulders.

"He could. Just that I said I'd be back by then. What time is Kim expecting you?" The constant shouting hurt the back of my throat. I longed for quiet. For the throbbing noise to cease.

"She doesn't know I'm out. Well she will by now. We had a row about the washing machine and I told her if she didn't shut up, I'd bugger off. So, when she went on and on about it, I did exactly that."

"Shona!" I felt terrible. What must Kim think of me for going off without her, even though I had no idea about the row. "You said she chose to stay at home."

"That's why I need the pic." Shona rubbed the back of her neck and winced. She pulled her hand away to reveal a sunburned strip. "She wanted to come out today to get a good photo of the kiln with the woodland behind. Let's just pop there quickly."

She eased the boat around and we set off towards Penfold Cove, skirting the rocks until we drew close enough to see the lime kiln tucked in a clump of bushes just beyond the pebble beach.

"My phone isn't good enough." I leaned forward but even with the zoom on maximum the kiln could barely be distinguished on camera from the limestone rocks which loomed behind.

"I'll get a bit closer," Shona said.

Boulders glistened inches below the boat. If I put my arm over the side, I could touch them. We couldn't go further in.

"No, don't!"

The boat rocked as I edged along the middle to the prow, where I knelt down to lean out as far as I dared to take a photo. Better that than we ended up scraping the hull or getting marooned. But as I stretched out, we became caught in the wake of a passing speedboat and our little boat lurched from side to side. I grabbed the edge to stop myself toppling in, horrified to find the phone slipping through my fingers and splashing into the water.

"Flamin' heck!" was Shona's helpful response.

The phone shimmered on the rocks below. I tore off my cardigan, gasping in shock as I plunged my arm into the freezing water. Just as I'd thought, the rocks were within touching distance and I managed to grab the phone, thankful to see it still had a picture. But no matter how much I jabbed, I couldn't make the touch screen work.

"I guess I won't be able to give Kim a photo of the lime kiln now," Shona said.

I wiped the phone across my jeans and pressed the screen again. Nothing.

"I guess you won't."

She gazed despondently at the beach. "May as well go then."

As she turned the tiller to manoeuvre the boat away, the engine spluttered and died. I watched helplessly as Shona yanked the pull cord again and again, until she slumped down, head in hands. For hours we'd lived with the tang of petrol and the noise. Now we could hear the slap of the waves, the gulls calling, the drone of a passing jet ski. I'd wished for peace and it had come true.

"Shit."

"What do we do?" I held up my broken phone.

Biting her lip, she gazed across the bay to distant Torringham. "Row."

"Seriously?"

"Have you got another plan?"

I didn't. I bent down and hefted one of the oars from the bottom.

"Put it in the bollocks."

"Rowlocks."

"Eh?" She glanced over the side and shrugged. "The fish'll have to wait until later. We haven't got time."

Not bothering to explain what I meant, I took an oar and slotted it into the rowlock. She sat next to me in the centre of the boat.

"Follow what I do," she said. "We've only got a few hours until dark. I hope you've got muscles."

I gritted my teeth, arranged my cardigan over my lifejacket and followed her as she sank the oar into the sea. As my oar forged its way through the heavy water, I realised I was about to discover muscles I didn't know I had. No way would we be making it back in time for the check-in. Jason would kill me. That's if we made it.

♦

My muscles burned. Pain shot up and down my arms and my neck ached, but I couldn't stop. Each time one of us called a halt unable to bear it any longer, the tide seemed to draw us backwards. Then one of our oars – usually mine – would skim the water or I'd lower them too deep, so we'd waste time with the boat curling this way or that as we fought to coordinate ourselves again. We'd done well, pushing on past the cove where we'd seen the seal and now the outer harbour was in reach. Beads of sweat ran down my forehead, stinging my eyes. My only relief was to dab my face on my shoulders.

If I looked behind us to see how far we had to go, I could make out the silhouette of Shadwell Point, framed by an apricot sky. Stunning. Except it meant we had little time before we were left to navigate our way in the dark past the many buoys and moored yachts – or worse – the trawler boats that could be heading back with their catches. They'd be lit but we wouldn't. We kept going, forward, back, forward, back. My shoulders ached, the muscles in my neck screamed with every jerk.

Shona touched my arm. "Hold on."

As I slowed, she steered us away from the hull of a yacht. I hadn't even noticed it.

"Can we help you girls?" A smarmy voice rang out.

Above us stood two figures, one smoking. When one of the men chuckled and flicked his cigarette into the sea, I recognised him from earlier. My heart sank. Could this day get any worse?

"Ignore them," Shona said. We fell into sync again, this time with renewed vigour.

The din of a motor cut through the air and minutes later the men appeared in another boat, not much bigger than ours, except it had a working engine. They slowed alongside us.

This time the other one spoke. "That dud engine gone? Let us tow you."

Shona shook her head. Panting, she said, "Not likely! You'd probably take us back out to sea again."

"Why? We'll take you to the town pontoon. You both look knackered."

This was the sailing version of hitching a lift from strangers, but Shona and I were too exhausted to argue as the man, who introduced himself as Eric, took the rope and instructed Shona what to do when they towed us. Ten minutes later we were back at the pontoon.

As Shona tied up the boat, she said, "Sorry about giving you the bird earlier."

Eric laughed. "Next time a wave will do. Or you could buy us a beer."

"Don't go overboard," Shona said.

With relief I dragged my lifejacket off and stashed it under the seat. My arms trembled and my legs wobbled. I could barely climb out of the boat and onto land. As I waved goodbye to Eric and his friend, the church bells pealed nine times. Great! I'd missed the promised check-in.

"Jason's going to kill me," I said.

"You think that's bad. Kim's temper is deadlier than a volcano. I'm done for and I haven't got a photo to give her either. I wish you hadn't dropped your phone."

A chill ran through me. With all the effort of trying to row back, I'd forgotten about my mobile. Jason would be worried sick, unable to call. Not only did I have to confess about dropping it into the sea but, worse, it still had a year's contract left and I hadn't insured it, even though I'd promised to do so. As we headed back, we both fell silent, each contemplating our fates when we reached the B&Bs.

Chapter 10

LIKE JEKYLL AND HYDE, JASON SMILED or glowered his way through the morning. But his behaviour had nothing to do with a potion. More the sight of my face. Put a guest in front of him and he bellowed jovially. Nothing could be funnier than the joke they told. Need something doing? No problem. But when he turned to me, his expression would darken. Like any couple we had our ups-and-downs and a good row would usually clear the air but that was impossible in a guesthouse filled with two dozen pairs of ears, especially as I've never been one for a hissed argument. I could imagine the TripAdvisor reviews: 'Flotsam offers the authentic seaside fish-wife experience'.

I spent the morning gritting my teeth. Each time I lifted the breakfast plates or took the tray laden with teapots out to the guests, pain streaked my arms. When I talked to guests, I turned my body rather than risking the agony of moving my neck.

We stood together smiling as we said goodbye to guests. When the last couple drove away, Jason retreated to the kitchen, which seemed to be getting the deepest clean it had ever had, leaving me to get on with the rooms. I gazed at the new zip-and-link bed we'd bought: two single beds that joined together to become one large bed. Currently set up as a twin, the people arriving later that day wanted a superking bed, but this meant lifting the mattresses to zip them together and then hefting the one huge mattress back onto the divan base. My shoulders throbbed at the thought. Placating my grumpy husband seemed the only option.

I hovered at the kitchen doorway, while Jason knelt with his back to me, scrubbing the inside of the bottom oven.

"Please can you come and help? I can't do this bed on my own."

"So, it was okay for me to deal with the Savells last night. No paperwork, no way of contacting you. Nothing." His voice was muffled by the oven but then he knelt back, a blackened cloth in his hand. "And you just happened to change the password, so I couldn't get into the booking system. How am I meant to book people in if I have no idea who they are and what they are paying?"

I flushed. That had been stupid but when I'd received the email saying our account may have been compromised, I'd changed the password without thinking to tell Jason. Usually I did the bookings, so it had gone unnoticed for over a week. Thankfully, yesterday's guests had brought their booking confirmation with them.

"I've said I'm sorry," I paused as guests clattered across the hallway, waiting until the front door clicked shut. "I would have called if I could. You know I wouldn't willingly have left you worrying like that."

"I know you've wrecked a new phone."

"I can get a second-hand one."

"That's not the point."

I sighed. "I know. But I can't take back yesterday. Please help. It's agony to lift my arms."

He threw the cloth aside and led the way upstairs. We put the mattresses together in silence, but when we moved onto making the bed he made sure that he took the duvet, leaving me with the easier pillowcases. As I made a start polishing the sides, he disappeared and came back with a tray laden with the mugs, spoons and glasses. We'd be servicing the rooms together. I was forgiven.

♦

As I closed the door on the final room after cleaning, I felt the same relief I always did. Later I'd do the washing and iron the bedding, empty and refill the dishwasher and set up the breakfast room in preparation for breakfast tomorrow, while Jason would get on with tiling the ensuite in room six. But with breakfast done and the kitchen and guest rooms serviced, we could stop for lunch. My stomach rumbled in anticipation.

I went through to our tiny storage area next to the utility room. The only space on the floor had been taken by the full bag of dirty laundry – we sent the sheets out to be laundered – so I had to put the cleaning box down in the hallway, while I shifted the bag and a few bits around. As I bent down, something trickled down my neck. Water! Puzzled, I gazed upwards to be rewarded by a splash in the eye, followed by another, this time on my cheek. Worse, my shoes squelched into the rug and I realised the laundry bag was soaked, its sides stained like blotting paper. I shot into the kitchen to find Jason but he wasn't there. He wasn't in the lounge either, nor in the breakfast room. I found him in our ensuite upstairs.

"Jason, come quick! There's a leak."

He took his time drying his hands, probably thinking I meant something small like a dodgy washer on a tap. He strolled downstairs, while I raced into the kitchen in search of a bucket.

"Look!" I pointed to the ceiling by the doorway, where the water piddled through a large bulge in the plaster.

"Great! That's all we need."

Jason rushed off in search of the stopcock, leaving me to gaze in concern at the swollen ceiling, praying it would hold until the leak was fixed. Moments later he came back.

"I've turned it off. Just make sure you keep an eye out for guests. It's really important they don't run any water."

I got out the ironing board, switched on the TV and jammed the lounge door open so I could hear guests coming through the front door. From above came scratching, followed by banging. Whatever he was doing, it sounded serious. While I ironed the pile of duvets, I watched a repeat of *Come Dine with Me* with the subtitles on. I couldn't hear anything above the banging. My mouth watered as the contestants tucked into a delicious lamb dinner. I hoped Jason would hurry up as we couldn't have lunch until he finished. From above came a loud splintering sound and the ceiling juddered alarmingly. I sighed with relief when the noise subsided. On TV they had moved from dinner to dessert and huge slabs of chocolate cake with homemade ice cream were being handed out. The smell almost wafted from the TV. As my stomach growled and my mouth watered, I set the iron into its holder and snuck off to the kitchen to steal a few biscuits.

With chipmunk cheeks and a mouth so full, I couldn't chew without spilling crumbs, I opened the lounge door to a deafening crack. I leapt back in shock. Grit and pieces of rubble showered down, followed by a trainer-clad foot. To a hat-trick of 'shits' the foot disappeared through the hole in the ceiling, leaving a cloud of dust suspended in the air. Pieces of brick, stone and plaster littered the carpet where, moments earlier, I'd been standing. Thank goodness I'd moved. But then I spotted my ironing board and – worse – my ironing pile, blanketed in a century of dust and grit like a grey moonscape.

"Are you okay?" Jason's voice trembled with pain. The top part of his face was visible through the ceiling, while a thick pipe obscured the rest.

I couldn't speak. The biscuits had become a solid lump clogging my mouth. I swallowed, grimacing as they tore at my throat. It took me a few moments before I could stammer, "W-what are you doing? The leak's the other side."

"The water's running down the pipe. I took up the floorboard to check where it started and, well, I had a bit of an accident."

"You're telling me." It felt odd talking to half his face.

"I'll help clear up once I've sorted this. It's a nightmare job. I've got to drain the system, then we'll have to check the water in the rooms. Ouch! I think I've busted my foot."

Not more work. In shock, I absorbed the devastation. Jags of plaster hung from the ceiling, ready to fall at any moment, while the only way to sort the ironing pile would be to wash every bit again, including the ironing board cover. Not that I'd be doing much ironing for a few hours, as I couldn't use the washing machines until Jason turned the water back on. My neck and arms ached from the previous day's rowing. They wouldn't be getting a rest today.

I picked up the small lumps of brick, turning them in my hand. When Jason had told me about the debris under the floorboards, I hadn't expected to see it for myself. I heaped them and the bits of stone and plaster outside the lounge door, fetched the broom and bin bag and got to work.

A while later, Jason hobbled into the lounge as I wrapped up the cable for the hoover. Everything – apart from the ceiling – had been cleaned. His arrival meant we could have a quick sandwich before we checked the water supply in the rooms.

He slumped onto the sofa. "That was a pig of a job."

"Sorry to bother you." John, our guest from room two, stood at the open lounge door wringing his hands. He cleared his throat. "But the water's dribbling out of my tap. I'm parched and can't even get a brew."

In all the chaos, I'd missed him coming in. Jason sat grim-faced while I ushered John into the hallway, hoping he hadn't spotted the ceiling.

"I'm really sorry. We've had to turn the water off to fix a problem. Give us five minutes and we'll get it back on."

Jason followed me out. I felt for him. Exhaustion etched his face and every bone in his body seemed to creak.

"I'll turn the water back on. We better pray the leak is fixed or your promise of five minutes may be a tad optimistic."

While he headed to the kitchen, I went through to the storage area. The leak had stopped but a bubble of sodden plaster remained. Nothing in comparison with the crevice in the lounge. From the kitchen came a whooshing sound as Jason turned on the stopcock. As I waited, unable to move my gaze from the bubble, relief crept through me. Jason had sorted the leak; our guest would get his cup of tea and I would get my lunch. Then, to my dismay, a droplet appeared, mocking me as it clung to the ceiling. It wobbled as if caught in an invisible thread until, ever so slowly, it fell to be followed by another and another. Like lemmings its stupid comrades poured down. Faster than ever they smashed to the floor, taking with them all hopes of food anytime soon.

♦

The following afternoon, with the guesthouse back to a semblance of normality, I shot across to Jetsam Cottage. Kim opened the door wearing a flour-dusted apron but her hands were clean, her fingernails polished with a perfect French manicure. She'd tied her hair in a vibrant silk scarf knotted at the back, showing off her elegant neck and gold hoop earrings. A slight raise of an eyebrow showed her surprise at seeing me, but she welcomed me in with a warm smile. If it hadn't been for the water leak, I would have bitten the bullet and apologised to her yesterday. While it wasn't my fault Shona had gone off without her, it felt as if I'd unwittingly taken sides in their row.

"Shona's out," she said, as she led the way through to the kitchen.

A ceramic mixing bowl sat on the side, just like the one my mum used to have, beige with a white inside. For a moment I was back in her kitchen, scraping as much of the tasty mixture as possible from the bowl.

"Baking?" An inane comment but I didn't know what else to

say.

She grinned. "How did you guess?"

"I'm sorry about the other day. I had no idea you didn't know we were going without you."

She frowned. "Oh, you mean the boat. Shona can be a daft mare at times. She got her karma though, especially when I left her with the rooms to clean while I spent yesterday shopping."

"I got my karma too."

She took the jar from the cupboard and popped a teabag into each mug. "I heard about your phone but don't be silly, you weren't to know."

"Not just the phone. We had a disaster yesterday."

I told her about Jason coming through the ceiling, about how we couldn't stop the leak until late in the afternoon, so I'd plied our guest with bottled water which he could use in the kettle to have all the tea he wanted.

"And guess what?" I didn't wait for her to respond. "He gave us a terrible review. You should see it. Apparently, we ruined his afternoon as he couldn't drink anything."

"But you gave him bottled water."

"When I took the bottles up to him, he was fretting about the cistern not refilling, but why he couldn't use the loo and wait until water was back on to flush it, I don't know. You should see his review. He must have written it last night."

Kim wandered into the lounge and came back with her tablet. "Let's have a look."

The light from the screen danced in her eyes as she chuckled. "Is he for real?"

"Sadly, yes."

She put her hand to her mouth to suppress a gurgle of laughter. "Oh my, this is good." Putting on a pompous voice, she proceeded to read the review:

Water, water everywhere but not a drop to drink.

A pleasant stay was ruined by the lack of water all afternoon, when I found out by accident that the owners had turned the water off. They seemed to think that handing over half a dozen bottles of water was sufficient, although there wasn't any water for my toilet needs. They simply told me not to use the loo, which meant I could not drink anything. The couple are new to the hospitality industry and it shows. Next time I will stay in a place with owners who understand that what goes in must come out.

She squealed the last few words and burst into howls of laughter. "The other B&Bers will love this," she shrieked. "I think you'll make the top ten of strange reviews with this one."

When I'd first read the review, I'd felt hurt. All our guests had left lovely reviews so far but while this was peculiar rather than nasty – well, apart from the score – it was disconcerting to know it would be there for years to come. I could respond, but it would look as if I was passing the blame. Sod's Law that the one guest who decided to spend the whole afternoon in his room was the moaning type. Other guests had come in to find we were still fighting the leak, but they'd been happy to accept the bottled water and wait until it was all sorted by four o'clock.

"I didn't tell him not to use the loo. Just that he wouldn't be able to flush it yet."

Kim brushed tears from her eyes. "The most difficult guests often leave the worst reviews. Don't worry about it. Anyone who reads it will think he's plain odd. And anyhow," she added. "You've made it to the start of July before getting your first weird review. It won't be your last."

Chapter 11

UNCLE BERT SAT ON THE EDGE of the settee, as if anticipating a speedy getaway. At first, I'd found it disconcerting but, in the two or three visits since I'd met him outside Kim and Shona's B&B, I'd come to understand that this was one of his many quirks. Even now I found myself scrutinising his expressions or actions for reminders of my mum. He found my gaze off-putting as he'd stutter to a halt mid-sentence and ask if there was anything amiss. I couldn't help it. Some of his mannerisms were uncannily like hers. It was over twenty years since I'd seen her scratch her chin when deep in thought or when she made that odd he-he-he chuckle, like he did now, just like Muttley from the Wacky Races. My thoughts sped back to when we laughed at Mum for sounding more like the dog than Penelope.

His warm blue eyes – Mum's eyes – crinkled as he chuckled. He took a sip of tea. "So, we had all these lads leaping onto the scaffold because they thought it were an adder."

"Was it an adder?" I asked.

He gifted me with another bout of Muttley and shook his head. "The idiots! It were just a grass snake. I told them an adder's got zig zags but you know these lads, they think they know it all."

"So, what happened?" I asked.

"Well it disappeared into the woods next door." His shoulders shook as he laughed. "You should have seen those lads, looking around all afternoon in case it reappeared. I'm sure we lost half an afternoon's work from them."

He put his mug on the coffee table and heaved himself up with a grunt. "After the day I've had I can tell you that was a welcome cup of tea, love. I best be off now."

We walked to the door, where a Shona-shaped silhouette

appeared through the frosted glass pane. She rang the doorbell twice in quick succession. As I pulled the door open, she stood finger in the air ready to jab the bell again.

"You've *got* to help me," she said. This sounded ominous.

"Mend a boat engine, deliver more packages to the post office?"

"I've got a mouse," she whispered.

"A mouse! A pet one?"

She mouthed 'shush' at me and looked furtively around. Spotting Uncle Bert standing behind me in the hallway, she signalled for me to come outside.

"It's only Uncle Bert." I couldn't help but point to his watch. "You must remember him."

Blushing, Shona gave Uncle Bert a little wave. "Sorry about that."

Grabbing my arm, she dragged me onto the driveway between two cars. A spot of butter sat in the corner of her lips and toast crumbs speckled her blouse. Kim must be out or she'd have words with Shona about having late afternoon snacks.

"It's stuck in the mousetrap. It's one of those humane things but the mouse isn't moving. Maybe it's died from shock."

"I'm not touching it. What about Kim?"

"She's out. I can't wait for her to come back."

Live and let live might be my motto when it came to creatures but that didn't mean I wanted to touch them. In the guesthouse I used a glass and card for the spiders but, thankfully, I'd never had to consider what I'd use to extract a mouse from a trap.

"I'm off now, love." Uncle Bert tried to slide between us.

Uncle Bert! He could handle it. He'd mocked the lads on the building site about a snake, so a mouse must be nothing to him. I blocked his escape.

"Are you in a hurry to go or have you got a minute?"

He gazed at his watch and then looked at me with an air of

resignation. "If it's urgent, I've got ten minutes, at most."

Shona gave us a running commentary as we walked through the guesthouse: Kim had gone out for the afternoon to a course at the library, leaving her with a pile of ironing. Feeling a bit peckish, she'd decided to get some toast when, all of a sudden, she remembered the thing by the back door – she didn't mention the mouse trap by name in case her guests overheard her – which she'd forgotten to check for almost two whole days, which meant the thing stuck in it may be dead.

"Thing?" Uncle Bert asked.

"What Shona was talking about outside," I said.

"I weren't listening," he said.

The smell of damp hit us before we'd even stepped from the utility room. Shona's tiny yard had the feel of a prison cell, due to the huge retaining wall which towered to the first floor of the property. I hadn't been out here before. Our yard was larger and also less oppressive, thanks in part to Jason's recent coat of limewash, whereas Shona's wall was buried beneath a dark-green paste of algae, which also carpeted the concrete floor. A dozen steps led to a small garden surrounded by a high stone wall, where an assortment of lilies, lupins and other cottage garden flowers jostled for space in the raised flower beds. In the centre, Kim and Shona had crammed a patio table and four chairs.

None of this could be seen from her yard below but I'd gazed at her garden many a time when cleaning the rear guest bedroom windows. Often, I'd wished the previous owners of Flotsam Guesthouse had cared for our patch. Instead self-seeding valerian jutted from the crevices of our stone wall, fighting oxalis and dandelions for control of the few concrete-lined flower beds.

What would I do if I had a whole day in which to turn our garden from pigsville to paradise, but our spare time and money had to be spent on improving the guest rooms. Jason had just finished the ensuite in room six and the new furniture we'd ordered to replace the old melamine bits in room four had arrived this morning. The oak bedside tables with dovetail joints and an open-style wardrobe had made a huge difference to the room's look and feel. I hadn't been sad to see Jason smashing up the old stuff before hauling it off to the tip. With a start, I realised he'd been gone ages, probably via Mike's for a pint at the pub.

"So here it is." Shona pointed to a small plastic box that sat outside the utility room door. "Do you think it's alive, Bert?"

"Eh?" Uncle Bert backed away to be corralled by the wall. "Oh no, I'm not touching that. I don't do mice."

"Well someone has to, or it'll die," Shona said.

The narrow box didn't have any air holes, a bit odd for a so-called humane trap. Shona was right. If the mouse wasn't already dead, it wouldn't last long in that horrible coffin-thing. With Bert planted by the wall and Shona standing there, arms folded, I had no choice.

"Fetch me a bucket and something to put on top and I'll do it."

The sound of toppling cans and a heavy clanking came from inside and moments later Shona appeared with a mop bucket and a lump of melamine. I guessed it was a cupboard shelf from the utility room, as it was decorated with half a dozen rust-coloured rings where old cans and aerosols had sat for years.

"We need something heavy, so this should do."

I caught Uncle Bert shaking his head. Like me he probably wondered why she needed the dead weight of a shelf to contain a mouse. Carefully, I lowered the mouse trap into the bucket and heaved the ridiculous shelf on top.

"You'll have to hold it, so I can put my arm in," I told her. "Somehow I've got to get the lid up on that thing."

Shona turned to Uncle Bert, but he crossed his arms and slunk further into the shadows. Sighing, she edged towards the bucket and, like a weightlifter readying herself, she opened and clenched her fists before tentatively grasping the edges of the shelf.

"Slowly!" I hissed as she slid the shelf out. "Not too far or else the mouse might jump out."

"Yeah, like it's a bionic mouse," she tittered but she watched me warily as I eased my arm through the gap.

It's terrible to admit but when my fingers touched the lid I half-hoped the mouse would be dead or at least unconscious. What if it bit me or scrabbled up my arm and leapt into my face? Ridiculous I know, but the vibes radiating from Uncle Bert and Shona made me more nervous.

I flicked the lid open and yanked my arm clear, leaving Shona to shift the shelf back in one fluid move. She smiled and dusted her hands together. Job done. Except with the shelf stuck over the bucket, we had no idea whether the mouse was alive or dead. It must have dawned on her too as she groaned.

"Who's brave enough to check it?"

"I've really got to go, love," Uncle Bert said. "I'll let myself out."

I grinned at him. "Next time we'll only call you when we've got snakes."

"Snakes?" Shona said as he slipped past. Her face whitened. "Have you got them next door?"

"Bert had one at work." When the front door clanked shut, I added, "He was telling me that he was the only one on the building site not scared of this snake. But I've a feeling it's because he was at the top of the scaffold the whole time."

She chuckled. "I've got to release this somewhere. Maybe we should take it to his work. Then again, I don't want it to become snake food. Not after all this effort."

Gazing at me, she added, "So, who's going to do this?"

Not only did she expect me to check on the mouse, but I had no doubt I'd be co-opted into driving to some remote location to release it. Jason would come back to find an ironing pile the size of Mount Vesuvius. At least he couldn't blow his top, not after he'd disappeared goodness knows where.

I decided to turn the tables. "I'll lift the shelf and you check on it."

She gave me a dubious look but knelt down while I lifted the top just a crack.

"I can't see," she said. "It's too dark. Lift it a bit more, but not too much. That thing better not jump at me."

As I inched the shelf higher, Shona screamed and fell backwards, her foot smashing into the bucket which shot from beneath the shelf and toppled over. I'd kept hold of the shelf, but its unsupported weight took me by surprise and it slipped from my grip to smash side-down on the ground. A blur of brown darted from the upturned bucket and bounded up the dozen steps each ten times its size. It paused at the top, its huge black eyes taking in its ruined prison and jailers below. Then it fled.

"For fricks' sake!" Shona said. "I don't know which is worse, Kim killing me when she finds out I let it go or not being able to go in the garden again knowing it's there."

I regretted giving her a hand up when she left my palm smeared in green gloop. While she staggered into the utility room to clean her algae-coated hands and jeans, I tidied the area. Back inside, I pointed to the droppings scattered at the bottom of the bucket. "It left you a calling card."

"Flippin' mice," she said. "I hate them."

♦

Later that evening, I retrieved the laptop from under a mound of paperwork. It may have been a fortnight since she sent me to the post office with that sex toy, but I'd finally had an idea for pay-back. 'Fake furry mouse' I typed and scrolled through pages of joke mice until I found something much better: a rat which popped out when the box was opened. If it looked as life-like as it did on the screen, it would be perfect.

I paid and typed in the address details for Jetsam Cottage and sat back grinning.

"What are you up to?" Jason slurred. He'd spent the past two hours snoring on the settee after finally coming home after an afternoon down the pub with Mike.

"Just arranging my own special package for Shona," I said.

A few days later I got the text I'd been waiting for. 'You cow!' it read. 'Not only did you freak me out. You've just set Kim off moaning as I had to confess about the mouse'.

In return I sent a 'crying with laughter' emoticon, because I was.

Chapter 12

JASON CAME INTO THE DAY ROOM where I sat with Daphne and Gloria who were staying again for a few days. I'd been thrilled to receive their booking email, as I'd wondered if they'd be too embarrassed to return. As I folded their registration form, I reminded them about breakfast times and a few standard house rules. I didn't mention the midnight stair Olympics but, with sheepish grins, they volunteered to go straight to bed without hurdling across the landing. Although I'd promised myself I wouldn't embarrass them by saying anything, I couldn't help but tell them what Emily had thought they'd been getting up to. Emily! I missed my beloved daughter so much.

"She thought we were doing *that*?" Daphne blushed but her eyes sparkled with amusement. She wore the same stripy top from when she'd stayed before, but today she'd paired it with a pair of linen trousers and deck shoes.

I smiled at her. "She had no idea who it was. Just that there was a thumping noise."

Gloria twirled a strand of hair between her fingers. Her silver bob carried a warm tinge the colour of heather. Unusual but very pretty. "It's been so long since I've done that, I've probably forgotten the basics."

Jason leaned against the doorway, chuckling and shaking his head. "Now isn't the best time to offer to take you to your bedroom, so I'll just take your bags and let Katie do the honours."

Laughing, Gloria popped her pen into her handbag and clipped it shut. She pushed herself to her feet and ran her hands down her A-line skirt to smooth out the creases.

"Lead the way."

With Gloria and Daphne tucked in their room and no other

check-ins, we had a free afternoon. After finishing a few necessary jobs, we headed into the warmth of a beautiful July day. Sunglasses on, sunscreen lathered and water in hand, I linked my arm through Jason's, although this gave me a lop-sided feel with Jason being taller. We meandered along side-by-side, with the gentle breeze on our faces and the cries of the gulls above.

"I'm so glad we didn't ask Shona and Kim. We haven't spent an afternoon out alone in ages."

When Jason didn't respond, I nudged him. "Don't you agree?"

"I should have said." He cleared his throat. "Mike called earlier and mentioned going out, so I invited him and Josie to join us."

My mood darkened. Silly, I know, but it was a rare treat for the both of us to have leisure time alone. Worse, what if it was like the last time I'd bumped into Josie? She'd bought a new camera, so I'd asked her how she found it. Great or okay would have sufficed. Instead she all but recited the technical manual, outlining its improved performance and the latest features, engulfing me with acronyms and initials. I had no idea what she was talking about.

Apart from her detailed interest in camera mechanics Josie was a lovely person, but I wanted to spend the afternoon walking with Jason. I'd even harboured secret hopes of ending up at a cosy restaurant, especially after one of the guests had made me drool when he'd told me about the amazing meal he'd had the previous evening: local mussels in cream followed by the freshest bass and a superb bottle of wine.

"I wish you'd told me. Now I'll have her rabbiting on about her photography, while you two talk about cars."

I sounded petulant but so what? I didn't feel reasonable. If I'd been a child, I would have vented my frustration by stamping my feet or squealing in fury.

"Her photography's good."

"It's great but I don't understand about this lens or that, or this shot, or care that she stood at Shadwell Point for four hours to capture a bat pic. Just show me the pic of the bat – not fifty pics each taken a second apart – and don't give me a minute-by-minute rundown on how you got it."

Jason frowned. "You're being a bit mean."

He was missing the point. I wanted to spend this valuable leisure time with him, not them. I yanked my arm from his. "You listen to her then. And he's no better. Anything with an engine."

We continued in silence, using the need to get around clusters of sightseers as an excuse to move further from each other. We were on different sides of the street by the time we reached Josie and Mike at the harbourside shellfish stall. The aroma of crab hung in the air. Not a smell I savoured. Forcing a smile, I headed over, dismayed to see a bulky camera dangling from around her neck. Strange how everything electronic seemed to have diminished in size except for professional cameras.

Beside the stall a man forked jellied eels from a small white pot, slurping noisily. With his bare arm, he wiped the oily film from his lips, leaving a slimy trail on his skin. Behind him, an elderly man sat on a bench, his back to us as he watched the boats in the harbour, his dog taut on its lead as it vacuumed chips from the pavement.

Hands shaken we paired, Mike and Jason in the lead while Josie and I traipsed behind, skirting the family groups crabbing by the harbour wall as we headed towards the Lord Mountfield pub. Josie fingered her camera as she chatted.

"I've brought it as I heard there's a pod of dolphins in the area. A friend texted from Shadwell Point as they might be heading this way. If they do, I hope you won't mind if I shoot off. I'd love to get some good pics."

Dolphins? I'd love to see them in the open sea. Some of our guests had seen them but I'd not been lucky enough. Without thinking, I found myself saying, "Could I join you?"

She gave me a warm smile, which made me feel like a traitor for being so mean earlier. "Of course!"

As usual the pub was packed with people enjoying views of the marina and the bay beyond. The one free bench was littered with finished beer glasses, the gaps between the boards crammed with empty crisp packets. Jason took a few empties when he went in to order our drinks and I pushed the rest to the side of the table. When Josie disappeared off to the loo, Mike decided he would check if Jason needed a hand.

A gull stood on the gutter above, cocking its head as it surveyed the potential menu options. There were plenty as most visitors were unused to safeguarding their food. On the neighbouring table a ruddy-faced couple sat eating, while beside them sat an untouched burger and chips, its young owner too busy doing figures of eights around the tables. He gambolled past almost tripping over a terrier snoring by my feet. Joined by a giggling friend, the boy headed back for a second circuit, so I shifted round and stretched out my leg to protect the dog, forcing the children into a larger course. Unaware, the dog's owners continued to saw their way through steaks buried beneath a mound of chips.

Decision made, the gull swooped down to snatch the boy's unsupervised meal. To yells of surprise, it sailed off with half a bun in its beak, having dropped the burger on the floor and scattered half a dozen chips over the table.

Jason plonked a cider in front of me and placed Josie's white wine on her side of the table. Mike followed holding two dripping pints. The bench creaked as they sat down.

"How's it going with the car?" Jason asked Mike.

The boy's parents had settled him in front of what was left of his lunch, the ruined burger and chips piled on the other side of the table. I gave it five minutes before the gull returned with its friends.

"You should come with us," Josie said.

Attempting to work out what she meant, I reeled the conversation back, but failed. As I started to apologise, a group of lads in wetsuits stripped to the waist jeered as one of their friends necked his lager. Her attention diverted, Josie swung round, tutting.

When the lads quietened, she said, "Katie was just saying she'd like to see the dolphins. She should come on this sea-life watch we're doing tomorrow."

Puzzled, Jason looked at me but, getting no reaction either way, he shrugged. No doubt he expected me to turn her down, but I'd loved the seal Shona and I had seen the other day and wild dolphins would be incredible. Not that I had any idea what a sea-life watch involved. Sitting and chatting while we waited would be fine, but if it meant standing in silence for hours on end like birdwatchers, I'd rather pass.

"Check your diary for tomorrow afternoon." Josie handed Jason his phone, as mine was safely tucked in my pocket out of her reach. "Are you massively busy then?"

Jason didn't bother to unlock his mobile. "If Katie wants to go, I'm sure I can do the check-ins. As long as I can get into the computer."

Josie grinned. "Great."

I returned her smile, until she added, "So that's settled then. A stake-out at Marsham Beach."

Marsham Beach? I closed my mouth, aware I might be impersonating a goldfish. How on earth had I co-opted myself onto a trip to a secluded beach only reached by a five-mile hike along the coastal path? If that wasn't bad enough, guests who had undertaken the walk had all told me the same thing: going down was hard work but the climb back from Marsham Beach was twenty minutes of leg-burning, thigh-killing torture just to get to the top of the hill, followed by three-and-a-half miles of rolling countryside. Never had 'rolling' sounded so fearsome.

◆

Josie's friends seemed a friendly bunch. As we strolled along the South West Coast Path towards Marsham Beach, Josie and I walked beside Laura and her border collie, Bessie, who kept a steady pace, while the rest of the group drifted behind. Up to Shadwell Point we were on familiar ground but once we stepped over an old stone stile and onto an unmettled footpath, I let Josie and Laura take the lead or – more accurately – Bessie, who padded ahead, not reacting to gulls screeching above or even a yapping dog.

"She's very good." I pointed to a copse a few feet from the path, where a dog stood on its two hind legs straining to reach Bessie, its owner clinging tightly to the harness.

"She's deaf," Laura said.

"She does doggie sign language," Josie added.

The determined dog forged ahead, unable to hear the birds and the sound of the sea crashing against the rocks below, not even stopping to sniff a rabbit hole. Maybe, like me, she just wanted to get the walk over and done with, especially the hill climb back.

"Has she been this way before?"

"Loads of times." Josie grunted as she lifted a post beside a stile, which Bessie slipped beneath. "But she prefers it when we go on our other walk through fields, as I'll let her off the lead there. She'll come to no harm in an enclosed field, especially as she can't hear me calling her back. But here." I followed her gaze to the grassy cliff edge dotted with swaying yellow and pink wildflowers. "It's treacherous in places. And she does have a tendency to wander off."

The coast path hugged Silver Bay, where the waves lapped over the grey shingle beach below and the expanse of sea glinted in the sunlight. We moved inland and into woodland, glad to be in the shadows and away from the warm sun, but soon we were back in the open and dropping down to Seacombe Cove, where we stopped to catch our breath. A few of the group took off their shoes and socks, gasping as they stepped into the clear but freezing water.

Half way up the hill that took us away from Seacombe Cove, one of our group shouted and pointed back to the cove, where a naked man stood by the waters' edge. He must have been tucked behind one of the rocks when we were on the beach.

"Surely, he must know we can see him?" I said to Josie, who laughed.

"You can't see much from this distance."

Half an hour later we started the long descent to Marsham Beach. I'd brought four bottles of water in a rucksack, but I regretted the one I'd already finished as my bladder twinged with every step. I didn't know these people well enough to dive behind a bramble bush but, even if I did, someone could be nearby. We'd already passed several groups of hikers heading towards Torringham. I didn't want to feature in their coastal path memories along with that naked man.

Below us lay a strip of beach bordered by a small lake the colour of spring leaves on one side and a glittering Mediterranean-blue sea on the other. White-tipped waves rolled onto the beach, but in the centre there was a strip so clear I fancied even from this distance I could see individual pebbles shimmering beneath the water.

The steep incline meant we all but raced down the hill. A stumbling Laura made it to the beach first, having been dragged by Bessie who dashed to lap from a little stream that ran from the pond. The trickle was like Chinese water torture to a woman with a full bladder, especially with the waves rushing over the pebbles. I scanned the area, hoping to find a large rock I could hide behind but no such luck. A forest of reeds surrounded the algae-filled pond water, enclosed at the rear by a wire fence which marked the boundaries of a field set within the valley bowl. My only option was to ask everyone to turn around and set myself beside the rock face or climb back up and find a copse.

While the rest of the group littered the shingle with rucksacks, upturned shoes and scattered socks, I headed over to Josie and Laura who stood with Bessie.

"So much for a nature watch. They'll frighten everything away with that noise." Josie shook her head as her bare-footed friends tiptoed, yelping and laughing, over the pebbles.

Laura smiled. "I could do with a cool off too. Poor Bessie's wilting."

Bessie's steam engine puffs rose above the excited squeals and drool ran from her lolling tongue.

"First I need a pee." Laura crossed her legs as if to emphasise her point.

"Me too."

"Me three," I said, grateful they'd beaten me to it.

Laura took Bessie over to a pointed rock where she hooked her lead. She patted Bessie's head and held out her hand. Stay. "Won't be a mo, then we can paddle," she said, even though Bessie couldn't hear her.

We hurried away to a corner of the beach where we would be in full view of hikers heading towards Torringham but hidden from anyone going the other way. Hobson's choice, as no matter where we positioned ourselves we'd be on view. Laura and I stood side-by-side acting as a barrier from prying eyes as Josie relieved herself. The noise made me ever more desperate and I begged to be next.

When it came to Laura's turn, she groaned. "Why, oh why, did I think dungaree shorts were a good idea? How I'm going to do this, I don't know."

I chuckled. Facing away, I couldn't see what she was up to, but I could hear the chink of shingle and grunting and guessed she'd decided to take her dungarees off rather than risk splashing them. Josie rolled her eyes and we giggled silently at each other. It felt like forever before I heard Laura peeing and even longer until her knees cracked and she announced she was done.

"Finally!" Josie said. "I thought you'd settled in for the duration."

Just two hardy women remained calf-deep in the water, chatting. The rest had decamped to the beach, where they unloaded cameras and food from their rucksacks.

"Bessie?" Laura said.

I looked over to where we'd left Bessie, but she wasn't there.

This time Laura shouted louder, panic clear in her voice. "Bessie! Has anyone seen Bessie?"

She rushed over to where she'd left her dog and stood frantically scouring the beach. Josie and I hurried over. I couldn't see Bessie racing up the hills on either side, nor was she near the lake. I couldn't imagine she'd gone through the reeds, not with all that algae. Which left…

"She's in the sea!" One of the paddling women pointed to a black and white head about thirty feet from shore.

"Bessie, Bessie!" The women chorused but, of course, the dog kept heading out to sea with the same determined air she'd shown when walking here.

Laura sprinted to the water's edge and threw off her shoes. Ignoring calls to wait, she hurdled the surf until it reached her waist when she dived in. Her head bobbed up and her arm curled into the water, then the other. Thankfully she didn't have to battle the waves as she swam through a calm channel. Strangely, Bessie's pace seemed to match Laura's. About forty yards out, Laura turned and waved to us. Except she wasn't waving, she was calling for help. And, although she'd stopped swimming, she appeared to be moving further away.

Oh no! Was this the riptide I'd heard about? I pulled my mobile from my rucksack, dismayed to see no signal. Josie did the same, as did a few of the other women. Their worried looks told me all I needed to know. Without thinking, I shot up the hill, pausing a quarter of the way up, my breath rasping, my heart pounding. Still no signal. This couldn't be happening. If I didn't get a signal soon they'd be in serious trouble. My legs shook as I belted onwards, while someone pounded behind me. Below, Bessie had become a speck in the sea and Laura a larger, pale dot. I pulled up again and checked my phone. One bar. I dialled 999.

Wheezing and gulping for breath, I shouted, "We need the coastguard. There's a woman out at sea. And her dog."

Dust in my throat made me cough. One of the women from the group had reached me. Panting, she grasped my shoulder – whether to support me or hold herself up, I didn't know – as I answered the emergency operator's questions.

"Marsham Beach. Just the one woman, Laura, and her dog, Bessie."

Eyes watering, I couldn't speak for coughing, so the woman took my phone from me to answer the final questions. As she ended the call, we both stared out at the vast expanse of sea.

"We've got to stay here," she said. "In case they need to call us back."

It seemed hopeless. Bessie had disappeared from sight and Laura had become the speck Bessie had once been. How would they last until the lifeboat arrived? Especially if it had to come all the way from Torringham.

The minutes ticked by. Each time we saw a fleck on the horizon, we'd pat each other and point, only to fall back into silence when it turned into a yacht or a trawler.

"I've left my binoculars on the beach," the woman said. "I could really do with them right now."

I didn't answer. It seemed impossible that Laura could survive this long. If it had been me out there, I would have been a goner. While I used to be able to manage a length of the pool – at a push two – that was the limit of my capabilities. I vowed to start swimming again, just in case.

A vessel came into view, the shape of the local lifeboat. It couldn't be, could it? That was quick. We hugged each other but drew away. It wasn't over yet. As the boat slowed to a halt, we shielded our eyes from the glare of the sparkling water, hoping to see a miracle: Laura and Bessie hauled on deck. But we were too far away. My teeth nipped the edges of my lip as we gazed out to sea, hoping, praying. The sun beat down but I found myself trembling with fear and cold. Overwhelmed by impotence, I clenched my fists, my nails digging into my palms. Again, I checked the time on my mobile. The lifeboat had arrived fifteen minutes ago at least. What on earth was happening?

Moments later, we spotted Josie struggling up the hillside, with a pair of binoculars. Red-faced, she arrived beside us, gasping for air. She clutched her heaving chest until able to speak.

"They've got Laura," she panted. "I don't know if she's okay, but they haven't gone back so they must be out looking for Bessie."

She handed me the binoculars, but I couldn't see more than the navy and orange lifeboat and a few figures on board. I passed them to my – still nameless – companion.

"I hope they find her," Josie said.

All I could mutter was, "That poor dog. Poor Laura too."

"Look!" The woman shook Josie's arm. "That looks like a dog!"

Taking a lens each and huddling close, Josie and I squinted into the binoculars. Sure enough, what looked like a black and white dog was being hauled on board an orange rib. Yellow-clad figures huddled round, obscuring her from our view. The rib joined the lifeboat but on the other side to us, so we couldn't see anything.

Minutes later, the lifeboat turned away towards Torringham, I sighed. We'd have to wait to find out their fate.

As the lifeboat ploughed through the waves, I slumped onto a grassy knoll and sent a little prayer for the determined dog and her lovely owner. Lost within my thoughts, I didn't notice the other women leaving the beach to clamber up the hillside. When they reached us, I smiled gratefully as one of them handed me my rucksack.

"We're heading back," a short woman said.

Subdued we continued to climb the rest of the hill. As we rounded the brow of the hill, my lungs bursting, my legs aching, I took a final glance at Marsham Beach. I couldn't imagine coming back here again, especially if anything terrible had happened to Laura and Bessie. Below the sea glittered and waves rolled onto the beach, while a yacht glided past, its sails bowed by the wind. The seductive beauty of the sea.

I followed the rest of the group along the track. Once again, the grass hanging from the hillocks brushed my legs and the same delicate blue flowers I'd admired earlier nestled by the dusty path. Incredible that when we'd passed this way not more than an hour ago, I'd looked forward to being at this point homeward bound, as it meant the long hill climb would be over. Now I'd give anything to go back and change things.

An hour or so later, as we rounded Silver Bay, Josie's phone rang. When she stuck her thumb up in the air, excited whispers ran through the group and we crowded round her. She put her phone down and grinned.

"Laura's okay. And Bessie too."

Chapter 13

THREE DAYS LATER I SAT in Jetsam Cottage with Kim, who'd taken out her laptop to show me the photographs of Laura and Bessie's safe return. One showed a bedraggled Laura being helped from the lifeboat, while a crew member carried Bessie ashore. Although Josie had phoned me with an update and to pass on Laura's thanks for calling the emergency services, I hadn't spotted these pictures posted on the Torringham Coastguard page.

"It says that the lifeboat was near Silver Bay at the time of the call. That explains why it arrived so quickly."

"Lucky for them!" Kim broke into a coughing fit. She wiped her streaming eyes. "This cough is so annoying."

"You poor thing." I waited until she'd composed herself and then clicked to another image which showed a lifeboat crew member's arms at full stretch as Bessie strained at her lead. "Bessie's off again."

"A bit like Shona. She's got a one-track mind when it comes to going out."

Had they argued again? I didn't dare ask, so I turned back to Facebook.

"It says that a woman called for help. That was you, wasn't it?" Kim said.

"Me and this other woman," I said. "I have no idea what her name was. We were too busy worrying about Laura to think about introductions."

The next photo showed Bessie being offered a dog treat.

"Definitely like Shona. She only thinks about food too," Kim said.

I didn't like talking about Shona – or Kim – behind their backs, so I deflected the barbed comment by pointing at the screen. "Amazing how dogs seem to recover so quickly."

Kim sank back into the sofa and sighed loudly. "We haven't got any money and Shona keeps wanting to go out to eat as she says we deserve it. But we won't make it through winter if we fritter it all away."

I closed the laptop screen. Kim needed to get this off her chest. "Where is she?"

"Apparently, she's too tired to cook or wash up here so she's dining alone at Caspian's." She broke into a second bout of coughing, choking up a globule of phlegm which she spat into her hanky. It didn't bother me. I'd seen worse in my previous job. A glass of water sat on the coffee table, so I handed it to her along with a clean wad of tissue.

I couldn't imagine Shona choosing to dine in a restaurant alone, even if she wanted to prove a point to Kim. No doubt she'd called one of her other friends en route or, more likely, she was sitting with the regulars at the Fisherman's Friend with a pint of lager and a plate of chips. After all, six o'clock was happy hour.

"I must remember to buy more cream." Frowning, Kim stretched out her manicured hands. "I think we're both shattered. The cleaning, the breakfasts, not a single day off for months. It can't be good for us. At this rate I'll end up a wrinkled old hag and we haven't hit August yet."

Only that morning, I'd looked in the mirror and thought my skin looked like tissue paper that had been screwed up into a tiny ball and then pressed flat. The creases would never disappear. I'd pulled the edges of my face taut, imagining myself with a face lift but when I let go everything drooped back into place, my jowls, my crow's feet, the crepe paper lines. I'd scowled and stuck out my tongue. Even Jason had bags under his eyes. It was 58 days since our last lie-in with another 75-day stretch before our next day off, when we could go and see Emily and Lucy again. Okay, we had the odd afternoon of freedom, but each morning felt like Groundhog Day. The alarm clock beeped and we'd roll out of bed. Once dressed, we'd head downstairs to set up for breakfast, where I'd serve guests while Jason cooked, then we'd clear up and say goodbye to guests checking out. I'd go up and clean the rooms while Jason finished the kitchen, when he'd join me to finish the rooms. We'd stop for lunch and do the washing and ironing. Depending on how many arrivals we had, our day could be anything from seven to fourteen hours.

Kim and Shona's B&B may be half the size of ours, but they'd been doing this job much longer than our three months or so. It must be exhausting to keep going day-in day-out. I was beginning to see why they said the average B&Ber around here lasted about six years.

"Have you got a full diary? Can you block out any time?"

She treated me to her throaty chuckle but her eyes didn't sparkle as they usually did. "We haven't got a clear day until October. I'm just worn out, that's all."

We were in the same boat – clinging on while we were pitched into the relentless summer season – but when we'd spotted a few days free at the start of October, I'd blocked them out. I'd got carried away then, closing out the calendar for a few weeks in November, the whole of Christmas – although that depended on how well our summer went – and a few weeks more in January. It felt decadent to do so, although I suspected I wasn't being ruthless enough.

"Well, if we can help, do shout." I'd tossed her a platitude. We both knew there was little Jason or I could do to help with the day-to-day workload at Jetsam Cottage. We had more than enough to do with sixteen breakfasts each day and eight rooms to clean, before we even started the laundry.

The more she spoke, the thicker and claggier her voice became. "Just ignore me. We hit this point last year and no doubt we'll be here moaning next year."

Like them, Jason and I were bickering more lately. Tiredness shortened our tempers, especially in the heat of the breakfast kitchen. I couldn't remember our last meal out together. Perhaps I should ask him if we could go somewhere and have an evening away from the B&B. I still dreamed of mussels and bass. No Mike, no Josie. Just the two of us.

I checked my watch and swigged the last of my tea. "I better get going. We've got a check-in coming soon and I don't want to leave Jason to it. I hope you and Shona get things sorted soon and you feel better too."

"We'll be fine. We always are. B&Bing has its ups-and-downs, just like us."

And like Jason and me too, I thought. But I didn't say as much.

As I stepped from Jetsam Cottage, I spotted Jason in the car park over the road, hefting suitcases from the boot of a guest's car. I crossed over to greet them. The man's firm handshake made me wince, but the woman gave me a warm smile and air-kissed my cheek. Her fragrance smelled like vanilla; a lovely fresh aroma rather than synthetic. I made a mental note to ask her what she wore.

"I'm Lisa and this is Ja... Matthew."

Matthew shot her a look and frowned as she giggled, "Listen to me! That journey was so mind numbing, I can't remember my partner's name."

"I can," he said drily. "It's still Matthew."

She smiled at him. While he turned back to shut his car boot, she pointed to the church next door. "I've been watching that lot come out. You're a God-fearing bunch down here, aren't you?"

Confused, I gazed to where she pointed. Did she mean we had

a lot of churches in Torringham? But then I spotted the groups of people heading away from the church hall, leaving a dozen or more mingling outside.

"Not God-fearing. Fat-fearing." I pointed to the slimming club sign.

She blushed and ran her hands over her flat stomach. "I should go there. I need to watch my weight too."

Jason handed me a small case, while he took the two larger suitcases. We followed him and Matthew across the road and into the guesthouse. As I took Lisa inside, I told her where to come when they were ready to check-in.

"I think James will want to come straight down. We missed lunch, so we'll have an early dinner," she said.

Puzzled, I didn't respond as I took her up to her room. Had she got memory issues or was there another reason why she kept getting Matthew's name wrong? Back downstairs, I found Jason in the day room setting out the registration forms.

"Have you noticed she keeps calling him James?" I whispered.

"Maybe she thinks he's her chauffeur." He grinned but clamped his mouth shut as the stairs creaked and Lisa and Matthew appeared. While Jason took them through to the day room to check them in, I headed for the lounge and the ironing pile.

Jason took ages. After dealing with Lisa and Matthew, he bumped into two guests in the hallway who'd had a wonderful time visiting Dartmoor. I could hear their laughter above the TV and the hiss of the iron. As he wandered back into the lounge, smiling to himself, I decided to broach the idea of a romantic night out.

"You want to go out for a meal?" He scratched his head. "I'd love to but what with buying those mattresses and needing to sort the roof, we're running on fumes. Plus, I thought you wanted to put minifridges in the rooms when we had a bit of spare cash. We could just about manage a pint at The White Hart if you're desperate."

Shrugging, I turned back to the ironing board so he wouldn't spot my disappointment. He was right. With the recent dry spell, I'd completely forgotten about the leaking roof. Jason and Mike had put in a temporary patch which had worked so far but we were looking at a couple of thousand to fix the small area of flat roofing so the general room improvements – and fancy evenings out – had been put on hold.

He came over and hugged me. "You look so down. How about I make you a nice cup of tea?"

With as much enthusiasm as I could muster, I said, "Sounds wonderful."

Leaving his arm resting on my shoulder, he added, "Then leave the ironing for me and you can have a rest while I rustle up a spag bol."

"No garlic. You don't want to stink out the guesthouse again."

He grinned. "Lesson learned."

♦

I rushed back into the kitchen with the next order, to be hit by the smell of burnt toast. At this rate I'd run out of bread. Jason darted between the cooker and the griddle, flustered and red-faced. As a tomato rolled onto the floor, he cursed and kicked it away. I snatched the toast from the toaster and threw them and the tomato in the bin.

"Two more full Englishes and an Eggs Benedict."

To the sound of clattering pans, I put the order form on the side, just as the telephone shrilled. I glanced at the clock. Eight thirty. Who on earth would ring a B&B at this time? As it rang on and on, I fought my irritation and answered.

A well-spoken man's voice responded, "Hello, can I speak to Lisa?"

Jason gestured me to get the plates. When he saw me on the phone, he threw his arms in the air and stomped over to the hot plate.

"Can you give me your number and I'll call you back when we've finished breakfast."

Jason ran a finger across his throat. Cut the call. Now.

"I want to speak to Lisa," the man repeated.

"I can't get her right now."

"I know she's there. Just put me through to her."

Did he think we were a massive hotel with a switchboard? The only switchboard we had was my legs as I ran up two floors to hand the phone to her. That wouldn't be happening at this time of the morning. Not only did his tone unnerve me but I couldn't leave Jason to plate up the four breakfasts, especially when he needed to get on with the next batch. I hung up on the man.

"Why you answered, I don't know." Jason tonged a sausage onto each plate while I filled the ramekins with beans. When the telephone started to ring again, he snapped, "Ignore it."

I hurried out with two of the plates.

"You're busy," a guest said as the telephone rang on and on. I shook my head to let her know what I thought of the caller.

Returning for the other two plates, I pulled out the phone socket rather than switch the answerphone on. Now he could ring all he liked. With a fixed smile, I headed out with the other two plates. "Your toast is just coming," I promised. "More coffee? No problem."

I dashed back into the kitchen, flicked the kettle on, grabbed the butter dish and the toast and put the four halves in the rack, rinsed the cafetière, refilled it, and disappeared back to the breakfast room, ignoring Jason's call for help with the scrambled eggs. Two guests wanted extra toast and tea and another two were waiting to order, so I took their empty cereal dishes – promising to return with the pad and pen – and stacked the bowls by the dishwasher, refilled the kettle, popped on more toast, before heading back out to take orders, ignoring Jason's cry for plates.

♦

Lisa and Matthew didn't make it down to breakfast. A relief as it hadn't been one of our finest services and two fewer guests lessened the crisis. After we'd cleaned up the breakfast room, I'd gone up to tell her about the caller, but they'd already gone out. By now, I felt guilty for hanging up. What if the man had been trying to get hold of Lisa to tell her about a death in the family or something? But why hadn't he called her mobile? Even if hers didn't work, he could have called Matthew's. Maybe they'd turned off their phones or neither had a signal.

The phone call played on my mind while I serviced the rooms. Even when I sat down to lunch with Jason, I felt ill at ease.

"That man was odd."

"What man?"

"The one who called this morning."

Jason shrugged and pushed the rest of his tuna and lettuce sandwich into his mouth. He slapped his hands together, so the crumbs fell onto his plate, and got up. We had little time to waste lunching with a busy day ahead including four check-ins.

Gulping down the last of his sandwich, he picked up the shopping list. "Give Lisa a ring if you're that worried."

He picked up the car keys and headed out the door, leaving me to the washing and ironing. I wondered if I should call Lisa, but I told myself this morning's caller would have got hold of her by now. Instead I turned on the TV, picking an old favourite: a series of Friends I'd seen countless times. Jason wasn't a fan of the show, so each time an episode finished I flicked to the next recording, making the most of him being out of the house. Ross was talcum powdering his legs in a vain attempt to get a pair of leather trousers on, when the guesthouse doorbell rang. Three o'clock. Probably someone checking in. Not bothering to press pause on the TV – I knew the ending – I switched off the iron and hurried out.

A man stood under the door canopy, his large Range Rover parked across two of the driveway spaces. There was no one in the passenger seat and we weren't expecting a single person. Crimson blotches stained his cheeks and sweat prickled his forehead. His chest heaved as if he'd sprinted here. Perhaps that wasn't his car.

"Can I help?"

"My name's James. I've come to see Lisa."

He sounded familiar. But we never had people calling for guests without warning. "Lisa?"

"Don't play games. I know she's here. I can see that bastard's car over there for a start."

As he leapt forward, I tried to slam the door shut but he rammed it open. No way was he coming in. I held my arms wide, barricading myself between the wall and the open door. Close up, he stank of alcohol.

"For goodness' sake. I just want to talk to my wife." Scanning the dark hallway behind me, he shouted, "Lisa! Lisa!" and shouldered my arm aside.

I blocked his way. Looking down at me, he grinned, clearly thinking I was a little woman he could swat aside. Okay, he could, but fury made me strong and I shoved as hard as I could. "Go away! Or I'll call the police."

Taken by surprise, he staggered back, grabbing the door jamb to stop him tripping over the ledge. As I slammed the door shut, he screamed, a high-pitched shriek of pain. Shocked, I wrenched the door back to find him clutching his fingers.

"You bitch!" Hands between his legs, he bent over, gasping.

"You've broken my fingers!"

Trembling, I watched him. What would he do? Probably sue me.

A young couple stood in the middle of the road, waiting for a break in the traffic. While they stood there, I felt safe. But soon they'd be gone and I'd be left with this man. Red-faced, James gazed at me, gritting his teeth and clutching his hand. Should I call them? When a white van slowed to let them cross, to my relief the woman headed over, leaving the man by the edge of the driveway speaking urgently on his phone. I could hear the odd words: 'stranger, breaking in, still here'.

The woman turned to me. "Are you okay?"

"Her?" James spluttered. "What about me?"

She ignored him. "We saw him trying to force his way in."

A witness! Thank goodness! She turned to James, who'd turned a plum colour. "Chris is on the phone to the police."

"The police? What the hell for?" He shook his hand.

The woman kept calm. "We saw it all. If you got hurt, it was your own fault."

Kim appeared from behind the Range Rover. She looked drawn, as if she'd just woken up. "Is everything okay?"

"No, *I'm* not," the man said.

"I don't care about you." Kim draped her arm over my shoulders. She broke into a coughing fit, stopping for breath before she could speak. "Is he a guest?"

I shook my head. "He just barged in screaming for Lisa."

"My wife!" said the man.

"He tried to force his way in," the woman said. "We saw it all."

Chris cut off his call and looked at his watch. "They're on their way. The station's only around the corner, so give them…"

From the opposite direction, a police car pulled up on the road outside, blocking the Range Rover. Great! We had four check-ins and Jason arriving any moment. This would be a lovely welcome to new guests. One of the policemen spoke to James, while the other addressed the young couple who'd gone over to the police car. Heart thumping, I stood by the door wondering what would happen – would I get in trouble for injuring him? – while Kim wheezed beside me. Soon the officer left the young couple and headed over.

"They say he tried forcing his way in."

Kim hugged me tighter, as if I needed protecting. While the confrontation with James had shaken me up and I could do with a cuddle, her height meant I was planted on her right boob. I extricated myself from her grip.

"I wouldn't let him come inside but he barged in. I pushed him back out and he hurt his hand when he tried to stop me closing the door." Not a perfect summary, but it would do. "Apparently, his wife is here but that doesn't give him the right to do that."

Kim coughed and banged her chest. Her eyes watered.

"That sounds nasty." She looked terrible too with black smudges beneath her eyes and an ashen tinge to her skin. She flicked her hand, brushing my concern aside.

"I don't want to take it further," I told the policeman. "I just want him to go and not come back."

On the other side of the driveway, the man had started shouting about his rights. Flinging his arm in the air, he narrowly missed the policeman. His colleague left us and hurried over to the commotion, blocking much of our view but we caught glimpses of the man's swinging arms and heard him bellowing 'You don't tell me what to do', 'She's my wife' and 'What do you mean drinking?'. Before we knew it, the man was being handcuffed and led to the police car.

"Oh no!" I said.

"He'll learn not to start on lone women."

"But his car. It's taking two spaces."

With a voice thick with phlegm, Kim said, "Selfish twerp."

I sighed. Now we'd have to pay for the guests to park across the road until James was released. They wouldn't be happy, expecting a driveway parking space. As the police car pulled away, he glared at me from the back seat. Not usually one for swearing, I stuck two fingers up at him. And I meant it.

Chapter 14

HOURS LATER JAMES'S HULK OF a Range Rover still hogged the drive, telling me he was probably spending the evening in the police station, if not the night. What had he said or done to the police to cause them to arrest him? Perhaps drink driving, as he'd smelled of alcohol. When they did release him, I prayed he would slip away quietly or else he risked coming face-to-face with a furious Jason.

Lisa and Matthew didn't arrive back until six o'clock, tanned and smiling after their ferry trip to Berrinton. But when they spotted James's car and learned about the day's events, they insisted on packing and leaving immediately, even though they'd paid for four nights. The worry about James diminished Lisa. Her petite features sunk into her bones, her shoulders sagged and even her blonde hair dulled. As we stood on the driveway, a jittery Matthew bobbed up and down like a meerkat scanning the road.

"We should go," he said, as Lisa apologised for the tenth time for leaving early.

She placed her hand on my arm. "It's just that you don't know him like I do."

One dose of James had been enough for me. Who cared whether she was having a weekend liaison with Matthew or if she'd left her husband for him. It wasn't my business. Anyone married to a bully like James had my sympathy.

As we helped them across the road with their suitcases, she glanced back to the Range Rover. "We came down to give ourselves breathing space from him. For the past week I've seen that thing sitting outside my workplace. I've been having to leave the back way. But how did he know we were here?" For a moment I thought she was accusing me of giving out guest information, but her eyes widened and she clamped her hand to her mouth. "He must know my email password."

A tear rolled down her cheek. "It's too much. I don't think I can cope with this anymore. I'm sorry he caused you so much bother."

I gave her a hug. "Please don't worry. Just look after yourselves.".

As we waved goodbye to Lisa and Matthew, I thought about going around to Shona and Kim's. I'd taken a bottle of wine to the young couple who lived in the cottages across the road and thanked them for their help, but Kim had snuck away when Jason arrived home and I hadn't had a chance to thank her. But now my feet ached and my head pounded and zonking out in front of the TV with a glass of wine was all I could manage. I'd thank Kim tomorrow after our check-ins arrived.

♦

Shona answered the door. With the blonde tips almost grown out, her hair looked more like a hedgehog than usual. Two sharp grooves sat between her eyebrows and weariness oozed from her. Putting a finger to her mouth, she ushered me through to their lounge where we found Kim asleep on the sofa, arm dangling so her finger tips curled into the carpet. The room smelled of sweat and sour milk. Kim had a strange grey pallor and her chest whistled as she breathed. Although she'd looked a bit off-colour yesterday, she hadn't sounded like this. Shona signalled for me to follow her through to the kitchen, where she carefully shut the door, so it didn't click.

"I'm really worried about Kim. She's been grotty for days, really moany, but her cough's got a lot worse and this morning she could hardly manage doing the breakfasts, let alone the room servicing. She even agreed to have a lie-down. That's not my Kim.

Look at her! She's so poorly. What should I do?" She gasped the last part as if she'd forgotten to breathe.

"Have you spoken to the doctor?"

"She wouldn't let me. Even after she was sick."

That explained the strange smell in the lounge.

"I don't think you have much choice. What about that NHS Direct?"

Shona bit her lip and opened the kitchen door a fraction to gaze at Kim. Without saying a word, she crept into the lounge and carefully lifted the handheld phone from the coffee table. A moment later I heard the stairs creak above the sloped ceiling in the kitchen. She'd gone upstairs so Kim wouldn't hear.

I gazed around. Like ours, Shona and Kim's kitchen had the sign about washing your hands by the hand basin, a fire extinguisher and blanket by the door, as well as a noticeboard pinned with temperature readings. But theirs was in a much better condition with sleek underlit units and matching floor and wall tiles. The expression about polishing turds came to mind each time we scrubbed our kitchen. I couldn't wait until November when we'd promised to replace it.

A grim-faced Shona came back five minutes later. "The doctor's calling back. I hope it doesn't wake Kim. Although you ringing the doorbell somehow didn't."

As she said that my mobile beeped. I mouthed an apology and turned it to mute before checking the message. Jason. 'Just shooting down the pub with Mike.' I glanced at the time. Six o'clock. A bit early.

Shona put the kettle on. Its hiss echoed round the room. She opened the fridge and the bottles and jars stuffed in the door chinked together. The mugs clunked against the worktop. She turned to me, smiling.

"Silence isn't my forte either."

At that the phone rang and Shona snatched it from the side and hurried through the utility room into the small courtyard, where we'd tried and failed to catch the mouse. Was it still roaming free in the garden? Shona hadn't mentioned any further forays, but she was unlikely to advertise the mouse's extended stay.

She returned with a worried expression. "They want me to take her to the out-of-hours GP at Berrinton Hospital. What if she won't go? People think I'm cranky, but she should've been born a mule."

"Go and fetch the car," I said. "I'll wake her."

"What about breakfast tomorrow?" Shona said. "If she's too ill."

We both looked at each other. With Jason and I doing sixteen breakfasts tomorrow, I couldn't help. What did small B&Bs like ours do with just two owners and no staff if one of us became incapacitated? This was something that often played on my mind, especially since Emily had left. Then I remembered Shona telling me that she and Kim still got on well with the old owners of Jetsam Cottage who lived just up the road.

"I could help with the rooms, once I've done ours, but what about your old owner? Could she come in?"

Shona's face brightened. "I'll give her a quick ring. If Maggie can't, maybe Jeff can."

Shona returned with a smile and a thumbs up, until her gaze dropped to Kim. She snatched her car keys from the side and shot off to retrieve her car. Like us, in addition to their driveway parking, they stumped up for passes across the road. But these luxuries were for the guests and they parked their own car in any free space they could find, usually on the side of Moreton Hill, where only those with the hardiest of handbrakes would park. Not that Shona and Kim's car was in the best condition, but Shona always said the car in front would stop it rolling too far. I hoped it wouldn't be ours.

I headed over to Kim and gently whispered that she needed to get up. Bleary, unfocused eyes met mine, until they flickered shut. I shook her.

"Kim, you have to get up."

Again, she blinked and her lids drooped shut. She let me wrap my arms around her to draw her into a sitting position, where she gazed around blankly. I brushed against her skin. Damp. I touched the back of my hand to her forehead. Too hot. She broke into a coughing fit, but she didn't seem to have the energy to choke up whatever her body needed to expel. Once she quietened, I helped her up. She leaned heavily on me, rasping as she shuffled out of the room.

We met Shona in the hallway. She went to take Kim's arm but I stopped her.

"She needs shoes."

Shona took the stairs two at a time while I stood with Kim by the Buddha statue and the fake trailing ivy. Panting, Shona hurried back, clutching a pair of crocs. They didn't match Kim's summer dress, creased after an afternoon on the sofa, but Kim slipped her bare feet into them without an argument.

After we bundled Kim into the car, I pulled Shona aside. "If you need me to help you when you get back, just call."

Pale faced, she gave me a brief nod. Then she clutched my arm. "Thank you. We have our ups-and-downs but I love her."

Her eyes welled. The thought of Shona crying shocked me – she must be worried beyond belief – but she forced the tears back with a loud sniff.

Within seconds they accelerated away, heading at speed past the corridor of houses and B&Bs, until they sailed through the green traffic lights at the top of the road and disappeared round the bend.

A strip of light alerted me to the open front door, so I headed back into Jetsam Cottage, where I found both the back door and the one to their private quarters open. I locked both and put the landing lights on for the guests in case Shona and Kim didn't arrive back until after dark.

As expected, Jason was out. I settled down to read the thriller I'd started the week before, but my mind wouldn't absorb the words and I kept having to go back to the same passage. Kim's distress and Shona's upset troubled me. I hoped they were okay. In the end, I picked up the laptop and played mindless games on Facebook.

At ten o'clock, I texted Shona but didn't get a response. At eleven o'clock I headed to bed, putting the mobile phone beside my bedside table in case Shona needed me. Jason hadn't returned yet. Odd, as he knew we had a busy breakfast service the next day.

Awakened by a beep, I opened my eyes to a blue-tinged room. A text from Shona. In my sleepy state the bright screen hurt my eyes, blurring the text. It took me a while to focus on the message which read like a telegram. 'Kim on a drip. Staying overnight. Pneumonia. I'm coming home. Don't worry. Maggie is coming at seven.' Too tired to think, I typed three kisses and pressed send. I turned away from the phone and its brilliant screen and burrowed into the pillow, puzzled to find the bed empty beside me. Shrugging to myself, I let my eyelids droop.

It seemed just moments later that the front door slammed, shaking the building and shocking me from sleep. A drunken guest? Jason would know better than to make a noise. I leaped from the bed and padded across the carpet to unhook my dressing gown from the back of the door. The stairs thumped, not an orderly pattern but a thud and a pause, followed by several thuds and a loud creak, as if someone had fallen against the bannister. My arms snagged through the dressing gown sleeves and my fingers trembled as I knotted the belt. I hated the idea of confronting a loud guest on my own, especially after yesterday's episode with that drunken man,

James. The landing floorboards groaned. I took a deep breath and yanked the door open. Jason crashed to his knees, arm outstretched.

"Ouch," he slurred in a belligerent tone. "What did you do that for?"

I clenched my fists and gritted my teeth, the only way to fight the bubbling torrent of anger. If we didn't have guests, I would have spewed fury. What was he thinking getting into such a state? We were in the middle of our busiest period and look at him crawling across the carpet like a baby. After a few failed attempts, he clambered onto the bed, rucking up the duvet. I left him to it while I padded downstairs to turn off the hallway light. I returned, slinking into bed to find his dead weight pinning the duvet under him. If we lived anywhere but a guesthouse, I'd be shouting at him while I tugged the duvet free. But all I could do was pray he hadn't woken our guests – especially lovely John and Agnes in the room nearest ours – and go to the laundry cupboard to fetch a spare sheet.

♦

The morning alarm went off and I rolled out of bed, eyes stinging with tiredness after a night spent elbowing Jason to silence his snores. As I tugged my trousers on, I noticed a receipt lying on the floor. He'd withdrawn sixty pounds last night! After he said we didn't have enough money to go for a meal.

Jason arrived in the kitchen seconds before the first guests came into the breakfast room. On tortoise speed – his sickly face looked like one too – he messed up orders, blamed the frying pan for overcooked eggs, sent out almost raw tomatoes, bounced the scrambled eggs onto the plates and, somehow, burned the baked bean pan. I maintained an icy silence: if words could kill, he'd have been murdered in the most savage way possible. He wasn't being let off though. There would be a 'discussion', but now wasn't the time. Not unless we wanted an audience.

After breakfast, I sent a text to Shona and received hers by return. 'Maggie great help. Waiting to hear about Kim.'

My hare-like efforts to race around the guestrooms were thwarted by Jason's lack of coordination. The morning echoed to the chink of glass and the clatter of dropped spoons.

"For goodness sake, hurry up!" I moaned, when I found him on his hands and knees stretching to reach a loo roll which had rolled beneath a bed. "I need to get round Shona's."

He knelt clutching his head. "Don't shout!"

We didn't get finished until two o'clock, when I swapped my cleaning clothes for the ones I'd worn that morning. They reeked of greasy food, thanks to the breakfast service being undertaken without the hob's extractor fan being switched on, but I couldn't waste more time changing again.

Jason met me in the kitchen clutching two plates, one with his usual ham sandwich, and the other my favourite, tuna mayonnaise. Buttering-me up wouldn't work.

"Where are you going?"

"Out."

"But, your lunch!"

I slammed the door, almost as hard as he'd done the previous night, safe in the knowledge our guests were out.

♦

Maggie bustled around the kitchen as she emptied the dishwasher. A short, plump woman, she had a lifetime of crow's feet formed by her ready smile. While I put the kettle on, she fetched the antibacterial spray from the utility room to give the cupboard doors a wipe. It seemed odd seeing a stranger so familiar with everything at Jetsam Cottage, but she'd lived here for eight years. She and Jeff had put in this lovely kitchen a year before they sold.

"So, you're one of the new people from next door," she said. Unusually for a B&Ber in Torringham she had a Devon accent. Most of the other B&Bers had come from the North, Midlands and South East of England.

It unnerved me that she would have known Flotsam's old owners, Maureen and Jim. How did she feel about Jason and me, considering what they'd told people about us? When I didn't respond with anything other than a brief nod, she ploughed on.

"I hear you get on well with the girls." She draped the cloth over the side of the tap. "We hardly spoke to Jim or Maureen but they seemed a nice enough couple. Jim wasn't one for handiwork, not like my Jeff, but that was their choice. I see you've been doing a fair bit of work."

I kept my expression neutral. "Bits and pieces."

She chortled. "There's an understatement if I ever heard one. Shona said you've done a right load of work on the place. I 'eard they weren't happy about the sale but that's not my business. Thing is, you'd have to be daft to take sides when you don't know the full story. Right, let's have that cuppa and see what else needs sorting."

Over a cup of tea in the lounge, she told me that she'd made Shona go back to the hospital as soon as the breakfast service finished. "It only took me a few hours to whizz round the rooms." She'd forgotten to ask for Shona's mobile number, so would I be so kind as to see how Kim was getting on.

Of course, I would! A few moments later, a text came through. 'Kim better but still poorly. Staying in another night. Is Maggie okay?' I relayed the message to Maggie who looked concerned.

"How long can you help out? I asked.

"I'm here for as long as those poor lovelies need me." Her eyes crinkled as she smiled. "Although I won't pretend I'm not glad to have sold up. It's blessed hard work."

I couldn't argue with that. "Are you sure you don't need me to do anything? I've no reason to get back anytime soon."

"Well, if you're offering, I'd love a hand with the ironing. My back could do with a rest."

As I slid from the stool to head through to the lounge, I smiled at her. "The more the merrier."

I'd do anything – even six hours of ironing – if it kept me away from Jason.

Chapter 15

WITHOUT A ROW TO CLEAR THE AIR – difficult with a houseful of guests – Jason and I grated along for the next few days, chafing at each other's misdeeds. His drunken state had been annoying and he should have been more considerate around the guests, but the money rankled more. I couldn't explain why I felt so hurt, not even to myself, so I let the pile of petty annoyances become an unsurmountable mountain. After Jason sauntered into the lounge one evening and turned the TV over without checking whether I was watching the News, I'd had enough. I slammed down the iron, told him to get on with it and stomped out of the guesthouse.

Once outside, I regretted my haste. When I'd popped round to Jetsam Cottage earlier that afternoon, Kim had been in bed asleep and – although Maggie had been helping her with the guesthouse – Shona had been exhausted. She needed an early night.

With nowhere else to go, I headed into Torringham. People wandered in and out of brightly lit convenience stores but further down the street had a desolate air, with a few souls strolling by or browsing through estate agent or gift shop windows. But, as I rounded the corner into the inner harbour, I stepped into another world. One which bustled with people strolling along arm-in-arm or lazing outside the pubs and restaurants. Children skidded to a halt with cries of 'Perlease!' by the doors to the ice cream parlour. Of course, the summer holidays had started. We didn't accommodate children, so I hadn't realised.

With the tide out, a dozen boats littered the harbour bed. I leaned against the metal railings enjoying the warm breeze buffeting my face. Two men in shorts, t-shirts and matching yellow wellies, inspected the twin keels of one of the small yachts, while gulls strutted between the boats and pecked at flattened strands of seaweed. Behind me a motorbike thrummed as it weaved past the holidaymakers who ambled across the road, laughing and calling to each other. A Babylon of British accents passed by, with the exception of the quartet who strolled along clutching their cameras. German. Fab! I loved listening to all the different dialects and languages. What had made this group chose to come to Torringham? Not the peace and quiet, that's for sure. Above the cacophony, bursts of hammering reverberated from one of the trawlers on the other side of the harbour, amplified by the natural bowl that rose in layers of colourful cottages.

The smell of fish and chips wafted from a nearby restaurant and my stomach rumbled. I fingered the tenner in the pocket of my jeans. Should I succumb? The idea of sitting by the harbour, filling myself with delicious stodge and watching the world go by was irresistible.

My mind made up, I headed over to the Fish Bar, when I heard someone call 'Katie'. It couldn't be for me. I still didn't know many people in Torringham. But with the next shout I recognised Laura's voice. She sat across the road on a table outside The Anchor's Rest with two other women, her lovely dog, Bessie, panting at her feet. I went over to say hello.

"This is Katie," Laura said to the two women, who both wore dark sunglasses and easy smiles. "She was with me when, ahem." She blushed. "I had to be rescued."

I smiled. "It's great to see you again."

"I'm mortified about it. Especially as I should know about rip tides. After all I've lived by the sea long enough but." She patted Bessie. "When I saw her heading out to sea, I lost all sanity. Thank goodness for the amazing lifeboat crew. Are you stopping for a drink?"

A bottle sat on the table, surrounded by a triangle of glasses, empty but for shallow pools of red.

Did I want to drink this early and on an empty stomach too? I shook my head. "I best not. I've left Jason at home."

"Have the one," Laura urged as she bent over to drag a chair from the neighbouring table. It juddered against the pavement. She patted the seat. "It's my round."

I hesitated. Just one should be fine, even if I hadn't eaten yet. It would be lovely to stay for a chat with Laura and her friends.

"I'll get..." I clamped my mouth shut. My tenner wouldn't stretch to four people and especially not wine.

"No, you won't." She picked up the empty bottle. "This will be my thank you for what you did to help me. I'll leave you with Sarah and Erin."

As she disappeared with Bessie, the sound of music and laughter escaped from the pub, muted as the door clanked shut behind them. Sarah and Erin asked about the B&B and talked about their jobs – one owned an art shop and the other worked at Berrinton Library – until Laura reappeared with Bessie but no drinks.

"He's bringing them out. Do you read, Katie?" She'd caught the tail-end of our conversation. "If so, we all go to this book group. You might enjoy it."

The bar man brought out two bottles of red wine and an empty glass for me. It wasn't my drink of choice, but I could manage a small one – or even this large one – thanks to Laura upturning the bottle so the wine glugged into my glass. I took a sip. Not bad. The women were good company, talking about books, the local scenery and people. Before I knew it, I'd finished my drink. My head felt hazy while sound took on a strange resonance, as if my hearing had distorted.

Amused, I watched a man who appeared to have three eyes. His toad-like chin wobbled when he laughed, his cheeks etched by a road map of purple lines which warped like a stripey shirt on TV. Best of all, he had no idea his beer threatened to slosh over his pint glass. I gave it ten seconds. At thirty, I got bored and turned back to find Laura pouring more wine.

"No more," I pleaded when it reached half full. She stopped at three-quarters. I'd take a bit more care to sip this one.

My phone beeped and I glanced at the text which swam across the screen. Jason. 'Where are you?'

Should I ignore him? But I couldn't remember why I would. Our disagreement had drifted into the mist of time, fogged by delicious wine. I shrugged. It couldn't have been anything important. Poor Jason, stuck at home while I had fun.

Beside me froggy man spilled his drink – I knew he would! – swiping his hand up his sodden chin to slurp the dregs back into his mouth.

Half-watching him, I typed. 'At the harbour. Just met Laura.'. As the man smeared his hand down his trouser leg, I noticed my phone had autocorrected my text to "Ate the harbouring.Just met Laureate.' I giggled. Again, my phone beeped. 'Your dinner is here. Will put it in the oven.'

I'd forgotten I hadn't eaten. I knocked back the last of my wine and stood up, alarmed to find myself swaying.

"I've got to go." My voice sounded thick and blurred. Not mine. Red wine and I didn't go well together. Or, perhaps we went too well! "It's been ni-sh meeting you all again," I slurred. "Do shout about the book club."

I didn't stagger home. Instead, I meandered – like a stream bending along the road – I liked that one. A tinkling stream! That made me want the loo. I giggled to myself and a passing couple looked round and shrugged. Maybe I should pretend to be on my mobile, or else they might think I was mad talking to myself. I pulled my new mobile from the pocket of my jeans, but it shot through my fingers, crashing onto the cobbles. Oh no! I caressed the crack which branched like a tree across the screen. Poor little mobile, not even a week old. But what a pretty fracture.

I told Jason about my mobile when I stumbled into the lounge. He needed to know how it had suffered.

"Look, my poor little mobile. It's got an owwie." I leaned against the wall. "Do you want to kiss it better?"

"Have you got in this state to pay me back?" Jason spat.

"Nooooo." I stuck two fingers up at him. "I've just had one-two. Oh, that reminds me, I need the loo. One-two, I need the loo." I cackled and stumbled upstairs.

♦

When I made it downstairs the next morning, I found my congealed spaghetti carbonara in the oven. Until that point, I thought I'd done well to get up without a hangover, but the smell of rancid food made my stomach heave and bile rise in my throat. I clicked on the kettle. Only black coffee would do.

Jason came into the kitchen without a 'hello'. He tied his apron strings round his back – the picture on the front showing him holding a sausage cigar had started to peel away – and opened the fridge door to pull the packs of sausages and bacon out.

"I'm sorry about last night," I said. "I had no idea red wine would affect me like that."

"You went out to pay me back. Tit for tat."

"If that had been the case, I would have stayed out and rolled in at midnight like you did."

Yet again, we spent a breakfast service in silence other than to hiss orders at each other or toss the odd barbed remark. My face curdled on contact with his, but I made sure to plaster a smile as I entered the breakfast room. 'Delicious breakfast?' 'Yes, I am lucky to be married to a great cook like him.' Luckily, with Jason not speaking to me, he couldn't boast about all the compliments.

If I was honest with myself, it unnerved me how Jason and I had changed recently. In our previous jobs we'd spent much of the week apart, but we'd made the most of our free time taking leisurely walks in the countryside, visiting relatives and friends or simply getting a takeaway with a bottle of wine. Each hour together felt precious. Because it was.

Now, forced into a 24/7 relationship, we weren't as close or comfortable in each other's company as we'd assumed. Like those 'open all hours' convenience stores, we'd become tired and in need of a refresh. But didn't that describe every B&Ber in high season? Shona and Kim had arguments too and they loved each other. Shona had even become the devoted nurse maid since Kim had come home, refusing to let her get up, let alone make a cup of tea.

It was early days for Jason and me. We just needed to give ourselves time to get used to this new life.

"Are you planning on doing any work this morning?" Jason thrust two plates into my hands. "Or do I need to do everything myself?"

♦

By five o'clock we had two of our three couples checked-in. I'd texted the missing couple that morning to confirm their arrival time, but they hadn't responded. It was my turn to do the check-in. Knowing my luck, they'd arrive seconds before our final arrival time.

Occasionally people complained about our latest check-in time being eight o'clock, but we worked seven days a week from early morning through to the last arrivals. That's unless there was an issue, when we had to be on hand day and night. In the first month, we'd allowed two guests to arrive after midnight, due to terrible traffic. But after realising how exhausted we'd become if this happened too often, I started to monitor traffic issues on Google. It meant we could be lenient if there had been an accident, but refuse an eleven o'clock arrival to people who'd simply chosen to leave London at six pm. After all, there were manned 24-hour receptions at hotels in the area that were better suited to late arrivals.

By seven pm, I became worried. Our missing guests hadn't answered my earlier text message and phone call. We'd waited up before for someone who'd chosen not to tell us they'd decided not to come. Like these guests, they'd ignored us too. I tried the number again, but the phone rang until it went through to an answering service. Instead, I texted to remind the guests of our latest check-in time. By eight fifteen pm, I decided they must be 'no shows' and went to charge their card but, as I typed in the details, the doorbell rang.

Two lads stood at the door, reeking of alcohol, each clutching a carrier bag. The taller lad's shirt hung down on one side, masking his hand which I assumed he'd tucked into the pocket of his jeans. He reminded me of Shaggy – the cartoon character from Scooby Doo rather than the pop star – with his lank hair curling around his ear lobes and tufts sprouting from his chin. Cream-tipped spots stained his cheeks, two threatening to erupt any moment.

"Donovan. For our booking."

I didn't reprimand them about being late. But they'd been drinking, so how had they got here?

"Where's your car?"

"We've come by train."

I sighed. Why had they booked parking? If I'd known, I could have used the parking pass rather than find the only space on the brow of Moreton Hill.

"Come through. I'll check you in and then take you to your room."

They flicked hesitant glances at each other. "Can we make this quick? We came back cos of your text, but we've left our drinks in the pub."

Now wasn't the time to tell me they'd been in Torringham for hours, while I waited for them to arrive. "You have to check-in and pay before you get your keys." I pushed the form in front of them. "Put your details, names and address. Then read the bit about loss of keys and times. We charge for damage."

Until now, all our young guests had been lovely and well-mannered, so these lads' ages weren't an issue, but something about them unsettled me. It wasn't so much their drinking, as most of our guests enjoyed a drink at night. Or even their thoughtlessness about the arrival time and parking, as many older guests could be the same. But it didn't bode well, especially when they stood rifling through their wallets as if struggling to find the payment amount.

"We usually pay when we leave." The taller one snapped his wallet shut as if it was his choice.

"The booking information clearly states payment on arrival. If you want to go elsewhere, fine, but we charge your first night regardless."

"How about we pay tomorrow?" The other lad swept his fringe aside to display pink-rimmed eyelids and bloodshot eyes.

It was eight thirty and my temper was shortening by the second. "How about you stay elsewhere?"

Incredible how they'd found the money for drink but not for their board. It was best they didn't stay. They weren't the type of guest we wanted. I could guarantee the card they'd booked with would fail if I processed it, no doubt insufficient funds. I headed towards the door.

"No wait!" The taller one held out a bank card. Not a type I'd seen before. "I'm sorry. We didn't know we had to pay today but there's enough on here."

I gave them the payment receipt, explained about breakfast

times and handed them the keys. Their one question related to the latest time they could come in.

"You've got a key," I said. "Just make sure you don't wake our other guests and you shut the front door."

When I took them up to the small double they'd booked, the taller one hit his head on the door frame but laughed it off and fell onto the double bed, bagsying it for himself. Their beers seemingly forgotten I left them to it and headed back to the lounge, to be blasted by the sound of gunfire as I opened the door. Jason lay across the sofa, arm behind his head, legs outstretched across the armrest. He kept a tight grip on the remote control, most likely to prevent me taking it.

"I've just told those lads to keep the noise down," I said. "And here's you with the volume up full."

"Speak up!" Jason kept his eyes on the TV. "I didn't catch what you said."

I sighed. It was going to be one of those nights.

Chapter 16

A STRANGE NOISE WOKE ME. The doorbell or had I dreamed it? In the darkness, I patted the bedside table to find my mobile phone. Its harsh brightness made me squint. Four o'clock. I groaned and slumped back onto the pillow, my tired eyes flickering shut. The sound of the doorbell pierced the sleeping guesthouse. No doubting it this time. Heart pounding, I shot out of bed and dragged on my jeans in the half-light of the mobile phone. Had something happened to Emily? Why else would someone be calling at this time? I debated whether to wake Jason but decided against it. I couldn't risk the caller going for a hat-trick, especially with a houseful of guests. Slipping my arms through a cardigan to conceal my pyjama top, I padded down the stairs into the hallway.

The shorter of the two lads who'd arrived the night before stood at the door. Behind him a car idled, its hazard lights flashing, the nearby street lamp casting a glow across its bonnet. I couldn't see anyone in the car. Had he driven it in his state? His crumpled shirt hung loose and a dark stain ran from below his crotch to the thigh of his shiny trousers. Hopefully, just a spilled drink.

"Do you know the time?" I hissed. If guests had slept through the doorbell, I didn't want to wake them by shouting, even though I could have wrung his neck.

A large man stepped from the shadows making me jump. The hallway light reflected on his bald head and his neck spilled over the collar of his shirt. My eyes were drawn to his thick fingers gripping the lad's shoulder. My heart thumped. What on earth was going on? I glanced back into the guesthouse. Should I call Jason? A car drove past, the sound of tyres on tarmac scouring the night. Its headlights lit up the car blocking the front of our driveway, a taxi by the look of the door plate.

"Sorry to wake you but this man's friend did a bunk, leaving him asleep in the back of my taxi." Like the lads, he had a London accent. "This one reckons his friend has the cash to pay."

"He's inside," the lad said. "He took the keys to the room. I could get the money if you let me in."

I pushed him back. While he hadn't been the one to run off without paying for the taxi, I didn't want to do anything that might disturb our other guests. "You're going nowhere and keep your voice down."

"I'll be a few minutes," I told the taxi driver. Jabbing my finger towards the lad, I added, "You better hope you haven't woken my guests. Stay here while I speak to your friend."

It wasn't a case of going straight upstairs. Being in a guesthouse, the doors were locked for all but the day room. I closed the front door on them and headed to the cupboard where we secreted the breakfast room key in a box accessed by a code. As I inserted the key into the breakfast room door, I fumbled and it clattered onto the laminate flooring. I tried again – this time keeping a tight grip – grimacing as the door creaked open. The light from the street lamp filtered inside, so I could make out the tables and chairs, albeit in shades of grey. I padded through to the kitchen to unhook the spare set of guest room keys and tiptoed upstairs to the second floor. The creak of the floorboards echoed through the landing and I winced, certain I would be fielding a mass of complaints from exhausted guests the next morning.

Not wanting to make more noise, I didn't knock but carefully opened the lads' door to be hit by the stench of stale alcohol and sweat. Flicking on the light, I gazed in distaste at the fully clothed lad, stretched star-like on his back across the covers. I hooked my pyjama top over my nose and headed over. The sharp tang of spirits oozed from him. I prodded his scrawny arm but he didn't respond, so I tapped his face. He gave a loud snore and his foul breath moistened my hand. Yuk! I wiped the back of my hand on the corner of the pillow but, unable to rid the feeling of it being tainted I looked round for the box of tissues we usually kept in the room. That's when I spotted the wallet jutting from his pocket and plucked it out, not caring if I woke him, although I had a feeling nothing would rouse him from his drunken stupor. Apart from the card he'd used earlier, a railcard and a driving licence in the name of Carl Donovan, the wallet was empty.

I took it outside, where I handed it to the taxi driver. "I can't wake his friend."

"I could!" The lad's voice ricocheted off the walls.

"What and wake my guests?" I snarled. Above us, a window had been left ajar. Great! That would be Alan and Sharon, a youngish couple with perfect hearing, unlike hearing-aid users Joan and Norman whose neighbouring windows were firmly closed. Like buttered toast my luck never landed the right way.

I dropped my voice to a whisper, "Unless he knows his mate's pin it won't be much use."

"It's the police then," the man said.

"I might know it." The lad went to snatch the wallet. "He usually writes it in biro on the leather. Look under the light and it'll be there. Two numbers on either side."

The taxi driver hauled him off to his car where I could make out their faces under the interior light. The man held the card in the air and a walkie-talkie to his mouth, it's tinny sound faint in the air. Why on earth hadn't I listened to my instincts and refused to let the lads stay? Yawning, I leaned against the building, the ripple of the render cool on my back. Lucky Jason. I envied him his ability to sleep through a storm. If only I could crawl into bed, roll myself into the duvet and drift away. I jerked upright, shocked at how close I'd come to nodding off.

The taxi driver and lad were getting out of the car. I went over to them, wanting to keep them and their noise away from the guesthouse.

"His card won't work," the taxi driver said. "Apparently, it's a prepayment card and his mate must have spent all the money."

"What now?"

The driver looked at me and shrugged. "One for the police, I'm afraid."

Appalled, I gazed at him. The police here twice in as many weeks? Not only that but they'd wake the guests, especially as they'd have to go inside to fetch the other lad. No doubt, he wouldn't go quietly either. I shuddered. This could end up costing us a fortune in ill-feelings and bad reviews. All because of two idiots.

"How much do they owe?"

The taxi driver frowned. "Forty quid."

"You don't deserve this." I stabbed my finger at the lad. "I'll pay but I want you and your friend out first thing tomorrow morning. No breakfast. No refund. You don't deserve this."

The lad smiled. "Thanks!"

"Oh, shut up!"

I headed inside to unlock the lounge door, certain I'd last seen my purse on the coffee table. At least I hoped I had, or else it could be in the kitchen, bedroom or the glove box of the car. Heaving a sigh of relief, I dragged it from where it poked from beneath the bookings' diary. It contained thirty pounds but, by hoovering up all the loose change on the sides, I made the required forty.

"I need a receipt," I told the taxi driver. "Give me your name and phone number too, in case I need to contact you."

As he handed me his business card and a receipt, I grasped the lad's arm, yanking him towards the guesthouse.

"You make the tiniest bit of noise and I'll be the one to call the police. And don't think I'm joking."

♦

When the alarm went off at seven o'clock, I lay there in dismay wishing for a few hours more sleep. My eyes burned with tiredness and kept flickering shut. It took all my willpower to pull myself upright, rather than snuggle back into my cosy duvet. Beside me Jason lay mouth open, snoring gently, his face lined with tiredness. Stubble grazed his face and chin, wisps of hair peeking from the v of his white top. I shook him awake and relayed the previous night's events. Without warning, he leapt from the bed and stomped out of the bedroom, the bottoms of his checked pyjama bottoms flapping round his bare feet. I caught hold of him on the landing en route to turf the lads from the bedroom.

He tried to shrug his arm from my grip, but I hissed, "Leave it for now!"

With my finger to my mouth, I nodded in the direction of the guestroom neighbouring the lads'. The strip of darkness under their door told us they were asleep. I prayed the one under the lad's door meant they'd already left, although I doubted it. We couldn't find out though. After last night's episode, we couldn't risk waking our guests. The eviction would have to wait until later. I towed Jason by the arm back into the bedroom.

"I told the lad they had to go first thing and he agreed."

"First thing is now. We might not have time later."

The snooze on my alarm sounded. I'd set the tune to 'By the Seaside'. Corny but apt. I rushed over to the bedside table to turn off the jingle, Jason's remark forgotten.

I'd hoped to find a set of keys in the box in the hallway but no such luck. Thankfully, none of the guests mentioned hearing anything untoward the previous night and I didn't plan on inviting comment by asking how they'd slept. When Alan and Sharon came downstairs relaxed and looking forward to their planned fishing trip, my worries subsided. Stifling my yawns, I smiled and made sure everyone left well fed and happy.

After we'd cleared up the breakfast room, Jason gave me a kiss on the forehead and stretched behind me to lift the car keys from the rack.

"Where are you going?" I asked.

"Have you forgotten my hospital appointment?"

I gazed at him in confusion. "But that was Friday morning."

"It is Friday."

"I'm going mad. There's me thinking it's Saturday, what with those lads partying until the small hours." Then it dawned on me. "You're leaving me with them?"

"I said we may not have time if we didn't do it then." He sighed and checked his watch. "Come on, we'll have to be quick. The traffic's going to be terrible."

I couldn't risk him missing his hospital appointment. It wouldn't be fair. He'd waited weeks to see the specialist to get his mole checked. He'd be gone from the guesthouse for a couple of hours, three at most. With check-out less than an hour away, it wouldn't be long before those lads would be on their way too. I could handle it.

"Go," I said. "It'll be fine. Good luck."

As I cleaned room four, guests passed by in their shorts and sunhats. Apart from the lads, no one was leaving today, so servicing the rooms was a breeze, even on my own. Wishing each group a lovely day, I moved onto another room and another until by eleven forty-five I had just the one room left: the lads. After their behaviour last night, I couldn't believe they had the audacity to hang around. But any anger I felt was dampened by anxiety. Should I deal with them or wait for Jason to come back? There were two of them, after all. But they hadn't come across as aggressive.

From where I stood on the landing, I could hear muffled snores.

146

I clenched my fists and took a deep breath. After two loud knocks I slid the key into the lock and shoved the door open. The stench of vomit overlaid the smell of stale alcohol. The tall lad, Carl, still lay spread-eagled over the bed, while his friend huddled on the floor. In the half-light I took care clambering across – making sure I didn't step on him or on anything he may have done on the floor – and opened the curtains to inspect the room. I couldn't spot sick, thank goodness, but the smell turned my stomach. Rancid. I prayed they'd made it to the loo.

I'd check once they'd gone. I clapped my hands together.

"Come on! You've got to get out."

"Whaaa?" Blinking in the bright sunlight, Carl lifted his head. "We've paid for today."

"And I paid for your taxi last night, so you and your friend are leaving."

He wrenched the duvet cover over his head and curled into a tight ball. I tugged his arm, but he didn't budge.

"Get up!" I screeched, furious with myself and them. Why was I such a weakling? Jason would have sorted them out. I jabbed the lad on the floor with my foot. "Get out. What sort of people do you think you are stealing from a taxi driver? I don't want you here. If you're not out in five minutes, I'll call the police."

From beneath the covers, Carl sniggered. "Yeah, right. We've paid, we stay."

"The form you signed said you had to behave or else you lose your money."

I didn't bother going on. I wasted my breath.

I stomped out, snatching their room keys from where they sat by the tea tray and jammed the bedroom door open. I had no idea what to do. Call the police or wait for Jason? I paced up-and-down the landing. Perhaps I should tip a bucket of water over them. Except that would wreck the bedding. Stuff it! I would call the

147

police. Those lads deserved it.

As I headed downstairs to grab the phone, a figure appeared through the other side of the opaque door pane. Hoping it would be Jason, I flung the door open, to find Shona holding a jug.

"I don't suppo… Fricking heck, you look fed up!"

"That's an understatement."

When I recounted the story about last night and how I couldn't get them out of bed, her expression became grim. Shoving the jug into my hand, she stomped off in the direction of Jetsam Cottage, shouting, "I'll just be a mo!"

Minutes later she shot back with Maggie who held a spray gun, while Shona had armed herself with a saucepan and wooden spoon.

I stared at them. "What are you planning to do?"

"They sound like right nasty pieces," Maggie said. "If this doesn't work, I've called Jeff and he's on his way with Ozzie."

Puzzled, I turned to Shona.

"Their dog." She grinned. "Jeff used to be a police-dog handler."

"Ozzie wasn't his dog but an ex-colleague's. When they moved abroad a few years ago, we agreed to take him as we no longer had the guesthouse. Anyhow, let's get to it." Maggie grinned. "This should be fun."

I didn't know what to think about an ex-police dog being used to help evict our unwanted guests. Would it drag the lads out with its teeth? But I didn't have a chance to ask as Maggie took the lead, holding the spray gun in front of her as if it were a real weapon. She looked so ridiculous, it took all my willpower not to laugh. She didn't ask if she was heading in the right direction but carried on up the second flight of stairs. Maybe the sound of snoring gave it away. When we reached the landing, she pointed towards the open door. Through there? I nodded. She stood with her back pressed into the landing wall and took a deep breath as if readying herself for battle.

As she swung through the doorway, she screeched, "Get up!" and sprayed water – or, at least I assumed it was water – all over the face of the lad sleeping on the floor.

He barricaded his face with his arms. "Go away!"

Maggie moved onto Carl who lay in the bed, while Shona stayed with the lad on the floor banging the saucepan centimetres from his ears.

"Are you lot mental or something," the short lad shouted. Shona gave him a swift kick and he yelped.

"I'll do it again! Get out!"

As she drew back her leg, ready for another boot, I touched her arm to warn her against it, but I didn't need to worry.

"Alright, alright!" The lad crawled towards the door. I grabbed his arm to help him up, but he shook me off, snatching his rucksack as he got to his feet. Once in the landing he shouted, "You coming, Carl?"

"These old biddies don't frighten me," Carl's muffled voice came from beneath the duvet. The only visible part of him was his fingers pinning the duvet down.

"But Ozzie will," Maggie laughed.

"A police dog," I said.

"The police? Carl!" he shouted. "They've called the pigs."

Carl didn't move. But his knuckles had become the colour of bone.

"I'd go if I was you," I said to the lad, who shot a glance at Carl and fled down the stairs.

Moments later, ferocious barks reverberated through the guesthouse and the lad's voice echoed up the stairs, "I'm going, I'm going!" He must have met Ozzie and Jeff at the door.

Maggie smiled in satisfaction. "Ozzie's arrived. Shona, be a love and show them up."

As Shona disappeared, Maggie bent over to bellow at the mound. "The dog's called Ozzie because he bites the head off things! Don't think I'm joking either."

I gazed at her in horror. If Ozzie bit Carl, we could be sued. The stairs creaked and a strange snaffling noise rose, like someone or something was being strangled and fighting for breath. We could hear Jeff's voice, urging Ozzie to be calm.

"I don't like this," I said to Maggie. "He won't bite, will he?"

Maggie winked at me. "He's trained to bite on command. Jeff and Shona will be our witnesses that this lad went to attack you and Ozzie stopped him."

A German Shepherd dog rounded the corner, straining at his lead, followed by a stocky, balding man who kept a tight grip on the leather handle. He shot Maggie a brief smile without taking his eyes from Ozzie and wound the lead round his hand to draw the dog closer. Shona smirked, clearly enjoying this. I should have known better than to involve her. This would end in tears. Most likely mine, when I was arrested for allowing guests to be mauled. The furious barking started again. I prayed all our other guests were at the harbour enjoying the sun and nowhere near this hell hound with its snapping jaw and fearsome teeth. Froths of saliva coated its mouth, making it appear rabid. Perhaps it was.

"Let him go, Jeff!" Maggie hollered.

"Okay, okay!" Carl shouted. He tossed the covers aside and leapt from the bed. "Just keep that thing away from me."

Skirting the wall, he kept as far away from Ozzie as possible. I couldn't blame him. From where I stood by the door, Ozzie was an awesome sight on his two hind legs, twisting and tugging, dagger-like fangs aching to get hold of Carl's skinny arm. By the look of it, those long canine teeth would pierce through to the other side.

I stepped back to let a white-faced Carl past. "Silly bitch," he muttered and shot down the stairs, taking them two at a time. I went to follow but Ozzie's hot breath on the back of my calf made me rethink my position and I stepped aside to let him and Jeff through. I met them moments later on the front drive. In the distance, arms pumping, Carl sprinted away towards the harbour, while a disinterested Ozzie munched on a dog biscuit.

Jeff laughed and hugged Maggie. "Oh love, I haven't had that much fun in ages. Reminds me of the olden days."

"Thank you," I said, relieved to see the back of Carl and his friend, but worried about possible repercussions. Hopefully, Jason would be here if those lads came back.

Maggie chuckled and held out a wallet. "I found this on the stairs. Mind if I hand it in at the police station? It'd be nice to have an excuse to pop in to see them all. Imagine those boys' faces when they have to go there to collect it."

I doubted they'd go to the police station for a wallet containing a driving licence, railcard and empty prepayment card. If they did though, the police might not be happy to hear what we'd done.

"But what would the police say about an ex-police dog being used on those lads?"

Maggie laughed. "Ozzie? He wasn't a police dog. He failed to get in so Barry, Jeff's old colleague took him on till he moved away. That's when we had him. He looks and sounds vicious, but Jeff'll tell you, it's all show."

"A right softie. He'd licked them to death." He patted the large dog. By way of thanks, Ozzie slopped his long, dripping tongue across Jeff's face.

I knelt to stroke Ozzie's silky head. His wet nose nuzzled my cheek – I made sure to keep away from his tongue – and his gentle brown eyes met mine. Hard to believe that moments before, I'd thought him capable of hurting those lads.

"That's one for the book. They won't be doing that again in a hurry." Shona slapped her forehead. "Duh! I almost forgot why I

151

came round. I don't suppose you've got some spare milk. Kim needs a cup of tea and we've run dry."

I grinned. "I did wonder if the jug was a gift."

We both stood for a few moments watching as Maggie, Jeff and Ozzie left in the direction of Torringham Police Station with Carl's wallet. Unconsciously, Shona tapped the wooden spoon against her thigh, the saucepan dangling from her other hand. Had she used them to get rid of guests before? They had made a terrible racket; one as loud as Ozzie but not quite as frightening. Then I remembered her kicking the poor lad on the floor and I amended that thought. Ozzie *looked* scary, whereas Shona *was* scary.

Chapter 17

BOOK IN HAND, I SAT on the rock, letting the clear water lap against my toes. Children's voices echoed from the nearby outdoor pool. Before making my way down the steps to the tiny cove, I'd watched them jump feet first into the water, laughing. Rather them than me. It had taken a full ten minutes for my feet to adjust to the temperature of the sea, let alone the rest of my body. As if to prove the point a wave rolled in, splashing my calves and making me wince. In the past hour, the tide had turned. Soon this rock would be submerged and much of the cove too. I checked my watch. Two thirty. Half an hour before I needed to head back for the new arrivals.

Beneath the shimmering water, my feet appeared pale but from the point my calves jutted above the waterline my skin was lightly tanned. Quite odd. Especially as I spent more time within the confines of the B&B than outside. As another large wave headed my way, I shuffled onto a higher rock shaped like a chair and, placing my book in my lap, leaned back against its craggy surface and closed my eyes. Without the cooling water to temper the heat, the sun prickled my skin. It felt decadent lazing here but strange too being alone here while Jason was stuck at Mike's fixing his macerator for the second time. Why didn't they get a new one? Who wanted constant toilet issues at a B&B?

I'd wondered if it had been an excuse to spend the afternoon with Mike, especially as we'd finally agreed to take a few hours off and go for a meal by the harbour. Instead, Jason's lunch had been a ham sandwich stuffed into his mouth while standing in the kitchen, aided by loud gulps of coffee. I'd turned down Josie's invitation to join her for a cup of tea. As much as I wouldn't mind a chat, especially now we'd found a joint love of books, it was ten days since I'd last gone anywhere other than food shopping and I didn't want to sit indoors. Not when I could spend a couple of hours beneath an azure sky, listening to the waves lapping the rocks.

Clumps of lime-green and russet-brown seaweed blanketed the boulder-strewn cove, while gulls lined the limestone outcrops, taking turns to lift into the air, cawing and circling in the sky. As much as other people found them a nuisance, I loved their cries. On days when I was trapped inside the B&B ironing and waiting for guests to arrive, the only thing that reminded me I lived by the sea was the sound of the gulls. For that I forgave them their five o'clock wake-up calls. Although, if they ever stole my food, I might revise my opinion of them. I checked my watch – not time to leave yet – and settled back to listen to the waves, the gulls and the screeches of excited children.

Fifteen minutes later, I packed away my towel and book and pulled on my deck shoes to hop across the rocks to the concrete steps. As I reached the quieter top road, which steered around the bustle of the marina, my mobile beeped.

'We're at the guesthouse,' the message read. 'Where are you?'

I sighed. Our check-in time didn't start for another thirty minutes. Then another notification popped up. Two missed calls from the same number, one at two o'clock and the other at two fifteen. I must have been out of signal range. What sort of mood would the guests be in? If I'd got the message I could have told them they were early and advised them to go for a stroll but ignoring them – even unintentionally – wasn't going to be the best start. I typed back to say I would be back for the check-in time and picked up speed. Soon my fast walk became a jog and before I knew it, I found myself sprinting through Torringham harbour, hurdling dog leads and slaloming between clusters of tourists.

By the time I reached the guesthouse, fifteen minutes ahead of our usual check-in time, I gasped for breath and sweat poured down my face, plastering my fringe to my forehead. My nose had become a waterslide upon which my sunglasses slithered, no matter how many times I pushed them back.

The guests sat in their car, tight-lipped and arms folded, with all the windows wound down. As I bent down to say a cheery hello, a blob of sweat fell onto the grey plastic door interior and dribbled inside. The man looked from the door to my face.

"I ran." My chest heaved as I fought to talk and breathe. "Even though check-in doesn't start until three thirty, I saw you were here and rushed back."

"Good to see you get time off running a B&B. On TV they reckon it's a full-time job."

What on earth did the TV have to do with running a B&B? If anyone thought taking a few hours off in the middle of a twelve-hour day made it anything less than a full-time job, they needed their head testing. I hid my irritation beneath a smile – after all, they had been waiting in a sweltering car – and stepped back to let him open his car door.

"Mark Potter. That's my wife, Belinda." He held out his hand.

Surreptitiously, I wiped my hand across the back of my knee-length trousers before I shook his. His smile couldn't mask his grimace. As I slid my sunglasses back into place and headed round to Belinda, who stood by the boot of their car, I spotted him pulling a tissue from his pocket to dab his hand. I took her case and took them to their room where I gave them the usual rundown of where to find the guestbook, fan and spare sheets, the latter if they got too hot at night.

"Come down when you're ready and I'll check you in."

I rushed off to my bedroom to have a quick wash and change into more formal clothing. We had two more couples to check-in later. At least they'd be greeted by someone who could talk rather than pant and didn't look as if they'd staggered from the finish line of a marathon. I gazed at myself in the mirror, horrified to see my t-shirt mottled with dampness, the area above my cleavage the only dry patch. It could have been worse as, beneath the t-shirt, my skin all but swam in a river of sweat.

When the stairs creaked half an hour later, I grabbed the registration form and met Mark and Belinda in the hallway where I ushered them through to the day room.

"Is everything okay with your room?"

They glanced at each other. Mark cleared his throat. "There's a stain on the bed."

I'd made that bed and the sheets and duvet had looked pristine. I'd ironed the duvet and pillowcases too, so I should have noticed any marks. But these were the customers and if they'd spotted something, I had to deal with it.

"I'm sorry about that. Where is the stain?"

"On the mattress topper."

Of their own volition, my eyebrows shot into my hair. My surprise laid bare for them to see. The mattress topper? What on earth had they been doing to see that?

"Let's have a look."

I led the way back to the room to be met by an explosion of furnishings. The new tub chairs had been turned around while the coffee table sat in the centre of the room, buried but for one peeking table leg beneath a mound of bedding. The sheet had been ripped off the bed, strewn on the floor beneath the new cotton mattress protector I'd bought the previous week.

His stubby finger hovered over the white topper. "There!"

Squinting, I could just make out the tiniest hair. Not a pube, thank goodness, as this couldn't have been more than three millimetres in length and fair in colouring. He must have bionic vision. Like threading a needle, it took me three attempts to pluck it from the bed.

He moved to point at a faint mark no larger than his thumb. "And we found this too."

I wondered if I should explain that a guest had spilled some red wine on the sheets and a small amount had seeped through the mattress protector onto the topper. I'd been unable to remove it, even with two washes at high temperatures, so I'd given up worrying about this tiny blemish. But I couldn't be bothered.

"If it wasn't for this you would have passed the *Four in a Bed* test."

"The *what*?"

"You know, on TV. We checked your wardrobe, the top of your doors, skirting boards, under the bed. You would have passed until we found this." Belinda beamed at me.

"That's nice," I said.

I gazed at the woodchip wallpaper and the faded carpet, which had been scrubbed to within an inch of its long life and was destined for the skip at the end of the season, along with the melamine drawer unit and the chipped coffee table currently blanketed by bedding.

"Do you think you'd be better off somewhere else?"

They looked at me as if I was daft. "We're here now. We just don't want to sleep on a stained topper."

"I'll take the topper away. If you go to the room I showed you and make a start on the registration form, I'll be down soon."

Ripping off the mattress protector and topper, I stomped down to the utility room. I didn't have a spare topper and the cotton protector alone wouldn't stop spills ruining the new mattress. They may be fastidious about blemishes but that didn't mean they wouldn't create their own. Too short to reach without Jason's help, I climbed onto one of the shelves in the laundry cupboard and balanced between it and the wall to drag one of the old rubber-backed protectors from the top shelf. Stuff them. They could squeak all night.

Back in their room, I held the mattress protector up to the light to inspect it before putting it on the mattress. Perfect. I bent down to retrieve the crumpled sheet from the floor but changed my mind. They'd probably rip it apart again. Instead, I left the room and, fixing a rictus smile, I headed to the day room to find them sitting in silence, the form completed.

"All sorted! I haven't made the bed again as, no doubt, you'll want to check it before you put everything back where it should be." I smiled sweetly. "Right, that's one hundred and sixty pounds, please."

♦

The doorbell rang and I hurried out, praying that these arrivals wouldn't be as odd as our earlier *Four in a Bed* fanatics. Since those awful lads had gone, we'd been blessed with two weeks of wonderful guests. Strange how it worked out. The vast majority of our guests were lovely and often I found myself wishing they didn't have to leave, but it seemed that every two to three weeks we landed a difficult pair.

Something about the woman and man on the doorstep felt familiar, unlike the trio of children who huddled around them clutching ice lollies as they gazed, wide-eyed, at me. They couldn't be guests; we didn't take children, especially not ones coated in sticky gloop.

In the heat, strands of the woman's grey curly hair clung to her forehead, while the fleshy mound of the man's belly bulged from beneath his vest. He wore green nylon shorts, the same awful colour as the guesthouse door frame and window ledges. Then it hit me. Jim and Maureen! Not today of all days. Then again, not any day.

"The grandchildren wanted to see the old place." He caressed a little girl's head. She gave a gappy grin and stuck her lolly into her mouth. Pink drool ran down her chin and over her fingers, dripping onto the paving.

Most people would smile, say goodbye and close the door. But not me. Instead of being honest – after everything you've told people about us, I don't want you near me, my family or the guesthouse – I stuttered nonsense.

"I'm busy. With guests." Half an hour earlier it would have been true. Where were the *Four in a Bed* couple when you needed them? Right now, I'd kiss them if they came down to moan about something else.

The children gazed into the empty hallway.

"Look Nan! They've still got the carpets. They haven't changed them like Mrs Keep said."

Mrs Keep? That must be Ellie Keep from the White Hart. When she'd asked about the work we'd been doing, I'd mentioned we were replacing the carpets at the end of the year. I hadn't realised her interest lay in collecting a stash of gossip. I wouldn't be going back there.

Maureen and Jim didn't move. I checked my watch. If the next guests arrived on time, they'd be pulling onto the driveway any moment.

Jim propelled the little girl forward. "It wouldn't harm to let Lily pop in for a minute. She's been asking about it all week."

"I hope you're having a good holiday, but I must be getting on."

Behind them, a red-faced Jason turned the corner and headed across the drive. I heaved a sigh of relief. Finally, he'd made it back from macerator duty, no doubt after a swift pint or two.

Maureen hadn't spotted him. In a Brummie accent – stronger than I recalled, although I felt sure they'd moved to Norwich – Maureen said, "Too posh for the likes of us, are you?" She crossed her arms. "We let you have this place for nothing and look at you.

La-de-da."

Jason towered behind her. When our eyes met, he shook his head. Tracking my gaze, Maureen spun round, clutching her chest as she leapt back in shock.

"I think you should go, before I do something you regret." Jason said. Turning to Jim, he added, "And I would be very careful what you say about us in future. We have *a lot* of stories to tell. And the proof too."

As Jim backed away, shepherding the children, the little girl tugged at his vest. "Why can't we go in Grandad?"

"Cos they're…" Maureen met Jason's eyes and she clamped her mouth shut.

"Too busy working on the place?" Jason suggested. He folded his arms, mimicking her earlier stance.

He waited until they reached the pavement, before closing the front door. "Why didn't you tell them to go away?"

"I did!"

He met me with a look of disbelief. "Just once, it would be good to come back to find nothing has gone wrong."

I opened my mouth to argue, then changed my mind. He had a point. As he disappeared upstairs to shower, I decided not to tell him about Belinda and Mark and their fascination with *Four in a Bed*. He'd meet them soon enough.

Chapter 18

THE NEXT MORNING, BELINDA AND MARK came into the breakfast room as I chatted with another couple, Paul and Helen, who'd spent the previous day visiting the zoo. They hesitated by the door, so I invited them to sit down and help themselves to the buffet, pleased to see they did, although Belinda took the lid off the orange juice to sniff it while Mark shook the jar of muesli and held it up to the light, most likely to see how much fruit it contained.

Or maybe he was searching for hairs. Either way, he poured the muesli into his bowl, so it must have passed his test.

Paul watched them, faltering for a moment in the middle of his story. He shook his head and continued, "So as I was saying, these meerkats…"

When he'd finished telling me about their day, I headed over to Belinda and Mark.

"Your seagulls are loud," Mark said.

Yawning, Belinda rubbed her eyes. "They kept us up all night."

From the other table came a loud 'ha hah' and Paul leaned across from his table. "You need my gun." He held his fingers out in the shape of a gun and closed one eye as if looking through the sight. "Bang, bang. Problem solved."

Shocked, Belinda turned to him. "You kill them?"

"Nah! Course not." He shrugged. "It's the seaside, they're wild birds. What do you expect Jason and Katie to do about it? Shoot them?"

It took all my willpower to keep my face straight as I asked, "Tea or coffee?"

When I went back with their pot of tea, they'd finished their fruit and yoghurts and sat in silence. On the neighbouring table, Helen and Paul were wading through their bowls of cereal. Paul had taken so long to eat his Weetabix, it had congealed into stodge.

"Are you ready to order?" I asked Belinda and Mark.

They nodded. "A full English with a scrambled and a poached egg."

I scribbled on my pad. "One full English with scrambled and one with poached egg."

"No, a full English with scrambled egg and one poached egg and Belinda will have a cheese, tomato and mushroom omelette with bacon and a sausage. Oh, and beans on the side."

Pen in the air, I gazed at him. Was he joking? Occasionally, we had guests asking for extra mushrooms or tomatoes or even a rasher of bacon with their omelette, but it was always an 'or' and never as much as this. It wasn't buy one, get one free in restaurants, so what made our B&B any different?

From the neighbouring table came laughter. "That's three breakfasts," Paul said.

"You can't have that!" Helen said. "That's plain rude."

My heart swelled in gratitude. I could have hugged my helpful guests.

As Belinda and Mark fired angry looks at their neighbours, I said, "How about you have scrambled egg today and poached egg tomorrow with your full English and either a slice of bacon or a sausage with your cheese, tomato and mushroom omelette. We use three eggs, so it's a dish in itself."

"On *Four in a Bed* people get what they ask for," Belinda said.

"You do know that's a game, made up for TV?" Helen said. "Do you really think these small places can give people everything they want, regardless of cost? They'd be out of business in months."

I headed back into the kitchen with the downgraded order. Jason leaned against the kitchen worktop, head in hand, his shoulders shaking with laughter.

"The first order's in," I said.

He chuckled. "I heard. We could do with staying at this *Four in a Bed* place, especially if you are given everything you ask for, no matter what."

Later, I went over to thank Paul and Helen, who grinned at me. "We've got a confession to make. We didn't like to tell you as it can be a bit off-putting but, until a few months ago, we were guesthouse owners too. Thank goodness we've retired though."

◆

Later that afternoon, Jason put down the phone. He shook his head as if he couldn't believe what he'd just been asked and wandered over to where I sat surrounded by paperwork. I'd promised to sort the receipts before the carrier bag overflowed. That was a fortnight ago. Now the receipts and other bits of paper balanced precariously on the mountainous peak. Another one or two more and the pile would topple.

"Mike," he said. Like I hadn't guessed.

"You did tell him you had to sort the bed in room four?"

I knew the answer. I'd heard the whole call. And not once had he mentioned the stack of jobs here.

"He's in terrible trouble."

"And so are we if we don't mend that bed before the guests get back."

He picked at his latest injury: a scab on his arm from days earlier when we'd been clearing out the shed and he'd been attacked by a four-inch rusty nail poking through an old piece of wood.

"How about I help Mike with his leak and then come back to sort the bed?"

"How about you sort the bed first?"

He clenched his jaw as he stared at me, expecting me to buckle and say 'Okay, go'. But I couldn't risk him leaving without

163

mending the bed first, especially if Mike bought him a couple of 'thank you' pints. Where would that leave our guest? On the floor, that's where, while he and Mike cosied up at the pub. I pursed my lips and mirrored his gaze.

Finally, he broke. "His roof is leaking and it's pouring with rain. It's a two-person job and Josie isn't strong enough to do it."

As I leapt to my feet, paperwork cascaded to the floor. Where had Mike been when, legs wobbling and back breaking, I'd helped Jason carry several old storage heaters from the shed? The bricks inside had weighed a tonne. I snatched a handful of receipts from the pile on the sofa and thrust them to his face.

"This is our business. The bed is broken. Our guests pay us to sleep here not at Mike's."

I hurled the receipts into the air, where they floated like confetti to the carpet. I'd regret that later but – for now – stuff it! Keeping up the melodrama, I flounced out of the lounge and into the hallway where I met Belinda and Mark, thankfully heading into the guesthouse – so they couldn't have heard much – but if I didn't want to follow them up the stairs, there was only one place to go: the kitchen.

A red zero on the dishwasher told me it was ready to be emptied. I turned my back on it, unable to face my least-liked chore. Sodding Mike. Even if Jason did reappear before the guest arrived, it wouldn't be with Mike in tow. No way would Mike volunteer to mend the broken bed.

Sighing, I tapped my nails on the worktop. I had no idea what to do or say to make Jason put the guesthouse first. But was I being unreasonable? After all, if we had a roof leak in the middle of a downpour, I would hope someone would help. The one we'd had in the lounge had been a nightmare. Poor Mike and Josie. They must be frantic. Especially if the rain was coming into a guest room.

My mind made up, I headed back to the lounge to apologise to

Jason, but he wasn't there. From upstairs came the sound of banging. Following the noise, I found Jason hammering a length of wood onto the inside of the upended bed. Three nails poked from his pursed lips.

He spoke with a strange muffled tone through the side of his mouth. "This will hold it for now, but we'll need a new bed." He drew another a nail from between his teeth and hammered it into the wood. "This one's had it."

When he finished, he pushed down on the frame to test it and got to his feet. "Give us a hand."

After we hefted the bed into place, I told Jason to leave the bedmaking to me, but he shook his head. "And have you moaning about doing everything while I swan about with Mike?"

We made the bed in silence. As I went off to empty the dishwasher, I heard the bang of the front door. He'd gone to Mike's. What time he'd be back was anyone's guess.

♦

Jason arrived home two hours later but instead of coming through to the lounge to say hello, he headed upstairs. The water running through the pipes told me he'd gone for a shower. Around me, piles of receipts littered the coffee table and carpet, weighed down by an assortment of mugs and glasses masquerading as paperweights. No way would I be throwing these in a fit of temper again.

I'd had enough, my eyes struggled to focus on the numbers, my mind had turned to mush, but I couldn't stop until each pile was checked against the bank statements. If I hadn't found myself glued to a repeat of *Four in a Bed* I would be almost finished, but I'd thought it might be worthwhile research to assess what else we could expect from Mark and Belinda. The only item outstanding on their list seemed to be a lengthy review followed by a decision on whether they'd come back. Recalling breakfast this morning, I had a good idea what their response would be.

My phone beeped, so I picked it up. Laura. 'Book club tonight if you fancy coming. 7pm at The Anchor's Rest. Don't worry about not reading it. I haven't.'

Like the roll of a wave my heart leapt and sank. I'd love to go but we had two couples arriving around then. It wouldn't be fair to leave Jason with them both, especially after I'd moaned at him for doing the same thing. But the thought of going out and chatting, over a glass of wine, with a friendly group about books – even ones I hadn't read – gnawed at me and before I knew it I'd stashed the receipts away, ready to be retrieved the following day.

I headed up to the bedroom and into the ensuite, assailed by the fug of steam. The buzz of the shower and splatter of water masked my entrance. Behind the misted shower screen I could just make out Jason's pale back, his hair a mass of white foam. It was pointless trying to talk to him as he wouldn't be able to hear me, so I sat on the bed with my phone, flicking through my Facebook page while I waited. The shower door clicked and Jason hummed as he towelled himself dry. He'd brush his teeth next; he always did after showering, no matter what time of day. Sure enough, the whirr of the electric toothbrush filtered out. A few minutes more and I could tackle him. Hopefully, he'd be in a better mood than earlier.

When he spotted me, his eyebrows arched but he didn't speak. A few grey hairs lined his temple but unlike many of his friends, he sported a full head of hair – most of it the same colour as when we'd married – while I had a bottle to thank for my brown locks. He'd tied his towel around his waist. With all the work in the guesthouse, his office-job paunch had flattened so he looked trimmer than he had for years. But his face bore the signs of fatigue, with dark shadows beneath his eyes. We both had those.

I cleared my throat, unsure where to start. "I've been asked to go out tonight."

"Have you?"

"Laura's asked me to a book group."

"And?"

"We've got two check-ins." Optimism made me hope he'd offer to do them alone but I had no chance. Not after this morning.

"Strange how you've changed your tune. One minute the business has to come first at any cost and the next it doesn't matter as long as you can go out."

He took his towel off to dry his hair and turned away, leaving me to talk to his back. I glanced at the mole by his shoulder blade, thankful the consultant had said it wasn't one to worry about. My gaze travelled down. Now he didn't sit on his bum for most of the day, it had become toned. – his thighs too. My legs were more muscular – I could run up-and-down the stairs with ease – but my bum seemed to be like my stomach: lumpy and stubbornly holding onto the fat. In recent weeks he'd made a few gags about my 'chubbs'. They'd hit the target and stung. Maybe I should do something about it.

He pulled on a clean pair of boxer shorts and tilted his head as he squirted aftershave. The loss of weight made his jawline more defined. I pressed my fingers to my jaw feeling the plumpness which heralded the first signs of the dreaded jowls, one of my less attractive family traits.

"Go if you want," he said. "But stop trying to chain me to this place."

How was I doing that? When we'd agreed to run the guesthouse together, neither of us had realised how constricted our leisure time would be. But instead of working together to reach a compromise it felt as if he was manoeuvring for top dog position. He got to call the shots – any excuse to disappear with Mike – while I begged for scraps of time.

I folded my arms. "So, expecting the guest bed to be mended is wrong? You're at Mike's more than here. All I wanted was one night out. But don't worry, I'll flipping well stay in."

"Don't be—"

"Oh, sod off."

For the second time that day I stormed off and, yet again, I regretted it within minutes. Back in the lounge I threw myself onto the sofa. When Jason had peevishly told me to go out, I should have said a sarcastic 'thank you' and left it at that. Instead, I'd stomped off in my size five boots and squished all hopes of an evening where the only B&B would be books and banter. And there would have been wine, although I'd stick to white in future.

The doorbell rang. We weren't expecting our new guests to arrive until seven or eight o'clock and it couldn't be Shona and Kim. When I'd spoken with them the day before, they'd been complaining about never seeing the sun again, thanks to their odd decision to paint their bedroom as the summer holidays started. But, after spending so much time in bed when poorly, Kim had decided she couldn't stand the yellow flowery paper a moment longer. Frowning, I got to my feet. Hopefully, it wasn't a door-step seller or someone ignoring our 'no vacancies' sign and looking for a room.

Uncle Bert stood on the doorstep. He'd exchanged his boots for a pair of trainers but his dusty blue overalls told me he'd come straight from work. His fingers nipped the edge of his cap, turning it slowly as he spoke.

"I'm sorry for not calling ahead, love, but I were passing by."

I ushered him through to the lounge. "You know it's always lovely to see you."

"Yes, well." He faltered. Giving me a weak smile, he sat down heavily.

"Are you okay?"

Now I thought about it, he didn't look well. The lines on his face had deepened, while beneath his eyes his skin hung sallow and grey.

"Just a hard day at work. Every day is one closer to retirement."

I gave him a wry smile. Only weeks back he'd told me he had chosen not to retire as he wasn't one for gardening or watching TV. A building site may be hard work but he enjoyed the graft.

"I'll put the kettle on. Tea?"

Not waiting for an answer – Bert was a tea and two sugars man – I headed out to the kitchen, where I typed a message to Laura. 'Can't make tonight but will def make next time. x'

Minutes later, I headed back to the lounge with two steaming cups to find Jason settled on the sofa beside Bert, chatting about cricket. Jason wasn't a cricket buff but he talked easily about wickets, runs and bowling. He didn't meet my eye and I didn't bother to see if he wanted a cup of tea. We'd reached stale mate. A phrase that reminded me of our marriage.

My sour thoughts must have shown on my face as Bert said, "You alright love?"

I nodded towards the piles of stacked receipts. "Like you, just tired."

"Moaning is hard work," Jason said.

Flushing, I swallowed the barb I longed to fire back and shot Jason a 'just you wait' look. As Bert's gaze flickered between Jason and I, a jagged 'z' settled between his eyebrows. Humphing to himself, he sipped his tea, while the silence solidified around us. I searched for something to say, but Jason beat me to it when he asked Bert how it was going at the building site. Bert responded, but he wasn't his usual chirpy self. A quiver threaded his voice and when he smiled it flickered and dimmed in seconds.

He patted his knees and, gasping about his age, heaved himself to his feet. "I'll be off now. Doreen will be wondering where I am, especially with Callum stopping over at his girlfriend's place."

At the front door, Jason shook Bert's hand while I gave him a hug. Up close, the faint scent of Lynx barely masked the smell of dust and sweat, and a thin film of grime clung to his skin. Exhaustion oozed from him.

"We'll come and see you both soon," I promised.

He gave me a weary smile. "No rush. You've enough on your plate."

As he traipsed to his van parked across the road, he seemed stooped and much older. Weighed down by something. He'd wanted to get back to Doreen. Was he worried about her? Perhaps if Jason and I hadn't been so absorbed in our squabbles, I could have persuaded him to tell me what was on his mind. As he drove away, I gave him a small wave and shut the door. Strangely, it felt as if I was closing the door on him. We hadn't got to know each other properly. There were so many questions I wanted to ask about his childhood with my mum. I hoped, prayed, he was simply tired from work and nothing more sinister.

Chapter 19

FROM WHERE I KNELT CLEANING the drawers in room nine on the second floor, I could hear a faint ringing. For a moment, I didn't react. Jason could answer it. But then I remembered he'd had to rush off and, annoyingly, I'd left the phone in the lounge. Sighing, I placed the can of polish and duster on the carpet and sprinted down the two flights of stairs, reaching the phone just as the answer machine butted in.

"Hold on," I told the caller as my voice droned on and on. Finally, I stopped talking and the caller could speak.

Whoever it was chuckled. "You need a shorter message."

"I need to remember to take the phone with me," I said.

"I guessed you were on the top floor. Murphy's Law, that."

His voice sounded familiar and he knew the building too. "Have you been before?"

He hesitated. "Erm, no. It must be the accent. You get a lot of us Brummies visiting Torringham." He sounded defensive, but he had a point: a large number of our guests came from the West Midlands, with South Wales a close second.

"Are you looking for a room?"

He wanted a single occupancy room for the following week. With our only room available being a small double suiting one person, it was perfect. As I took his details, I became convinced we'd spoken before but while his unusual surname was familiar, when he gave his first name too – Max Manningtree – I knew no one with that name had stayed with us. He read out his card details and I input them into the system.

"We'll only use your card details if you cancel and then it's a one-night fee," I said.

"Take the money now."

"We usually take payment on arrival."

"I'd prefer it if you take it today. You can do that, can't you?"

I shrugged to myself. We rarely had guests begging to give us money, but he was welcome to do so. When I finished the call, I headed over to the card machine to process the payment. As the receipt spilled from the machine, I noted the address details didn't match. Perhaps I'd misheard his house number or postcode. Not that it mattered as the payment had gone through, but when he arrived I would make sure to confirm his address.

Something bothered me about the call, although I had no idea what. Before I headed back upstairs to finish the cleaning, I checked the diary system. An Alan Manningtree had booked four nights in April, but he'd cancelled the day before his planned arrival saying he'd been called into hospital for an urgent operation the following morning. I wasn't going to charge the cancellation fee – especially as Alan had been a regular with Maureen and Jim and might come back again – but Shona pointed out that charging a one-night fee was fair, especially as we'd lost four nights and we were unlikely to resell his room at this late stage.

"You're a small business," she'd said. "Why do people accept the likes of Ryan Air keeping their money when they cancel, but not little Flotsam Guesthouse. You have to toughen up or you'll go broke."

I felt bad pushing people for money. But Shona was right. After discussing it with Jason, I'd decided to take the payment but, thanks to an invalid card, it wouldn't go through. I picked up the phone to call Alan, then promptly put it down. It wouldn't be fair to bother him when he'd be preparing to go into hospital.

The next day Shona bumped into me in the driveway where I told her about my lack of success. She'd frogmarched me into the lounge.

"For frick's sake! You're too green for words. Give me his

number."

"I told you, he's in hospital."

She raised an eyebrow. "Well, he won't answer then, will he?"

I shouldn't have let her coerce me but, to be honest, I was curious to find out what would happen. I tapped out the number and handed her the phone. She hummed to herself while it rang.

"Alan!" Such was her enthusiasm, he may well have been a long-lost friend. "Good to hear you're up-and-about already. I'm calling on behalf of Flotsam Guesthouse. Yes, that's correct. I think there may have been an error when I took your card details and I'd like to check them with you."

Handing me the phone, she pulled a face. The dialling tone purred through the speaker.

"He got cut off?"

"Hung up, more like."

When I looked unconvinced, she snatched the phone back and pressed redial. It rang and rang, until she cut the call.

"I'll send him an email," I said. "When he booked he said he'd been coming here for years. I'm sure he'll sort it."

"Unless he's one of Maureen's stooges," Shona said, reminding me of the issues Maureen had created with guest payments and the diary. "Remember the hassle you had when she messed everything up."

Months later, I'd all but forgotten about Alan Manningtree until today's call from Max. Of course, Alan never paid and my email remained unanswered. Remembering Shona's ominous words about Maureen – strange how this Max had called days after she'd wanted to bring her grandchildren in – I felt compelled to check the two address details. Breathing a sigh of relief, I saw that Alan lived in Edgbaston, whereas Max came from Birmingham. No doubt about it. They were different people.

As Jason came through to the lounge and handed me the receipt

173

he'd got from the Post Office, I clicked the laptop lid shut. He'd left half an hour ago when a guest had phoned in tears after leaving her prescription medicines behind. With her train already whizzing through Bristol, it was too late for her to come back. Luckily, she had enough to keep her going until Monday, but her medication would have to be ordered in by the pharmacy. Being a Saturday, Jason had just ten minutes until the last post went at noon, so he'd sprinted down to the Post Office.

"Just made it. Are you finished already?"

"I've just taken a booking. There's still two rooms to do."

"That's a shame," he grinned. "I was hoping it would all be done and dusted."

As we headed upstairs, Max fleetingly came to mind but I didn't mention it to Jason. What would I say? A man who reminded me of Alan Manningtree is coming to stay, but while they share the same surname, he isn't Alan and they don't have the same address. I could imagine Jason's response: Alan who? Then he'd say I was going mad. He wouldn't be far wrong.

♦

A week later, Max Manningtree stood on the doorstep, a small suitcase in his hand. After his insistence about paying upfront, I half-expected this Manningtree to turn up with a partner in tow and claim he'd paid for two people. But he appeared to be your average, lovely person, just like ninety-nine percent of our guests. He led the way up the stairs, to the second floor, and stepped into his room, commenting politely on the spaciousness.

"You've changed the chairs."

"That's right." I smiled, pleased he'd noticed the improvements, until I realised he wouldn't know what the room used to look like. He solved this by adding, "It's a nice surprise to have a comfy chair

174

rather than those dining room ones I saw on the internet."

As he spoke, a loud smash reverberated from outside and I rushed to the window, gazing down in shock. A car had reversed into our wall. When I'd answered the door to Max, Jason had been checking in other guests in the day room, so he would have seen the accident. Sure enough, he raced outside skidding to a halt by the back end of the car.

"I have to go," I said to Max. "Come downstairs to check-in when you are ready, but there's no hurry. I think it's going to be one of *those* afternoons."

I galloped down the stairs and out to the driveway where a small crowd had formed. Somehow the driver had managed to embed his car on the small slate wall that separated our drive from the narrow lane which led to Moreton Hill. The car's rear wheels were about a foot in the air, while the metal pole, from which the sign for Flotsam Guesthouse had hung just five minutes before, jutted from beneath the bumper. Our poor sign had been launched into the lane.

Jason stood by the driver's side door, helping an elderly man out of the SUV, while on the passenger side two women aided a frail woman who clutched a hankie to her forehead.

The man's crooked fingers grasped Jason's arm for support and his voice trembled. "I don't know what happened." He pressed the heel of his palm to his eye. "I just don't know. I only got the car yesterday."

Jason ushered him inside to the day room, while I salvaged our wrecked sign from the roadside. After tucking it by the side of the house, I brushed the splinters from my palms and headed over to the women helping his companion, telling them to bring her inside. They cradled the woman between them, patiently mirroring her feeble steps. Now she'd removed her hankie, I could see an egg-shaped mark, the colour of veins, on her forehead. Someone would need to look at that.

Panic-stricken, Kim dashed over as I led them into the hallway. "Martha!"

"Is she your guest?"

"Shona's auntie." Holding out her arm she whispered 'thank you' to one of the women and took her place.

"Are you okay, Martha?" Usually Kim had a husky low voice, but she spoke loudly as if to a child. "Not hurt?"

"No, no," Martha's voice wobbled. "Just a bit of a shock, that's all."

While Kim settled Martha down beside the elderly man in the day room and inspected her bruise, I rushed off to get them all a cup of tea. When I came back with the pots of tea, mugs and biscuits on a tray, two paramedics were kneeling by Martha. The two women who had helped her from the car loitered by the bookcase chatting, while Jason and Kim stood beside the elderly man.

"That wall's dangerous. I couldn't see it," the man told Kim.

"Well, it hasn't moved in over a hundred years," Jason said. "But if it makes you feel better, we'll blame the wall."

Turning her back to the man, Kim rolled her eyes and mouthed to Jason, 'Don't worry, he's always moaning.'

"Now Derrick," she raised her voice. "You can't blame a wall when it's in someone's driveway."

His gnarled fingers clutched the arms of the chair. "I can and I will. It's too low. Something needs to be done so it can be seen."

Jason folded his arms. "Maybe we should put up an eight-foot-high sign just like the one you knocked down."

Max Manningtree stepped into the day room, surprised to see so many people milling about. When his eyes met mine, he smiled. "I can see it's not the best time for you. Do you want me to come back later?"

"Jason will check you in," I said, relieved to have an excuse to move Jason away from Derrick. With all the bodies in the day room, they'd have to do the registration form in the restaurant. I pointed to the door on the other side of the hallway. "Go through there."

Pleased to be released, Jason disappeared with Max, while Kim spoke to the paramedics about Martha, leaving me with Derrick who sat muttering to himself. When I handed him a mug of tea it shook violently in his hand, splashing his legs. As he shot me a furious look, I rescued the mug and placed it on the table. His face told me exactly what he was thinking. First, we'd attacked him with our wall and now with tea.

"Are you feeling okay?"

"Do I look it?" He jabbed his finger towards Martha. "And does she?"

While I appreciated he was upset, his indignation was misplaced. We'd had a long, tiring day and, thanks to his car being stuck on our wall, we probably had hours more work ahead of us dealing with a recovery vehicle and making sure everything was safe. My feet ached and I longed to sit down. But rather than moaning, we were trying to help.

I bent low so his eyes were level with mine and hissed, "No, she doesn't. The best thing you can do for Martha is to get your eyesight checked."

As soon as I spoke, I felt ashamed. No need for me to resort to spitefulness, no matter how much Derrick annoyed me. Shock did strange things to people. He must be embarrassed too. Outside, people mingled, chatting and taking photographs as they inspected the car's rear end resting on the wall, the rest of it blocking the footpath.

When someone called, "How on earth have they managed that?" a man hollered, "Evel Knievel's moved onto cars!".

Yes, Derrick would be mortified. No matter what he said.

Kim came over, frowning. "They're worried about Martha. Not

so much the bump on her head but she's got chest pain. Maybe her heart. They're going to take her in. When the ambulance arrives I'll go with her."

Kim placed her hand on Derrick's shoulder. His bottom lip quivered and his hands trembled, even though he cupped them in his lap.

"You'll be okay here with Katie until Shona gets back. There's only room in the ambulance for one."

Derrick glared at Kim. "I'll go with her and you stay here."

"That's not going to happen. You're in no fit state to be traipsing around a hospital. Shona can bring you over later if they keep Martha in."

Kim turned to me. "I'm sorry about this. Look after him for me."

I gave her my best impression of a smile. "It will be my pleasure."

The doorbell sounded and two stocky men in oil-smeared overalls wandered through the open door into the hallway. Had someone called for a breakdown truck? Before I could ask, Jason appeared from the breakfast room and shook hands with Max, who'd stepped between myself and the visitors. As Max disappeared outside, Jason turned to the men.

"Do you need a hand?" One of the men pointed to the car. "The lads and I could get it off, just so it's out of the way."

"You can lift the car off there?" Jason asked.

"We're old hands at it. You'd be amazed where grockles end up. They're not used to the lanes and hills, though…" He eyed the main road. "This one hasn't much excuse."

Jason scratched his head. "You've done this before?" When the man nodded, he said, "I'll just check it's okay."

He popped into the room, not looking to Derrick for approval but to Kim, who hovered by Martha and the paramedics.

"You heard that, Kim? Are you okay with it?" She bobbed her

head before turning back to Martha.

Leaving Derrick, I headed outside to see what they planned to do. I expected to see a tow truck arriving but instead half a dozen burly mechanics joined Jason and two other men. Oddly, I found myself wishing Emily and Lucy could be here to see this. They'd never believe it when I told them.

I gazed at the men. How would they lift the car when it was jammed on the wall? As the men bent to take their positions around its rear, the crowd hushed, and a man I vaguely recognised from the garage leaned through the driver's door and gave a thumbs up. To a shouted, "Go!" the grimacing men heaved the back of the car, sinews protruding from their necks. When the front wheels started to roll forward, they shouted instructions to each other and staggered behind somehow keeping the car's rear centimetres above the wall. I held my breath, praying they wouldn't drop it and cause further damage. Derrick would not be happy.

Before I knew it, they'd eased the car to the ground. The men gave each other high-fives and accepted handshakes from the crowd, until a siren shrieked above the cheers. In the distance an ambulance raced towards us, blue lights on, headlights flashing in turn. My relief turned to anxiety. Martha must be more serious than I'd thought.

A red-faced Jason strode over to me. Panting, he said, "Get the keys off Derrick. I'll drive it round to Kim's."

I found Derrick being placated by Kim, who turned imploring eyes on me. As he pulled himself to his feet, he staggered back into the chair. I doubted there would be room in the ambulance for both him and Kim. No matter how much he wanted to be with his wife, he would be a hindrance if he went alone. I laid a firm hand on his shoulder.

"Stay here until Shona arrives. Martha needs someone to help her." I touched his trembling hand to prove my point. "And you've had a bad shock. You'll be able to follow with Shona soon. Do you have your keys?"

When he gave me a confused look, I twisted my hand as if turning an ignition. "Your car keys. They've got it off the wall. You can get it looked at tomorrow."

Angling to one side, he pulled the keys from his trouser pocket. I handed them to Kim, asking her to give them to Jason on her way out. As Martha was tucked into the wheelchair, Derrick gave a low moan and started to visibly shake. He tore a hanky from his other pocket and dabbed beneath his eyes, but his gaze didn't leave Martha as she was wheeled out clutching her chest. We both watched through the window as she vanished into the ambulance, with Kim following behind. A few minutes later, the ambulance fired a short burst on its siren and sped away.

Jason appeared at the door holding two large boxes of Budweiser. "I'm giving those lads a drink," he said. "Most of them are from the garage but two are fisherman down the quay."

I nodded. With Martha gone, just Derrick and I remained in the day room. Outside, the crowds had dispersed, with just a few stragglers standing near Jason and the men who'd helped him. Between their bursts of laughter, silence filled the room, amplifying Derrick's sniffles. I had to distract him. Chatting wasn't an option – not unless I wanted my head bitten off – but the TV could offer some respite.

"Do you want to come through to the lounge?" I extended my arm in case he needed a hand out of the chair.

"I want to see Martha," Derrick muttered, but slowly he rose to his feet and shuffled through to the lounge with me.

After he'd settled into the sofa, I switched on the TV and handed him the remote control. "I'll put the kettle on and make a fresh pot of tea."

When I came back a little while later, I almost dropped the tray in shock. Mouth open, eyes closed, he slumped back. Had the day been too much for him? His face had an ashen pallor and his lips had become a purple-grey colour. Like death.

I shoved the tray onto the coffee table, not caring as milk spattered over the side of the jug and the cups clattered against the teapot. I grabbed his hand. His skin was paper thin over his bony fingers and cold to the touch.

"Derrick!"

Startled, his eyes flew open and he clutched his chest. Great! If he wasn't dead before, I'd done a great job of giving him a heart attack. At least he'd get his wish to be with Martha in hospital. His bleary eyes gazed around, until he focused on me hovering above him.

"What? Is it Martha?"

I shook my head. "I'm sorry. I thought…" How could I tell him I'd thought he'd died? "…you'd want your tea while it was hot."

Chapter 20

SHONA ARRIVED TWO HOURS LATER. Oddly relaxed for someone with an aunt in hospital, she laughed as she pointed to the damaged sign.

"A guest didn't like your sign either, I take it."

The sign dated back to the days when ensuite rooms were a luxury rather than the norm, so it said, 'some rooms ensuite'. I'd laughed at the 'some' when we first viewed Flotsam Guesthouse, but I'd been more amused by the centrepiece picture of a sinking ship. Hardly the best sales tactic. A replacement sign was on my 'to-do sometime this year' list, now bumped up to must-do.

"Didn't Kim tell you about the accident?"

Colour drained from her face. "Kim?"

"Derrick had the accident. He's in the lounge—"

She clamped her hand to her chest. "I thought you meant Kim. But Derrick? How is he?"

I'd made such a hash of a simple explanation. This time I ploughed on, ignoring Shona's interruptions. "Kim's taken Martha to hospital… No, she's okay. She had chest pains after the accident so they're keeping her in overnight… I don't think it's serious, just a precaution. She wanted you to drive Derrick over. Did you not get her message?"

She shook her head. "She must have forgotten I left my phone behind. I only came round to ask what had happened to your sign."

In the lounge, she attacked Derrick with a volley of questions, "Are you okay? What a shocker. Poor Martha. Are you ready to go? Do you need the toilet?" She paused and looked him straight in the eye. "Because you need to go now."

With a grunt he waved away my arm and heaved himself to his feet. "Hello to you too."

"I said are you okay. What more do you want?" She linked her arm with his. "And don't be telling me you need the toilet when we're driving there. Go now or forever hold it in."

She turned to me and whispered (although it was a Shona-style whisper, so the whole guesthouse would have heard), "You have to ignore his grumps or else he's a right pain."

Derrick pursed his lips but didn't say a word. Towed by Shona, he tottered into the hallway, both coming to an abrupt halt as the front door flew open and Max Manningtree stumbled in. Seeing the three of us, Max raised an eyebrow, his irises startlingly blue against his bloodshot eyes. A web of thin veins crossed his flushed cheeks. I didn't recall his nose being quite so bulbous, its lumpy tip looked like a head of purple broccoli. Without warning, he tottered backwards, flinging out his arms to steady himself.

"A welcoming committee!" he slurred, pulling himself away from the wall. Addressing Derrick, he said, "Still here?"

Shona glared at Max and strode past, dragging Derrick in her wake. Giving Max a brief smile – and praying he hadn't drunk so much he would be sick in the bed – I followed her out. She slowed her pace when we reached Jetsam Cottage's drive.

"You've got him staying?" she hissed. She flung a glance in Max's direction.

"Who? Max?"

"Max? That's not…" She frowned. "It'll come to me. Here, hold onto Derrick while I grab my car keys. I wish I'd known I needed to go back out or I wouldn't have parked up the hill."

She disappeared inside, reappearing moments later to dangle car keys at me before sprinting away. Derrick and I stood in silence, both in our own thoughts. Mine settled on Max Manningtree. How had he got that drunk in two hours? When Shona returned, I'd have to ask her what she'd been going to say. Judging by the state of him, he'd probably bumped into a lot of things on the way here.

Maybe one of them had been her.

"Martha loves that one," Derrick said. With my mind on Max, it took me a few moments to realise he meant Shona. "But I find her a bit, well, you know, tough at times. In Forrest Gump's box she'd be a sherbet lemon. Hard shell, sharp enough to make you wince but, if I have to be honest, sweet and lovely too. She's a wonder with Martha."

I saved my pedantry for another day and didn't point out that sherbet lemons wouldn't be found in a chocolate selection. He was right about Shona though. Her kindness and vulnerability were well camouflaged but beneath the odd acidic comment she was a great friend and someone to turn to, unless it involved vibrators or mice or boats. I had a feeling the list would grow.

Derrick shuffled backwards to lean against the boot of his car. His earlier grey hue had returned and he wheezed heavily. He opened his mouth to speak but all that came out was a rasping whistle which seemed to come from his chest. He held up a finger to tell me to give him a moment to regain his breath. Concerned, I gazed at him. He should be going for a lie-down rather than a trip to see Martha in hospital, but there was no point telling him that; he'd insist on going. I'd be the same in his shoes.

"But she thinks I was born yesterday. Reckons she and Kim are just good friends but my mum was good friends with my Auntie Jane. She wasn't our real auntie and she wasn't just good friends with my mum either. But who cares? I certainly don't."

I squeezed his arm affectionately. "No flies on you."

Shona's car screeched to a halt and she jumped out. While I shepherded a shuffling Derrick round to the passenger door, she raced round to open it. When we finally got him into the seat, she clicked her heels and saluted him.

He shook his head. "You're daft, you are."

After our short conversation I knew he didn't mean it, as did

Shona who grinned.

"You love me really. Now get your backside in gear. We've a hospital to get to."

As the car accelerated away, I could imagine Derrick clutching the door handle and nagging Shona to go slower, while she'd be telling him to shut up. Then I remembered I'd meant to ask her about Max. It would have to wait.

♦

I opened the breakfast room door to find four couples queuing outside and, within ten minutes, a further two couples sitting expectantly at the breakfast tables. As I raced about taking tea and coffee orders, handing food orders to a red-faced Jason who baked beside the hob and cooker, making teas and coffees and pushing more bread into the toaster, I felt the stirrings of rising panic.

Of the eight people who'd walked in as I opened the breakfast room door, only one couple was having cereal and fruit. Two couples who'd arrived moments later were settled with their cereals and yoghurts, but in minutes they'd have empty bowls and be wanting hot breakfasts. Even if Jason cooked four breakfasts each time – the maximum capacity on our four-ring hob – at least one couple would be facing a lengthy wait. That's if no one else arrived soon.

As I took toast and butter out to a table, Eric waved me over.

"Can I have another brew, love?"

I took the teapot from him.

"Me too." Owain from the neighbouring table held out his teapot. "And Gwen wants more coffee."

Holding a smile in place while I fought to dampen my anxiety, I hurried back to the kitchen to find the toast had popped up too early. I slammed it down and lifted the kettle. Empty! I refilled the kettle and rinsed the cafetière.

"Get me four plates," Jason said.

I threw my hands in the air. Did he think I was an octopus? "I'm busy."

Huffing, he stormed over to the top oven and snatched the plates and three ramekins out. The smell of burning alerted me to the toaster and I cursed as it shot out burnt offerings. I binned them and grabbed another four slices of brown, just as the timer beeped. Great! Gwen's poached eggs were ready but they wouldn't be sitting on toast for a while.

Jason glared at me. "What's the matter with you?"

I rushed back to the kettle and poured the water into the two teapots and cafetière and hurried back to the toast. Still not ready. Jason had dished the three full Englishes, so I took two out to a couple who wanted tomato ketchup and brown sauce. Moments later I rushed back out with the sauces, along with Gwen's poached eggs with toast and the full English, followed soon after by the coffee and teas.

Heading over to take two other orders, I realised I hadn't put the muffins on for the Eggs Benedict Jason was currently cooking along with another three full Englishes. I whisked away the empty cereal bowls and rushed back into the kitchen, where I threw the muffins into the toaster, along with two slices of white bread.

When I went back out to take more orders, I apologised for the wait.

"You've forgotten our presents," John said.

I frowned. "Presents?"

He glanced at his watch and laughed. "We've been waiting so long, it must be Christmas."

I forced a smile. They'd been waiting five minutes after finishing their cereal. What would they make of waiting a further ten to fifteen minutes for their hot food? My bubbling anxiety had reached boiling point. What on earth had made us choose this profession? My waitressing skills were zero and I couldn't even manage to cook toast without burning it. I flipped to a clean sheet on the pad and strode over to take an order from a table.

Eric called across the breakfast room, "Can I have more toast." He held up the empty toast rack.

"Won't be a minute."

My heart sank as Max sauntered into the room, bringing with him the stench of fermenting vodka. But his smell was at odds with his appearance, every inch the holidaymaker in his beige cotton shorts, pristine yellow shirt and a pair of sunglasses stuck on his head. Two tables were free, one in the centre of the room, the other near the kitchen and away from most of the guests. I pointed to the latter, dismayed to see him ignore me and cross the room to the other.

I shot back into the kitchen to hand Jason the orders and to butter the muffins before racing out with a round of toast for a waiting couple.

"Katie!" Eric hollered and waved the toast rack at me.

I took it from him. "The toasters can't keep up, so it'll be a few minutes."

"You just can't get the staff," John called across the room to Eric, who laughed.

I swung round to him. "Sadly, I only have these two hands." I waved them and the toast rack at him, tempering my outburst with a smile which no doubt appeared more like a grimace.

In the kitchen, Jason shook his head as he poured the Hollandaise sauce over the poached eggs. Sweat speckled his forehead, thanks to the furnace heat. Above him the extractor fan roared – all noise and little effect – while we couldn't entice the slightest breeze through the back door, even though we'd jammed it open.

"If it's not too much trouble, put the beans in the ramekins. That's unless you want to bite my head off too."

"Oh, shut up!" I hissed.

After serving the dishes, I went over to Max. As I got close the cloying scent of perfume hung in the air. Had one of the guests squirted it to mask the reek of alcohol? Max slouched, arm over the back of his chair, staring at John.

"You get a lot of arseholes in this business," he drawled in a voice so low, thankfully it was lost beneath the hubbub in the room. He shifted round to look at me. "Don't let it get to you."

I shrugged, hoping John couldn't hear us. "He's a nice man really. It's just one of those mornings."

"So, how's the old dear doing? Got over the shock yet?" Of course, he'd seen yesterday's accident.

"Martha's fine. They're hoping she'll be home later this morning."

"I meant the bloke."

I laughed, turning a few heads on the neighbouring tables. "He's okay too. Now what do you fancy having?"

He chuckled. "You should never, ever ask a gentleman that."

When I came out with his full English, I found him on the other side of the room, chatting to Owain and Gwen. I placed his plate on the table and went over to tell him.

"Max?" He didn't hear me, so I touched his shoulder. "Your breakfast is ready."

"Sorry, too busy talking."

The final two guests, arrivals from yesterday, hesitated by the doorway. A couple pushed their chairs back ready to leave, so I wished them a lovely day before showing the newcomers where to sit. My earlier panic had ebbed. As I cleared a table, Gwen gave me a warm smile while Owain munched his way through the last of the toast and gazed vacantly through the window. The workers – care staff in their uniforms, employees from the shops and cafés, and the mechanics from the nearby garage (I recognised two of them from Derrick's car accident) – I'd seen hurrying in either direction when setting up for breakfast this morning, had been replaced by a stream of tourists meandering towards the harbour, bags over their shoulders, mats or towels under their arms.

"Heavy morning?" Gwen took a sip of her coffee.

I nodded. "The heat isn't helping. It seems to have shot up ten degrees overnight."

She exhaled deeply and fanned her face. "It's roasting. Alan was just saying this heatwave is here for the next week."

Alan? I thought her husband's name was Owain. Knowing my luck, I'd been calling him the wrong name for the past few days.

"Shouldn't complain." I heaved the laden tray from the table. "It's better than rain. I hope you have a fab time on your boat trip. Everyone says it's a great day out."

"I know. When we came last year, we said we'd go on it."

I'd forgotten that Owain and Gwen used to come when Jim and Maureen ran Flotsam Guesthouse. After my efforts this morning, would they long for the good old days? I could only hope tomorrow morning would be different and everyone would come down in dribs and drabs rather than bunched together. It would be good for the new guests to see that not all breakfast services were like today.

Later, with just Max and another couple left in the breakfast room, I started to clear away the dairy and fruit on the buffet selection. As I headed back into the kitchen with the tray, a chair scraped as if being pushed back. I shot out to say goodbye to find Max already by the door. His sunglasses lay on the table, peeking from beneath a crumpled napkin.

"Max!" I rushed over to the table but he'd disappeared. Following him, I called again as he reached the turn at the top of the stairs. "Max! Your glasses."

He disappeared around the corner. Shrugging to myself, I turned away. I couldn't abandon the last guests in the breakfast room. Anyhow, he knew where to find me when he realised he'd left them behind. If not, I'd put them in his room later when cleaning.

Max must have gone out while Jason and I cleaned the kitchen, either not remembering he'd left his sunglasses in the breakfast room or he didn't need them, although I felt sure he would. The sun blinded me when I took out the bin. Under the bluest of skies, gulls shrieked and wheeled on outstretched wings. On busy days when we couldn't get out even for a short stroll by the harbour, I loved hearing their calls. The sound of childhood holidays.

Later that day, when I watered the hanging baskets in the cooler warmth of dusk, Gwen and Owain stopped to admire them. They'd been listening to live music at The Anchor's Rest but needed an early night after their packed day. Even in the half-light, their faces glowed. Gwen rubbed her reddened shoulder.

"Factor 30 and I still burned."

"I told you," Owain said. He sounded fed up, as if her sunburn had become a sore point. Literally.

Changing the subject, I said, "I don't suppose you've seen Max on your travels?"

"Max?" Gwen said. They both looked blank.

"You were talking to him at breakfast."

She shook her head. "Nope."

"Yellow shirt." I swallowed the urge to mention the smell of alcohol, even though it had been his defining feature. "He came over to your table."

"Oh! You mean… whatshisname…" She clicked her fingers. "Alan. That's it. We met him here last year."

Alan? No wonder he hadn't answered to the name Max. Then the penny slotted into place. That made him Alan Manningtree. But why had he lied about his name? Of course, the cancellation!

But why not just pay the fifty pounds, rather than go to the inconvenience of a name change?

"It was a bit of a surprise to see him again, to be honest. Him being Maureen's brother and all. You did know that, I assume." Gwen looked at me, probably to gauge my reaction.

I bit back the urge to point out that if I didn't know his real name, I was hardly likely to know he was related to the old owners. A chill ran through me. Had his last-minute cancellation a month after we started running Flotsam Guesthouse been one of Maureen's nasty tricks? If so, what was he doing here now?

Fighting to keep my voice light, I laughed, "Jason checked him in so M- Alan probably told Jason. I'll have to ask Alan how his sister is doing."

They smiled and disappeared off to their rooms. When their door closed, I shot off to find Jason in the utility room dragging a load of towels from the tumble drier. I jabbed my finger at him, ready to launch into the bizarre tale about Max/Alan.

"You won't believe it!"

He sighed, "What now?"

"What do you mean 'what now'?"

I didn't hang around to find out. Annoyed by his tone and the inference that I irritated him, I stomped off and threw myself onto the sofa. I ached with exhaustion. No doubt Jason was shattered too after what had been a long and challenging day. We hadn't had time to recover from the busy breakfast before a melee of guests from five rooms checked-out within minutes of each other. All their rooms had needed to be given a thorough clean and bedding change – rather than the basic refresh undertaken when guests stayed on – before the next arrivals. We'd stopped for a hurried lunch before Jason shot off to the butchers. When he got back, I'd checked in three couples on my own, so he'd agreed to look after the two evening arrivals while I prepared the breakfast room for the next day and emptied the third dishwasher load. If we hadn't spent so much time bickering, we could have been proud of our teamwork.

Carrying an armful of towels, Jason ducked through the door. I grabbed the remote control and turned the TV over, determined to ignore him. Big Ben chimed for the News at Ten.

"So, what is it?" He flapped a towel and folded it.

"I'm watching TV." I jabbed the volume button to make it loud enough to provoke him, but not too loud for our guests. "I haven't stopped all day."

He huffed. "And I have?"

Before we came to the B&B we'd heard tales of couples growing closer when working together. But the only thing we'd managed to grow was frustration. We nurtured it well too. I missed the old good-humoured Jason and our free time spent having fun and relaxing together. No doubt he missed my old self too, joking and laughing at silly things. It was in my power to make tonight better. If I was being rational I would simply tell him about Max/Alan. But tiredness sapped all reason.

I got to my feet. "I'm going to bed."

Chapter 21

I HAD MIXED FEELINGS WHEN Max/Alan didn't come down to breakfast. Half of me wanted to find out what he was playing at – was his change of name because he was related to Maureen or because of the cancellation fee he still owed us from back in April? – while the rest of me felt relief at not having to confront him.

After breakfast I left the servicing of his room until last, in case he'd decided to have a lie-in. When I knocked on his door no one answered, so I crept in. It's always a bit worrying if you're unsure whether a guest has gone out or not and they don't answer the door. A few months earlier, I'd found a man asleep in bed wearing ear plugs. Luckily, I hadn't woken him and just snuck a note under the door to say that I'd tried to clean the room but hadn't been able to do so.

I promised myself I'd order the 'Do not disturb' signs later, even though I knew that by the time I finished the cleaning I'd have forgotten about them. One day they would make it onto the shopping list.

Max had gone out, thank goodness. But then I realised he hadn't come in.

His duvet lay smooth and tucked in at the corners, the pillows plumped, while clean towels hung over the bathroom rail. Even his sunglasses sat on the bedside table where I'd left them. The room smelled fresh too, after I'd aired it yesterday. He hadn't slept here last night. Had he left? I flung open the wardrobe doors, holding my breath in anticipation of a gust of stale vodka but other than an underlying musty smell from the jacket, two shirts and pair of trousers hanging inside, he'd taken the stench of alcohol with him, wherever he had gone. With a final, puzzled glance at the unused bed, I left the room.

After two days without seeing the sun – which our guests informed me was very hot and yellow – I needed to get out of the house. After lunch Jason and I agreed to switch jobs: he'd do the ironing and I'd go to the butchers and shops. I chuckled. The highlight of my day had become a trip to see Tommy the butcher. When I arrived back all the guests were parked on the driveway, so I abandoned the car on the side of the road while I went inside to ask Jason to give me a hand. I found him in the day room with new guests filling in the registration form.

"This is Peter and June," Jason said.

June's hairstyle reminded me of a silver-haired Margaret Thatcher, although this appeared to be the only comparison, as the woman in front of me carried a gentle demeanour and wore a flowery dress, tied at the waist. Peter smiled and dabbed his forehead with a handkerchief, which he stuffed into his jacket pocket. Immediately, flecks of perspiration dotted his forehead. Why the jacket in this weather? Perhaps it masked the sweat stains on his shirt, which would be a vicious circle as he'd be drenched soon.

Jason added, "They've been before, about ten years ago. They were just telling me how much they used to like the bar that was once here. Do you want a hand with the shopping?"

June nodded. "We came because of the bar."

"You won't have to go far. There's a pub up the road." I turned to Jason. "You're busy. I'll be fine, thanks."

"Does this pub have a TV?" Peter said. "Because it has to have a TV. June knows how I like my TV. Don't I, June? We always get the TV listings. June makes sure she circles my programmes in red and hers in blue. Red for me, as she recognises I'm important. Don't you, June?"

Finally, he stopped for breath. I glanced through the window to where I'd left the car parked on the side of the road. I needed to get on.

"I don't know but there's one in your room and I'm sure you'll find a pub with a TV." Smiling, I said, "I'll leave you to it."

June patted her husband's hand. "We like different programmes. He likes a pint or two at night too, don't you, dear? One at The Oak and another at home. You can set your clock by him."

"That's nice." A toot came from outside, where a line of vehicles had built up waiting to get past my car. "I really must go. See you at breakfast."

I raced outside, staggering back with heavy bags and boxes which I dumped on the kitchen floor before sprinting back to the car. Each time I passed the day room, Peter and June paused their conversation for the few seconds it took to give me a wave. Once unloaded, I parked the car across the road before heading back to unpack the shopping.

"Katie! I was just saying…" Jason waved me over.

What was he playing at? He knew I had to unpack the shopping and get the meat and dairy into the fridge. I pointed towards the kitchen. "I haven't finished."

"I'll do that," he said. "Peter and June were asking me about the changes in Torringham since they last came. I know you look at those Facebook sites, so you'll be able to tell them about it." Scooting past me to the door, he gave us all a cheery grin. "I'll see you both at breakfast tomorrow."

Puzzled, I watched him disappear before I turned my attention to Peter and June. "So, what do you need to know?"

One of my flaws has been the inability to close a conversation. Whether Peter and June recognised this, I don't know. But four, maybe five times within what felt like an hour, I said 'I must be going', each time with more desperation. Now I understood why Jason had been so eager to unpack the shopping. I would have happily traded shopping, ironing and cooking the evening meal for a moment's respite.

When the phone rang, I headed to the door. "I must get that."

"Let your husband do it," June said. "If you're interested in history, you should see this. Peter, show her the map."

The phone stopped ringing – Jason must have answered – and with it any hope of escape died. Peter pulled out a leaflet. Once unfolded he spread it across the table, flattening it with his hand. It was a detailed map, showing historic sites in Torringham along with information on each. Usually I loved learning about the history of an area, but Peter's incessant drone made it feel more like a treble physics lesson. He didn't pause for breath, his sentences merging into one another until he gabbled rather than spoke. As he pointed at the various locations, he told me so much about each site it would take for ever for us to reach Shadwell Point and the end of the map.

My legs ached but I refused to sit down. Standing meant I could edge closer to the door, but each time I shuffled an inch from the table, Peter would jab the map and say, "And look at what it says here."

I'd bend over and smile and nod.

"This is where they kept prisoners. Several hundred of them put to work. And here." His finger moved a centimetre across the map. "This is fascinating. I mean you don't get history like this anywhere. Those prisoners, well…"

This was torture. I'd become his hostage and this room my cell. Through the window I watched couples strolling by, free to walk at will. Would he ever shut up? My stomach rumbled and my head ached. Hoping for support from my fellow captive, I gazed across at June who sat beside Peter, hands clasped in her lap. Like a grandmother watching little Johnny in the nativity play, a proud smile touched her lips. She might know the words and story by rote, but this was Johnny's moment on stage and she would savour it.

I could stand no more.

"I really…"

"I can't believe they shut the Torring Bistro. It was famous, wasn't it, June? On the site of the old gun emplacement, so it had miniature cannons by the doorway. Everyone who was anyone came to Torringham to eat there. We ate there once. What did we have?" He drummed his nails on the table.

I backed out of the room. "I hope you have a lovely holiday but I must go. I've an urgent call to make."

June's expression told me she knew I'd lied to get away. I swallowed and held her gaze, hoping she'd think me more honest if I looked her in the eye. But she tightened her lips and narrowed her eyes. There was no fooling her. But, if she was reasonable, she'd appreciate I'd spent ages with them. I needed a cup of tea and five minutes to myself.

Something about Peter's downcast gaze and the 'Oh…' wilting on his lips, made me say, "You'll have to tell me more tomorrow when I'm not so busy."

Peter stood up and folded up the map of Historic Torringham. "I'll find you after breakfast."

The thought made me want to cry but I managed a weak smile. "I'll be cleaning then. How about when you get back tomorrow afternoon?"

As I wandered into the lounge cursing and berating my stupidity, Jason leapt from the sofa to stand by the ironing board. He wore a smug grin.

"Don't bother pretending. I know you've been watching TV."

"I am capable of multi-tasking, darling."

"Well, do it then."

Instead of biting back at me, he smiled. "No problem. You made it out then? That man must have a blowhole in his head. He doesn't stop for breath."

I slumped onto the sofa and rubbed my face. "He wants to show you this map tomorrow. He'll grab you after breakfast. I said you'd love to see it."

Jason smiled. "Yeah, right! Knowing you, you've told him you'd love to see it tomorrow. Why can't you just walk away?"

"Like you did?"

His response was cut off by the phone ringing. When he held up the iron to show he was too busy to answer, I sighed and snatched the phone from the coffee table.

"Flotsam Guesthouse. How can I help you?"

"I'm sorry to call but I had no choice." The voice sounded familiar but I couldn't place it until he said, "It's Max."

"Is that Max or Alan?"

He fell silent, leaving me listening to the tinny chatter of people in the background. A café or a shop?

He sighed. "It's Alan. I'll explain later. Look, I'm sorry to ask but I need your help. I'm in hospital and they won't let me out unless someone picks me up."

I couldn't believe it. Had he really phoned to ask me to call him a taxi? Huffing loudly, I said, "You want a taxi?"

"I- I know you're not happy but I need you to pick me up. I've hurt my head and they won't let me leave unless I go back with somebody."

He might be in hospital, but the last thing I wanted was to go into Berrinton to rescue a man who'd not only lied to us about his name but also owed us money. The more I thought about it, the more annoyed I became. Apart from the noise in the background, silence filled the line until I said, "Did you tell them we're not a care home?"

"I told them you were family."

My sarcasm had bypassed him, so I added an extra dose. "That makes me Maureen, I guess."

"Well, sort of." He sighed. "I got mugged by two men and I bashed my head when I hit the pavement. The ward is short of beds and people are queuing for them, but they can't let me go unless I have someone. I'm well enough to leave, in case you're wondering. I know it's a cheek asking but *please* can you help?"

Before I could stop myself, I found myself uttering two words I knew I'd soon regret. "Which ward?"

Chapter 22

AS IT WAS RUSH HOUR, I took the coastal road to Berrinton Hospital, only to be frustrated by everyone else having the same idea. While I waited at another set of traffic lights, I consoled myself that at least this route offered sea views. Through a break between the trees and houses white-sailed boats leaned into the sparkling sea below, while a ferry cut across them as it made its final journey back to Torringham. On a hot day like this, it would be crammed with a full cargo of tourists, all heading back to the B&Bs and caravan parks. Further out, a trawler seemed to float lazily in the bay, but the arms – What was the word for them? That's it, derricks! – jutting out from the sides told me it would be moving through the water. Work done, another trawler chugged past, heading back to the fish quay to unload its haul.

The queue ahead moved, so I eased the car forward to find my view blocked by a line of houses. I sighed. Jason had been right to say I was crazy doing this. I gripped the steering wheel, imagining it was Alan's neck. I dreaded the journey back. What on earth would we say to each other? The jingle for the traffic news filtered into the car and I turned up the volume. Great! All roads into Berrinton jammed, this one by a removal lorry and, worse, there was an accident on the bypass. I bit my lip. Should I turn back? Not only did I face a long journey to Berrinton, but it didn't look much better on the other side of the road either. Knowing my luck, this meant a crawl back and more time stuck with Alan. I groaned. I longed to do a U-turn but, no matter how much I wavered, I couldn't. I'd promised to help him and I wouldn't back out.

An hour later and after finally finding a parking space at the hospital, I stepped from the air-conditioned car into the warmth of a sunny late afternoon. Or was six o'clock classed as early evening?

Ahead stood a tower block surrounded by squat buildings, typical of hospital developments in the sixties. I followed the signs to reception and then headed towards Ward D, as instructed by Alan.

A stone or nail must have embedded into the sole of one of my trainers as every other step clipped on the tiled floor, echoing down the corridor. Rather than pull off my trainer, I settled for tiptoeing on one foot, while walking normally with the other. If it looked like I limped, who cared? This was a hospital.

The distant sound of clanging pots masked my footsteps. Towards the end of the corridor, a smell like school dinners seeped from the wards. I hoped Alan wouldn't be eating when I arrived. I wanted a quick get-away. Ahead hung a sign pointing to 'Ward D' so I headed to the nurses' station, where I asked a nurse how to find Alan Manningtree. He ran his finger down a list and pointed down the corridor.

"Second door on the right."

I thanked him and set off on my half-walk, half-limp to Alan, my stomach churning. How would I greet him? While I didn't feel like being friendly, I couldn't be rude. He was a guest, albeit a lying one.

Open double doors led into a six-bed ward. As I headed inside, a nurse stopped me.

"I'm here for Alan Manningtree."

"You must be his sister. He's waiting in the patient lounge. Follow me."

Sister? What on earth was he playing at? If they made me sign anything, no way would I be joining in his lies and becoming Maureen. More than ever I wished I'd turned the car around. The nurse reached a door. She shouldered it open and stood with the heel of her shoe against the door, watching us. I clenched my fists and gritted my teeth, preparing for the meeting.

Alan didn't get up from where he sat on a low chair, a large square of white fabric taped to his forehead. He seemed shrivelled and sunken, no longer the man who'd arrived at the guesthouse a few days before. Brown stains splashed his yellow shirt – dried blood, I guessed – and a graze marked his bruised chin. My anger died. I couldn't think what to say – 'you look terrible', 'are you're okay?', 'what happened to you?' – nothing seemed to fit.

"Your sister's here. Have you got everything?"

The edge of Alan's mouth twitched. "Thanks for coming, love. I do appreciate it."

Grunting, he heaved himself to his feet and stooped to pick up a Burtons carrier bag. I felt guilty for standing there, clutching my hands together, especially when a real sister would jump to his aid, so I offered him my arm. He shook his head.

"No need, love. They bashed my head, not my legs."

The knees of his chino trousers were scuffed grey and a stain marked his crotch, as if he'd wet himself. I hoped it was beer or something. When I'd last seen him at breakfast, he'd been wearing the same yellow shirt he wore now, but he'd matched it with beige shorts. Now he wore chinos. Had he come back to the guesthouse when we'd been out? Not that it mattered but it was strange he hadn't picked up his sunglasses or moved anything in his room.

Thankfully, the nurse let us leave the hospital without asking my name as I wouldn't have known whether to say Katie or Maureen. With Alan's top speed not much more than your average zimmer-frame user it took a while to reach the car, where I stood patiently by the door while he folded himself into the passenger seat. When he put the carrier bag down in the foot well, I glimpsed something beige. As I got into the drivers' seat and clipped my seatbelt, my eyes strayed again to the bag. What was in it? I had no idea why it bugged me so much, but I had to know. While he fussed with his seatbelt, unable to find the slot, I pulled his carrier bag open.

"Your shorts?"

He nodded. "They insist on long trousers at the casino."

The casino? I didn't know there was one in Berrinton.

"Where's that?"

"The back of Albert Heights. It's in the old Hamilton Hotel."

I tried to place the location but failed. My knowledge of Berrinton was limited to the harbour, esplanade and the shopping area. I regularly got lost in the one-way system and ended up heading out of town. My lack of direction had proved useful once, when I'd stumbled upon a large M&S store tucked behind a row of furniture and carpet outlets and next to Sainsburys, although I'd need a sat nav to find it again without Jason's help. Luckily, Berrinton Hospital was well signposted or Alan may have faced an even longer wait.

"How did you end up getting hurt?"

"I had a bit of a win. Someone must have been watching me." Wincing, he rubbed his forehead. "They were big lads too. Took me down before I could get a look at them and stole my wallet. The police have been checking CCTV in the area, so I hope they get caught."

"I hope so too," I muttered.

We fell into silence. In contrast to Torringham with its colourful cottages rising in layers around the twisting streets above the quaint harbour, the seafront at Berrinton offered a mix of modern buildings interspersed with large Georgian and Victorian hotels. Tourists strolled along the promenade, while others ambled through the large park opposite. Berrinton, with its casino, nightclubs, bars and amusement arcades, seemed to suit Alan more than Torringham. Why had he stayed with us, especially when he'd had to use a false name to do so. Tiredness and hunger brought out the bluntness in me. Shona would have been proud.

"So why call yourself Max when you booked?"

From the corner of my eye, I could see him turn away to look out of the passenger window.

I couldn't stop myself. "It's just an odd thing to do."

"I just wanted to see Maureen's old place again. I loved coming down when she lived there. She's just been back with her grandkids and said they had a lovely week. It made me want to relive happy times."

Not wishing to get side-tracked, I decided against asking him about Maureen and Jim's brief visit to Flotsam Guesthouse with their grandchildren. "But when you booked you paid up-front. Why not have been honest and added the one-night you owed us?"

He looked down at his lap, picking at a fingernail, leaving me dangling. I didn't want to badger him, but I needed to know. I let the question hang between us. The tension grew until I felt one of us would surely surrender: me by asking again or him by giving an answer. He couldn't play with that nail for ever.

He cleared his throat. "I wanted to pay upfront as I'd won on a horse. It was just enough to cover the nights here, so I couldn't add any more."

"Let me guess. When you cancelled the time before, it was because you lost on a horse."

"The dogs. Promised a sure bet which turned out to have three legs."

I shook my head. Unbelievable. He'd gone through all the hassle of pretending to be Max for the sake of fifty odd pounds. Not much when you consider our loss had been more like two hundred if you took the whole booking into account. But the burning anger I'd felt before didn't materialise. Now I felt sorry for this man who'd wanted to come back to his sister's old place, who drank too much, gambled every penny and no doubt had more issues going on in his life than I dared to imagine. Strange that he'd lied about going to hospital when he'd cancelled that first booking, yet he'd ended up at one.

"I'll forget the cancellation fee."

"I didn't use my room last night, so you're in arrears with me."

Very funny. "Your clothes did."

"I didn't have breakfast either."

"Don't I know it! We had to wait until the end of breakfast to find out you weren't coming down."

"I'm a bit short at the moment."

His comment threw me. It didn't sound like he was joking any more. Surely, he didn't really think my offer to forget the money he owed us meant we were also going to refund him for the night he'd spent in hospital? I decided to keep my response light-hearted.

"It's a good thing I'm giving you a lift then. Saves you a taxi fare."

To end the conversation, I turned on the radio, using the steering wheel paddle to rachet up the volume to a level where he couldn't speak without shouting. From the look on Alan's face he didn't like Coldplay as much as I did but I kept my eyes glued to the road, leaving him to squirm beside me.

We passed the 'Welcome to Torringham' sign, surrounded by huge planters filled with bedding plants. Rounding a corner, we sped beneath a tunnel of trees before we glimpsed the first house in Torringham, the Old Toll House, with its wonderful sign giving historic toll costs. From this point, the countryside changed to townscape. Interspersed between the houses were the B&Bs, easy to spot with the signs hanging by the roadside and vibrant hanging baskets decorating their frontages. Even after Shona's party, I still knew most of the owners by the name of their property: Seaglade, Torringham Lodge, Arundel and so on, except for Raymond at Waves B&B who would remain infamous for his wandering hands. I'd got chatting with a few of the others as they passed Flotsam on their way to town. It would be good to get to know them better when business quietened down, perhaps at Jetsam Cottage as Shona had been threatening to have a barbeque. If she didn't, come winter we would hold a small drinks party. But, for now, it was all work.

Beside me, Alan waved to a couple walking up the street. He jabbed his finger in their direction and, over the din of a dog food advert, shouted, "Marge and Barry from…" He clicked his fingers. "Arndale or something. Friends of Maureen's."

I nodded. Of course, many of the B&Bers would be their friends. Although, the few I'd met at Shona's last party hadn't mentioned them. Did people still believe Jim and Maureen's stories about us forcing them to sell the guesthouse for a pittance or had it become old news? I gave Alan a sideways glance. Had he fallen for the tale of woe too? Or did he recognise the amount of work needed to put the place right? I didn't dare ask, especially as talk of money could lead back to him trying to wangle a discount on his stay.

I pulled up outside Flotsam Guesthouse. When Alan didn't budge from his seat, I hauled his carrier bag from beneath his legs and handed it to him. I jabbed the volume down.

"You need to get out, unless you want a long walk. I've got to park round the back."

"I'll wait for you."

"To make sure I get in safely?" I laughed. "I'll be fine. If you need anything, Jason's indoors. Just ring the bell."

Hesitantly, he pulled the door handle. Whatever he wanted to say, he didn't want to say it to Jason. As he stepped onto the pavement, I gave him a cheery wave.

"See you at breakfast. Make sure you get some rest."

As Alan trudged off, Peter and June stepped from the guesthouse. In my rear mirror I could see a line of cars. Unable to make a speedy getaway, I groaned as Peter tapped on the passenger window. What with rushing out to collect Alan, I hadn't had a cup of tea or a moment to myself. With a sigh, I wound the window down.

"We've put some booklets on the side for you," he said. "We're not doing much, so I can show you them now, if you like."

"I'm sorry." I gave him my best impression of an apologetic smile. "But I'm going out tonight. I just stopped to drop Alan off. How about we look at them tomorrow?"

Chapter 23

AFTER PARKING THE CAR ON Moreton Hill, I took my regular route down a set of steep steps to the back of Flotsam Guesthouse. On reaching the bottom, I groaned. I'd left my mobile phone in the glovebox. My legs ached as I made my way back up. No matter how many times I ran up and down the guesthouse stairs, I could never get used to these steps. Found throughout Torringham, they offered a shortcut between roads on different levels, and ranged in gradient from steep to almost vertical. The only way to avoid them was to take the circuitous route cars had to take along the narrow lanes and around hairpin bends where, invariably, there would be the constant jams and manoeuvring as cars reversed or squeezed into the tiniest of gaps to allow each other to pass.

As I climbed down, holding tightly to the handrail, I gazed at our little-used rear gate. If by some miracle it was open, I could sneak into the guesthouse unseen by Peter and have a comfortable evening on the sofa rather than another history lesson. I tugged at the latch but the gate didn't budge. What did I expect? We kept it bolted top and bottom to prevent intruders getting in.

With my mind set on an escape from Peter, I called Jason's mobile but he didn't answer. Sighing, I propped myself against the wall to think. If I used the front door, Peter would spot me and know I'd lied about going out. Then I'd have to listen to him talking about Napoleon Bonaparte or Operation Tiger, both interesting subjects but not when the lecturer was Peter and definitely not at eight o'clock, with my empty stomach growling like a ravenous bear. There could be double trouble too. What if Alan had decided to wait for me? The look on his face when he got out of the car suggested he had unfinished business.

Like ours, Shona and Kim's rear gate was set into a stone wall too high to climb. I tried their door. Locked. In desperation, I called Shona's number.

She answered before it rang, "Hello."

"It's me. Can you let me in your back gate? Jason isn't answering."

"Can't you…" She trailed off. "Won't be a sec."

A few minutes later I heard footsteps and the grind of the bolt as she prised it open. Puzzled, she ushered me into the small patio garden.

"Are you okay?" She swiped her hand through her blonde-tipped hair. Her eyes were rimmed red with exhaustion and the last dregs of colour had leeched from her usually pale skin.

I gabbled an explanation. "I'm sorry about this. I'm hiding from a couple of guests. After the day I've had, I really can't face them tonight."

As she ushered me down the steps into the dank courtyard, heading through the utility area into the kitchen, I told her about Alan and the trip to the hospital before moving on to Peter. I felt a bit mean talking about him, as he hadn't done much other than have a passion for history. If he'd come in low season, I may have offered to do some research for him, even welcomed the discussion, but he'd picked our busiest month when we were lucky to get an hour or two of waking time to ourselves. He'd left me with little option than to climb the wall between the guesthouses to get home, rather than endure his endless drone.

"Do you want a cup of tea?"

I took in the steam-filled lounge and the condensation on the windows. On the coffee table sat a laptop, surrounded by a mass of paperwork. Centrepiece in front of the TV stood an ironing board, draped with a half-ironed sheet while a twisted mass of pillowcases and duvet covers overflowed from a large basket on the sofa. On each armrest sat piles of folded towels, the only calm amongst the storm. It reminded me of our lounge, except Shona and Kim's was usually tidy.

"Busy day?"

She rubbed her forehead. "It's been a nightmare and then Kim's insisted on doing this yoga course her friend's been going on about."

"Yoga?"

"I know! Trust her to decide she needs to *learn* how to relax in the middle of August. Most people watch TV or read a book."

She stumbled over the leg of the ironing board. "We're up to our eyes in washing after the machine broke down this morning but she says she can't let her mate down. She went last week and reckons it helps her but what about *me*?"

I gave her a sympathetic but non-committal shrug, all too aware their relationship issues seemed to be mirroring mine and Jason's.

"I'm slogging away ironing and she's like 'I'm a tree'!"

She flung her arms in the air, Y-shaped, and raised her leg, promptly planting it back on the floor. Again, she attempted to lift her foot to the inside of her thigh. I'd seen the tree pose in yoga before and hers was nothing like it. After a few wobbles she pointed her hands together and raised them steeple-like above her head, grinning victoriously.

"Easy!"

Without warning, she lurched backwards, her mouth a circle of shock as she threw out her arms to stop herself from falling, but her hand caught the mantelpiece. I gazed in horror as her vintage paperweight – with its stunning depiction of a coral reef covered in vibrant anemones – wobbled and then in slow motion tumbled from the side, smashing onto the old tiles surrounding the hearth. As shards fired out like bullets, Shona crashed into the ironing board. I grabbed the metal legs to stop it from toppling over, but the huge steam unit and iron slipped from the stand and plummeted to the carpet. As water poured from the tank, I snatched the iron from the floor. Luckily, it had fallen on its side rather than flat on to the carpet, but molten fibres clung to the metal band and a dark strip marked the beige carpet.

"Ouch!"

Biting her lip, Shona clutched the back of her leg. Pulling her hand away, she gazed at the red smear and quickly clamped her palm back over her calf. She limped off towards the kitchen, a crimson line trickling down her leg, leaving me to turn off the iron and settle the unit back onto the ironing board.

As she pressed a bundle of tissues to her wound, she groaned, "Kim's gonna kill me."

While she dressed her cut, I took the dustpan and brush into the lounge and cleaned up the fragments of coloured glass. Shona hovered over my shoulder.

"I loved that."

"So did I."

She took the dustpan from me and hobbled back into the kitchen, returning with a cloth and a wire brush. The latter she handed to me.

"Do you reckon we can hide the mark?"

I gave her a doubtful look. "I don't know. Then there's the tile too."

Three large cracks snaked from a chip in the centre of the large ornate blue and green hearth tile. Glumly, I surveyed the beautiful hearth. I adored the cast iron fireplace with its ornate designs and often wished Flotsam Guesthouse hadn't been stripped of most of its features in the sixties. To think this one had lasted over one hundred years until destroyed by a 'tree'.

Shona slapped her hand to her forehead. "I'm well and truly done for."

While I knelt on the floor with the brush, taking care to lift rather than snag the damaged carpet fibres, Shona shot off. The front door clanged shut and, for a moment, my heart jumped into my mouth. Had Kim arrived home? When she didn't appear, I heaved a sigh of relief. I didn't fancy being the one to tell her what had happened.

By the time Shona came back clutching a pencil case, I'd done my best with the carpet, making the mark a bit less visible – although Kim would spot it immediately – and I'd scrubbed the melted fibres from the iron. Apart from the hearth, the cluttered lounge was almost back to how it looked when I'd first come in.

"Jodie gave me her Ellie's colouring pens."

She pulled out a navy felt-tipped pen and settled down to her colouring project, while I stood back. How on earth she thought Kim wouldn't notice, I had no idea, but I didn't voice my doubts. When she finished retouching the last of the white with a shower grout pen, which she'd found after rummaging under the kitchen sink when searching for trainer whitener, I had to admit she'd done a good job. It increased the time before Kim spotted the damage from one to ten seconds, or twenty at a push.

She got to her feet and slapped her hands together. "You were saying about needing help to get in?"

"I wouldn't worry. Alan and Peter would have given up by now."

Then I groaned. Jason would have seen Alan come in and expected me to arrive a few minutes later, no more than the time it would have taken to park the car. I should have tried to call again and let him know I was next door. Great! My plan to hide from our guests meant Shona faced a furious Kim, while I would have a worried Jason to contend with.

Apologising for bothering her, I left through the front door and cut across the gravel drive to slip into our guesthouse. At first all seemed quiet, but then I heard a low drone and my heart sank. I crept forward, hoping to avoid Peter but as I passed the day room,

Jason sat in one of the chairs, arms folded, pouring over a map with Peter. He threw me a filthy look.

Caught between escape and helping Jason, I hesitated by the door. Peter glanced up and smiled at me.

"You've missed me showing you the old cave system."

The chair scraped as Jason stood up. "You can show her now if you like."

"I'd love to, but I need Jason to give me a hand with something, umm, that needs sorting."

Peter smiled and folded the map. "That's sounds worrying. I hope you get it dealt with."

I hid my surprise. Was that all he was going to say? This was Peter who would never use two words if two hundred could be found. He stretched back and lifted his arms and yawned loudly.

"It's been a busy day. I'll show you tomorrow."

I said my goodbyes and followed Jason into the lounge.

"Thanks for that." He slumped onto the sofa and grabbed the remote control, jabbing it at the TV. "I really enjoyed listening to him for an hour while you disappeared goodness knows where."

"Round Shona's. We had a bit of an issue."

I headed off to the kitchen in search of food but came to a halt by the lounge door. "You don't want to be stuck with Peter but you're quite happy leaving me with him. If you noticed, I tried getting you out of there." Then I added one more moan because I could. "Stop being so thoughtless. Your time isn't more precious than mine."

Before he could respond I shot off.

♦

With breakfast being its usual manic affair, I managed to stop Peter each time he started to chat by pointing at another guest and saying

'Sorry, got to go'. One of the first to arrive that morning and the last to leave, he sat with June amongst the detritus of a finished service, craning his neck to attract my attention as I cleared the tables at the other end of the room. From the corner of my eye I caught him pointing at me to June. When he pulled himself up from the table, I grabbed the half-laden tray and shot into the kitchen, where I clattered around filling the dishwasher – although most of the plates and cups were on the tables in the breakfast room – and wiped the sides, while Jason discovered the oven required an urgent clean after an accidental bacon juice spill. Any meanness I felt about hiding from Peter and June was overlaid by relief when their chairs scraped on the floor.

"Have a lovely day!" I shouted from the kitchen door and waved my tea cloth at them to prove I was busy working.

Once they'd disappeared upstairs, I put the dishwasher on, locked the breakfast room door and grabbed a tray. Four tables, including Peter's, were laden with cafetières, pots, cups and side plates. I glanced at the clock. By now we should have finished and be heading upstairs to make a start on the guest rooms.

Jason appeared with another tray and together we settled down to clearing the tables. We didn't speak. Somehow, we'd got used to not talking to each other. Did he notice too? Okay, we sniped, made sarcastic comments, even laughed if something stupid happened, but we didn't talk. Not like we used to do. The only conversation I had each morning was in my head, which meant I had a lot of time to think. Right now, Peter filled my mind.

I shouldn't have treated him so badly. I'd apologise later and listen to his tales, even if he did go on and on and on and on and on. But why should he expect me to spend my precious free time learning about Torringham's history with him as the tutor. If I wanted to do that, I could read a book or go online. But it was mean of me to ignore him. He was a guest after all. I clamped my hands to my face and groaned. I'd have to bite the bullet and listen to Peter or else my conscience would eat at me.

As Jason passed with a full tray, he gave me a puzzled look. "Are you okay?"

"Just thinking about something."

He didn't stop to find out what. Not that it mattered. If I told him I was worrying about hurting Peter's feelings, he wouldn't understand. Not that I did to be honest. Any sane person wouldn't expect a receptionist, a waiter or a cleaner in a busy hotel to spend hours with them and, unlike us, staff in larger hotels had the luxury of going home to get a break from unusually needy people.

Jason came past carrying a full bin bag. "Is your face going to fall apart if you let go of it?"

Back in the kitchen, I ploughed the tray through the cups and plates on the worktop to make room. If we didn't get a move on, we'd be here all day. I turned to Jason. "You finish the kitchen, while I make a start upstairs. I saw room two go out earlier."

I stepped from the breakfast room to be hit by the stench of stale alcohol in the hallway. Alan stood there, his room keys dangling from his hand. In all the rush of the morning service and keeping out of Peter's way, I hadn't realised he'd missed breakfast. I'd even forgotten he was here.

"Are you okay?"

Swaying, he rubbed the plaster on his head. "Lucky that Maureen's sorted me a coach back home after those men stole my ticket, so I'm fine now."

His petulant tone made it sound as if *I'd* done something wrong. Strange how just a few days ago Kim and I had been talking about the challenges of running a B&B. One of her warnings had been about her recent experience with a guest who'd expected too much.

"Most guests are lovely and laid-back, but the really demanding ones are often the least grateful. You go overboard for them and nothing's good enough," she'd said.

Alan was proving her point.

A red-topped bottle jutted from the pocket of his jacket. Vodka. How Maureen had got the money to him, I didn't know, but thanks to her contribution towards his journey home he'd been able to treat himself to a half-bottle or more. From the state of him, this may be the second one. What condition would his room be in? I muttered a silent prayer for him to go quietly and quickly.

He dumped the key in my hand and I smiled. "I'm glad you're sorted, especially after yesterday. You've got your bags and everything?"

I opened the front door to let Alan out, thankful to breathe fresh air. As he veered towards the door frame, instinctively I grabbed his arm to help him but he shook me off.

"Do you want me to walk you to the coach stop?"

He waved me away. "I'm not an invalid, you know."

He staggered off. Three steps forward, one sideways, the occasional lurch backwards, like the drunks at the White Hart. Lovely old men who spent all day downing pints, not moving from the bar stools until the bell signalled time. Then they teetered out like marionettes being controlled by a child.

Would he be back within the next hour begging for a room, not allowed to board the coach? When he made it to the corner, I shot upstairs to check his room. My eyes smarted from the alcohol fumes, so I flung the window open and sprayed the room with odour neutraliser. The duvet lay in a huddle on the bed, a damp towel strewn across the pillow but there was nothing amiss. No underlying smell of sick or anything else to fire warning signals. On the side by the kettle sat a notebook. Rubbish? I flicked through it. In jagged handwriting usually seen in much older people than Alan, he'd scrawled figures interspersed with notes to himself. I flicked through the pages, ready to throw it in the bin.

Bailiffs coming Saturday. Need £250. (This was underlined twice). *Maureen? Elsie?*

Boris Lad. 10/1. (And beside it a huge tick).

Torringham £200. Paid.

Electric. Must pay. How?

Faster than Reason. 8/1. (This time a cross which sliced the paper).

Hospital. 27 August. Oncology ward. 10.15am. Mr Anderson.

I snatched the book, raced down the stairs and out of the door. Had he come to Torringham for a holiday before he went into hospital? I sprinted down the road – not thinking to tell Jason where I'd gone – and, not waiting for the little man to turn green either, dashed across the traffic lights, rounding the corner to the coach stop as the National Express pulled away. In a fug of diesel fumes, I juddered to a halt. The seats by the bus shelter were empty, which meant Alan had been allowed to travel. Sure enough, as the coach rumbled past he sat by the window near the back. Our eyes met as I waved the book at him, mouthing and signing to say I'd post it to him. He put his hands together and mouthed 'please' and gave me the thumbs up.

Yesterday's sun had been replaced by low grey cloud that promised drizzle at best, rain at worst. I felt that way inside too. I wished I'd listened to him the night before. But it wasn't my place to be giving him money. Or was it? I had no idea what I should or shouldn't have done, only that I hoped his hospital visit wasn't too serious. As soon as I finished the rooms, I'd get his address and post the notebook back to him.

♦

After finishing Alan's old room, I headed to the next door along and knocked. When no one answered I went inside, pushing the jamb beneath the door. The ensuite in this room could be seen from the landing – not ideal when I knelt to scrub the loo and guests walked past waving as they went out for the day – but wedging the doors open made it easier when I took out the used items and brought in clean towels, cups and beverages.

As I made a start on the sink, a shadow appeared in the landing. Peter. I waved my cloth at him, hoping he'd get the hint. My late start on the rooms followed by a failed attempt to return Alan's notebook, meant I would be lucky to finish before our new guests arrived.

"Have a good day!"

He stood by the ensuite door. "We're going to Berrinton Museum."

"That will be nice." I gave the taps a final swipe before heading over to the shower. "I'll see you later then. I can't stop now."

I laid an old towel in the cubicle and stepped onto it, surprised to find Peter in the ensuite when I went to close the shower door.

"This is someone's room," I said.

He cleared his throat. "I won't be long. Did you know the museum holds the largest collection of…"

Was he really trying to talk to me about history now? While I didn't like him being in the ensuite, thankfully there was nothing personal to the room's occupant on the sides. Ignoring him, I made a start on the side wall, moving round to spray and wipe the rear and shower unit. Noise spurted from his mouth but all I heard was 'blah, blah, blah'. Obviously, he didn't need an attentive audience, just a body in the room while he rabbited on. Hot and flustered, I moved onto the final section, scrubbing the tiles as fast as I could. In my haste, my elbow hit something hard and I gasped as a jet of water poured from the shower head. I punched the shower's off button and, gasping, smeared my hand over my drenched fringe and face, splatting the excess water to the floor. My top resembled a wet t-shirt competition, the lace on my bra peeking through the translucent material. At least the cold water had cooled me down. I made sure to keep my arms level with my bust when I finished. Oddly, I found Peter still droning on, with no mention or seeming knowledge of my accident. How had he missed what had happened when he stood just inches from the glass, his eyes now level with mine thanks to the shower tray being a foot higher than the floor.

"…so, I'll bring you back some leaflets. I know you'd like them. I can't believe you haven't been there yet."

"I can't get out."

"Oh yes." He stepped back, leaving me barely enough room to squeeze through the gap between the shower door and the wall. Would he ever get the hint and go? Keeping my arms at chest height to hide my soaked top, I waggled the bathroom cleaner in his face.

"I need to get on. Hope you have a good day."

"Well, yes, but that reminds me. June doesn't want to miss Emmerdale later but I've got my eye on this documentary."

Seriously, would this man ever shut up? I needed to finish this ensuite and then change my top before continuing with the cleaning. I walked into him, forcing him to retreat into the hallway. As forcefully as I could, I said, "I have to get on."

He reminded me of a fish, his wide bulbous eyes, his mouth dangling open. When I knelt to clean the shower tray, I could feel him there, hear him breathing. His silence unnerved me. What had Emmerdale got to do with anything? But I didn't dare ask. It might set him off again. When I looked up, he'd gone.

♦

We didn't finish cleaning the guest rooms, kitchen and breakfast room until after two o' clock, when Jason went shopping while I did the washing and ironing. By the time we checked in a new guest, it was gone five. With Jason slumped on the sofa, head back and snoring, I decided to see how Shona had fared after yesterday's 'yoga' accident.

She answered the door to Jetsam Cottage, grinning like a child at Christmas. Putting her finger to her lips, she waved me inside. Intrigued, I followed her. Why the need for quiet? All became clear when we reached the lounge. Kim sat on the floor, eyes closed, legs crossed, arms resting on her knees, her index fingers and thumbs together in the typical meditation pose.

After leading me through to the kitchen, Shona clasped her hand over her mouth in a feeble attempt to mask her giggles. She pushed the door shut and all but crumpled to the floor, while I gazed at her.

"Are you okay?"

She jabbed her finger in Kim's direction. "Didn't you hear her? Ommm. Ommmm. I mean, first yoga, now this. She's off her rocker."

"Isn't meditation part of yoga?"

Her expression became serious. "I dunno. I preferred it when she was a tree." She held up a mug. "Coffee? We'll have to drink it outside, unless you want to sit in silence while she ommms."

She bustled around making the coffees until for no reason she spun round, jabbing a teaspoon in my direction.

"If she's like this now, imagine what she'll be like in a few years."

"Maybe it's a phase."

She picked up the kettle. "She's flipping well fazing me."

I smiled, even though Shona wasn't joking anymore. The earlier churning and hissing of the boiling kettle had masked Kim's low hum which now filtered through the closed door.

"I tell you, she's gonna drive me nuts."

Although I would have felt the same way if Jason decided to hog the lounge and meditate each night, I didn't want to say so – if we could hear Kim, she would be able to hear us – so I changed the subject.

"Did she spot the tile?" As soon as I said it, I wished I hadn't, especially as I'd just been thinking about sound travelling between the rooms.

Shona's finger shot to her lips. Shush.

She grabbed a sheet of paper and pen and wrote, 'I told her you did it.'

Seeing the surprise on my face she burst out laughing. 'Only joking,' she wrote, but I had a feeling I featured somewhere in the telling of the tale. Lifting her mug, she pointed up to the courtyard garden. My cue to follow her. She snatched a packet of biscuits from the worktop and headed out.

Rarely did we go outside when I came around as either one of them was ironing or they were waiting for guests to arrive. Shona led the way through the dank courtyard – I resisted the urge to mention 'Mousegate' – and up the steps to their little garden, where she brushed the seat on one of the patio chairs before offering it to me. The metal chair grated on the patio slabs and I sat down, finding myself beside a beautiful potted bush with dainty red and white flowers. I twisted the label, 'Hot Lips'.

"Is this the plant version of the dog thing, where they say dogs are like their owners?"

Shona grinned. "Most definitely. Kim says my lips are very hot."

She puckered her lips just as I'd seen Emily and, occasionally, Lucy do on their social media profiles, but Shona definitely fell in the trout more than pout camp. As I took a sip of my coffee, she wrestled open the biscuits and offered me one. Above a herring gull – I'd been learning about the different breeds of gull – perched on the stone wall eyeing the packet.

"You can bugger off," she told it.

We chatted about guests and housework issues, moving on to talk about other B&Bs and the little snippets Shona had heard, which included Raymond who had been seen sporting a black eye. According to Shona, local gossip suggested his wandering hands had roamed around the wrong woman. If he behaved anything like the way he'd been when I'd met him at Shona and Kim's party months before, I couldn't blame someone for getting a bit fed up. But I pitied him too, as Shona said he'd been running his place alone for years after his wife died. His might only be a three-bed B&B, but that would be hard work for one person and he'd have no one to talk to about everyday worries. The conversation meandered along. Nothing too taxing as Shona hated debating politics, whereas Kim loved intense discussions.

My phone beeped. I glanced at the time, surprised to see it was almost seven o'clock. No wonder Jason was texting. We hadn't eaten yet. I glanced at the message and shook my head. *What?* I read it again.

"What's the matter?"

Perplexed, I handed the phone to Shona. She burst into peals of laughter. "Seriously?"

Still giggling, she read the message to me. "Why did you tell June she could watch Emmerdale in our lounge?" She grinned. "Is this your guest?"

I snatched back the phone and texted. 'I didn't.'

Shona and I both sat waiting for Jason's response, which came within seconds. 'Well, she's here and she said you did.'

A moment later, another message appeared from Jason. 'I woke to find her sitting there.'

Hearing Shona's cackles of laughter, Kim appeared at the top of the steps. "What's so funny?"

"You should see this." Shona handed her the phone. "It's their guest."

Kim broke into a wide smile. "Poor Jason. What on earth made her think she could do that?"

A chill ran through me. "Oh dear!" I turned to Shona. "You remember I told you about Peter stalking me in the shower this morning? Well, he said something about his wife wanting to watch Emmerdale later, but I had no idea what he was going on about."

Kim handed me the phone. "But even if she does want to watch Emmerdale, she's got her own TV in the room."

"He said he wanted to watch something else. Maybe he thought it was like the old days with the bar when people could have a drink and watch TV."

"They'd have to be pretty stupid to think your lounge is a bar," Shona said.

"They don't seem to have boundaries about personal space," I said, recalling Peter standing by the shower earlier. "Jason won't be impressed about this."

Shona's eyes sparkled. "I'd love to see him sitting with this June woman watching Emmerdale. Let's go round."

Kim laughed. "He won't thank us."

"He will when Emmerdale finishes and we help him move June. Or, if you want to annoy him Katie, I could invite her to stay and watch Corrie too."

"I'd rather you helped with the eviction. Nicely though."

Shona rubbed her hands together. "What do you mean? I'm always nice."

Chapter 24

SHONA STOOD AT THE FRONT DOOR, craning to look over my shoulder. When she didn't attempt to come inside, I turned to follow her gaze but, other than the full laundry bag I'd dumped at the back of the hallway, there was nothing of interest.

"I'm not coming in if they're still here," she said.

The penny dropped. "Oh them! They went days ago."

"Good thing too. I can't believe you left me talking to that bloke about history. I came over to save you and you landed me with him."

"Be honest, you came over to see Jason stuck in the lounge with June."

"As soon as it finished I got her out and look how you repaid me."

She'd forgotten the sequence of events. Kim had left soon after we managed to encourage June to leave the lounge, while Shona decided to stay on as she liked Coronation Street. When she finally left at nine o'clock, she'd bumped into Peter in the hallway. I'd heard his voice and, sensibly, didn't follow her out to say goodbye but instead stood by the door eavesdropping. When he'd asked Shona if she'd seen me as he'd discovered more information about the caves near Shadwell Point, she'd said 'Oh that sounds exciting'. Head in my hands, I'd all but wept on her behalf. Hadn't she listened when I warned her about him?

But, regardless of how she remembered it, I apologised and gave her a hug, even though I knew she didn't like public displays of affection – not that anyone was around to see – and pulled her inside. As I did, I caught a glimpse of our new sign swaying in the breeze. Derrick had done us a favour when he drove into our wall and knocked down our old sign, as this one looked sleek and modern. Gold lettering on black, with the F and G for Flotsam Guesthouse entwined around each other, and the addition of our website address taking us to the heights of modernity! The sign didn't match with the canary yellow and green guesthouse façade but come October we'd have paintbrushes at the ready and Norwich City's colours would be relegated to the past.

Shona eyed me with suspicion. The cuddle hadn't softened her.

"I'm sorry. I just couldn't cope with Peter again. Did you learn much about Torringham?"

She rolled her eyes. "I've blanked it out. It's too distressing. Gone ten o'clock before I finally made it home. You owe me big time."

"Okay, next time you find a vibrator, I'll post it for you again."

She grinned. "I'm sure I can think of something better. Anyhow, I've come to beg a favour from Jason."

"He's out with Mike."

"Again? Do you two actually plan it so you don't have to spend time together?"

She laughed as if joking but this was too close to home. Often Shona's words could be like precision bombs, smashing into the target and leaving a trail of destruction while she waltzed off rubbing her hands in satisfaction. But this must have been an unintended direct hit. I couldn't believe Shona would be mean about our marriage or, at least, not in such a snide way. Forcing a smile, I ushered her through to the lounge, where I lifted a pile of ironed bedding from the settee to make space for her.

"Can I help?" I folded the still-warm towels I'd taken from the tumble drier.

"Not unless you have a clue about clutches."

No need to answer. We both knew I didn't.

"If Jason's out, why don't you come out with me? Kim's at yoga tonight."

I pulled a sympathetic face. "Sorry, it's my book club night. With Laura."

She grimaced and fell silent. She looked so downcast I almost found myself offering to cancel but I held my nerve. If I turned it down for a second time, I risked not being invited again.

A moment later Shona slapped her thigh. "Stuff it! I'll join you. Laura's asked me to go before so she won't mind."

In all the time I'd known Shona, I'd never seen her hold a book, let alone open one. She must be desperate for a night out. Although we both knew Laura, I didn't like the idea of Shona arriving unannounced, so I said, "Make sure you let Laura know you're going as it's being held in the back room of The Anchor's Rest. They might need to know numbers."

♦

Late thanks to Shona being unable to find her door keys, we took a brisk half-run, half-walk down to the harbour. Through streets clogged with sunburned people with glowing faces, we dodged families clutching fishing nets and crabbing buckets and too many dogs to count. From nearby came the sound of tooting. The crowds parted and Mrs Hollacombe came through on her mobility scooter, her steering wheel set in a line as straight as her face. When a man stepped in front of her, she jabbed her horn again, but didn't slow. He hastily jumped aside and Shona grabbed my arm to make sure I did too.

"Twelve quid for two hours. That's cheap," Shona said.

"Eh?"

She pointed at Mrs Hollacombe's scooter and the laminated posters for mackerel fishing tours that had been sellotaped along its back and sides.

"Bob Langdon charges £16 so he won't be happy with Drew

dropping his rates. You watch there'll be mackerel wars."

"I see." Not that I did.

We turned into the harbour, stepping into the road to dodge a group of people who stood chatting on the pavement, and ended up continuing along the road as people spilled from pubs blocking the paths. Opposite a busker stood by the harbour wall strumming a guitar, while further along uniformed members of Torringham brass band were setting up. Shona led the way into the pub, angling sideways to get through the people queuing at the bar of The Anchor's Rest. I could see why everyone stood in the street enjoying the sun rather than in the gloomy bar which smelled of sweat and alcohol. To my relief, Shona headed out the back through a door marked 'toilets'. A long alleyway led to the loos, but she took an immediate right through a thick door that creaked when pushed open. We found ourselves in a small, musty smelling room.

A group of women sat round an oval table. I recognised Laura, Josie and one of the other women from when I'd joined Josie for a drink, but the rest were unfamiliar. Curled in the corner lay Bessie. Her tail flapped the tiled floor but she didn't get up. Laura seemed surprised to see us and when I spotted the one free chair I understood why.

"Hello everyone." Shona settled herself in the chair, leaving me standing. "I've come with Katie."

I smiled but inside I fumed. Not only hadn't Shona told Laura that she planned to come, but she'd also made it look as if I'd invited her. Before I could explain, Laura stood up.

"Have my chair. I'll find another one."

"I'll get it. Just point me in the right direction."

By the time I waded through the bar to commandeer the only free seat I could find – a bar stool – I found the book club in progress. They paused their discussion to clatter round, chairs banging and scraping on the flagstones, while they made room for me. Once a stool-sized space had been created, they watched in silence until I settled down and then, as if someone released the mute button, restarted their conversation. My stool was a foot taller than everyone else's chairs, so my knees butted the edge of the table. Worse, I felt more like the uninvited guest than Shona, who held court on the other side of the room showering us with her views on the book even though neither of us had read it. I debated whether to go and buy a drink but hemmed in on both sides I sat parched and unhappy, wishing I'd never mentioned the book club to Shona.

About half an hour later, the woman next to me picked up her own and her neighbour's wine glasses. She smiled at me and said the first words anyone had said since I'd sat down.

"We don't do rounds as it gets a bit expensive."

Taking the opportunity to free myself from my pen, I followed her out meaning to join her at the bar, but when I saw the size of the queue – even bigger than earlier – I found myself heading outside where I stood surrounded by a mass of revellers who bumped my arms and stepped on my toes, apologised and forgot me. Unable to decide what to do – should I stay or go? – I hovered by the doorway. If I went home, my unannounced departure would make it awkward to return in the future, but was this book club thing for me? On the other hand, could I really say that thirty minutes of discomfort was 'giving it a go'? I enjoyed reading, I liked chatting to people and this offered both. I should stay and try harder to be part of the group. Decision made, I headed back but as I did Laura appeared with Bessie. Had she come looking for me or, more likely, did Bessie need to get out for a bit?

"I was just getting some air," I said.

"We're leaving before it blows up in there." Laura shot a glance behind her. "No offence but Shona will insist on arguing black is white when it comes to opinions on books. She hasn't even read this one but won't let up about the heroine being the antagonist. It's Grace's favourite book, so she won't budge an inch either. All that jumping up and down is starting to upset Bessie."

My cheeks burned with embarrassment. I'd caused Laura to leave her own book group. As I started to apologise, a man stumbled through the door, spilling lager over the floor. The look on his face suggested it was my fault for blocking the entrance, so I stepped outside into the crowded street where Laura joined me.

"I'm really sorry." I had to shout above the laughter. "She said you wouldn't mind her coming, but I did ask her to check with you."

"I should have guessed. Shona is lovely, but we don't invite her to the book group anymore for good reason." She gave me a wry smile. "How about we go over the road for a drink? It'll be a bit quieter."

As we turned to go, a red-faced Josie rushed out. "Don't leave me! It's handbags at dawn in there."

Laura grinned. "That'll be interesting to see but I vote we stick to the safety of the wine bar."

We waltzed away relieved to be leaving. I felt a pang of guilt for abandoning Shona again. No doubt she'd let me know her feelings tomorrow. But it had been horrible sitting there a foot higher than everyone with no one to talk to and nothing to drink, while she didn't stop to draw breath. Had she noticed me stuck there unable to join in? Or had she been so keen to broadcast her opinion on something she hadn't read, she'd forgotten I was there? Either way, I was looking forward to my glass of wine in quiet company, while she continued to duel over a fictional hero.

♦

As I lay in bed that night, my head whirled like a helicopter. Round and round and round, faster and faster, down, down. Great! Frustrated, I twisted round to my side, hoping it would make me feel better, but the waft of Jason's alcoholic breath made it worse. I hung my head over the edge of the bed but soon the familiar spinning resumed. How had I managed to get this ill after three glasses of wine? Large ones admittedly, but I'd made sure to sip them, rather than make my previous mistake and guzzle them down. Then I remembered the rhubarb gin the barman had insisted we try – delicious – and how we'd agreed to each have 'a cheeky double' in a fishbowl glass filled with pomegranates, raspberries and goodness knows what else. I burped, rewarded by the foul taste of acidic gin, followed by a wave of nausea so strong I knew I would spend the night in the loo. Blooming gin. I couldn't be sick. Not tonight, please. Especially when we had a full house again for breakfast in the morning.

I staggered to the loo and sat there for an age, praying I'd be able to go to bed soon and not spin. My eyes stung, my back prickled with cold and my throat felt like a worm, coiling and straightening. Ugh. A worm. I dropped to my knees and head in the depths of the bowl, I plastered it pomegranate red. Minutes later, I sat back, eyes watering, mouth burning. Now was the hour for bargaining. Eyes to the ceiling, I prayed. If I didn't drink again, please let me get to sleep. Maybe that would be too challenging. Change of plan. How about I drink again but next time I won't have gin after three wines.

I brushed my teeth and stumbled back into bed beside a comatose, snoring Jason. How I longed to be like him: drunk, yet asleep.

A buzzing sound woke me. In my dream it had been a bee but when the noise continued, I woke with a jolt. My phone. Who would call at this early hour? *Lucy!* And at four o'clock too! Something must have happened. Scrabbling to pick up the mobile,

I knocked it from the bedside table to the floor.

I pressed the phone to my ear and kept my voice to a whisper, conscious of guests in the nearby rooms. "Is everything alright?"

Beside me, Jason groaned in his sleep and shifted round, dragging the duvet across him. I elbowed him. Hard.

"Katie, it's me. Listen…" She paused while something clattered past her. "Emily's been in an accident."

Heart pounding, I leapt from the bed. "Is she okay? What sort of accident?"

"She's unconscious. They're taking her for a scan."

"Where are you? We'll come up."

As soon as I said it, I realised the impossibility of the situation. Even if we hadn't been drinking, we were a four-hour drive away. Worse, we had a guesthouse full of people who we couldn't abandon to dash off to see our daughter. Maybe one of us could get up there but how would the other cope alone with sixteen people? Would they understand our situation? I'd seen the reviews when another guesthouse owner had learned of her mother's sudden death and she'd shot off to be with her father, leaving her husband to hold the fort. Instead of receiving sympathy and understanding, two couples had given appalling reviews even though they acknowledged the bereavement.

Stuff the reviews. OUR DAUGHTER NEEDED US. Emily was injured and unconscious, while we were miles away, stuck in our sodding utopian ideal of a guesthouse by the sea.

"Stay there," Lucy said. "At least until we find out more. There's no point you coming all the way here if you don't need to."

Jason wiped his eyes and pulled himself upright. "What idiot is calling at this time in the morning?"

Hadn't he heard anything? Or had he been too drunk to notice me elbow him? I'd been tipsy but at least I answered the phone, whereas he just lay there looking like a village idiot with his stupid mouth open in the 'What have I done now?' pose he favoured.

It took all my willpower not to kick him. Instead I mouthed 'Shut up!' and stomped into the ensuite. It reeked of sick and in the harsh LED light I could see crimson flecks littering the bowl. Ugh. I lowered the lid and sat on it.

"What happened? Have they said anything?"

In the background, I heard a muffled voice. Then Lucy spoke, "Hold on. I'll call you back."

She hung up, leaving me sitting in silence. When I went back into the warmth of the room, Jason had propped himself up on pillows. I couldn't stay in the bedroom, especially with other guests asleep nearby, so I headed to the door.

He smeared his hand down his face. "Are you going to tell me what is going on?"

"Our daughter. That's what." I kept my voice to a low hiss. "Lucy called. Emily's been in an accident."

He leapt from the bed. "What happened?"

"You heard as much as me. Lucy's phoning back soon. I'll be downstairs."

In the lounge, I sat with my head in my hands, overwhelmed and powerless. What could I do other than wait for a phone call? For all I knew Emily could be dead or dying. A sob wrenched my throat and I pressed the heel of my palms to my eyes as I fought to stem the tears. How would I live without my lovely daughter? Why had we moved so far away?

The door clicked open and Jason appeared, ashen-faced. He dropped onto the sofa beside me. "Any news."

I shook my head and checked the signal on my mobile phone. Three bars. How I wished it was a teleportation device rather than just a phone. I needed to be there with her.

It began to vibrate.

"Lucy! How is she?"

Jason planted his ear next to mine so he could hear too.

"They've brought her back from the scan. We're waiting on the results. She's still unconscious."

"Still unconscious?"

"They don't know if it's a knock on the head from the accident or something else."

"Something else?" I'd become a parrot but this was frustrating. Lucy needed to give us more information.

"The person driving has been arrested for drink-driving. Look, I wasn't there so I don't know much." She sighed. "And I haven't got much battery, so I'll call you when they've got news."

She hung up, leaving me staring at the phone. Why on earth would Emily have got in a car with a drink-driver? Also, what did Lucy mean by 'something else'? Emily would be unconscious because of a head injury. What other possible explanation could there be? Questions raced round without an answer.

Frustrated, I leapt to my feet. "We have to do something!"

"What do you propose?"

"Go up there. What if she gets worse? We can't sit here doing nothing."

Jason got to his feet and placed his hands on my shoulder, his blood-shot eyes scrutinising mine. Prickling with discomfort and unable to bear his scrutiny – we didn't get close anymore, not like this – I dropped my gaze to his chest, but not before noticing his hollow orbs, as if the grey-smudged skin had sunk into his sockets. Tiredness from the constant churn of the B&B, a night on the tiles or the fear about Emily? Probably all three. Like me.

"You know as well as I do that we have no option but to be patient. Once we know what we're dealing with, we can make plans."

A balloon of hurt expanded in my chest. As if someone was pumping it harder and harder, until it grew so full there was no room to breathe. I gasped in shock. I COULD NOT LIVE WITHOUT MY DAUGHTER. If I'd been alone I would have bawled my eyes out but not with guests just six feet above us. Even in my terror I thought of them. Why, oh why did we live so far away? And why, oh why had Emily got into a car with a drink driver?

We had no choice but to sit and wait. And breathe.

Agony. That's the only way I could describe it. A minute seemed to last ten, ten minutes felt like forever and we'd been waiting twenty minutes with no news. Anguish and fear stabbed me each time my thoughts turned to Emily lying there, hopefully alive, hopefully awake, although that seemed too much to hope for.

A car zoomed past, its headlights cutting through a crack in the curtains. Soon it would be dawn. In a few days it would be September. I pressed my hands together and prayed she would live another day, another year, a lifetime. I couldn't imagine living an Emily-less life. It mustn't happen. Please.

Jason's knees cracked as he got up. "I'll put the kettle on."

"Not for me."

As he disappeared, I checked my phone again. No missed calls and three signal bars, but I turned it from vibrate to full volume just in case. If I answered quickly we wouldn't disturb guests. My screensaver was a picture of myself, Jason, Lucy and Emily, taken years ago when Emily was a foot smaller than Lucy. They were about the same height now. Back then, Emily had worn a wide grin and her dimples cut into her cheeks. Her hair had been pulled back into a pony tail, while Lucy's had lain loose around her shoulders, in a centre parting, the fashion at the time. Jason stood in between the girls, his arms strung over their shoulders, and I stood at the edge beside Emily. Poor Emily. Please let her be okay. They must know something by now. What if Lucy's phone battery had gone and she couldn't call us? Should I call the hospital? As I hesitated, my phone beeped and a message appeared.

'She's woken up. Will call soon.'

Burying my head in my hands, I whispered, "Thank goodness."

When Jason came back a moment later, I handed him the phone. "It doesn't say Emily's okay, just that she's woken up."

The sofa creaked as Jason sat beside me and scratched his bristled chin. "But it's a step in the right direction."

While he went back out to make a coffee, I nestled into the cushions. A chill seeped through my flimsy pyjama top, yet my palm sweated from the heat of the phone which I couldn't put down. From outside, the faint chime of the church bells filtered in. Five dongs. I yawned and rubbed my eyes. Usually, in just over an hour I would be getting up.

The phone rang – Emily's number this time – and I hurriedly jabbed the answer button. "Are you okay?"

It was Lucy. When Jason shot back a moment later, I hit the loudspeaker button and her voice filled the room.

"They've given an all-clear on the scan. They've done blood tests, just to check and I'll let you know about them. But she's talking and, other than a bruise on her cheek and a cut arm, which they're going to stitch, she's okay. I've got Em's phone as my battery is knackered. Can you believe it? What a night for me to forget to charge it."

The squeal of an ambulance siren made her pause, which was probably a good thing as she hadn't stopped for breath.

"It's cold out here. Em's phone hasn't got a signal inside, so I'll call you back later."

As I cut the call, Jason smiled and gave me a cuddle. "I'm sure the blood tests will be fine. It's just a precaution. Changed your mind about coffee?"

The thought of coffee in a belly tender from the night before didn't appeal but my stomach rumbled. "Just water, but I could do with a piece of toast, please."

When Lucy called half an hour later, she sounded more buoyant. "Everything's clear. They're letting her home."

"Home? But she was unconscious not an hour ago."

"Umm." She paused. "That may have been something else. When they put her on a drip, she came round pretty quickly. She's confessed to having over a bottle of wine and quite a few cocktails too."

I mouthed to Jason 'They're letting her home' and frowned to let him know I wasn't happy about it. Being unconscious that long must be serious. He signalled that he wanted to speak with Lucy, so I handed over the phone. It was frustrating to catch bits and pieces of the conversation and even more so when Jason's expression darkened and he pursed his lips. I wished I'd put it back on loudspeaker. He hung up.

"First she gets in a car with a drink driver and then she's just admitted to Lucy that she was swigging cider while they drove to a party. It's unbelievable. She'd already had enough to put herself in hospital even without the car accident, but they think she may have become unconscious in the car and that may have contributed to the accident. Of course, the driver is at fault. Not only did he have a skin full, but the car was going so fast it ended up on its roof. But Emily's not come out of this well. What on earth made her behave like that?"

We fell silent. If we hadn't moved away, would Emily have done this? I couldn't say either way but at least we would have been at the hospital and having words about her behaviour. An image of me kneeling over the toilet bowl swam to mind, but I pushed it aside. There was a world of difference between getting tipsy and drinking to the point of unconsciousness. We'd have words when Jason and I called her. For now, we were thankful. Yes, we'd have to smile, forget our exhaustion and make it through a busy day, but it was one in which we still had our daughter. I got to my feet.

"I'll make a start on the breakfast room."

Chapter 25

THE WOMAN'S HANDS FLEW to her mouth. Bewildered, I fought to maintain a concerned appearance as she sank onto the pyramid of towels on the bed.

"You let him go on his own?"

"It's just over the road."

Margaret shook her head, leaving me under no doubt I'd done the wrong thing in directing a seventy-year-old man to the car park not more than twenty yards opposite. I gritted my teeth and refreshed my sympathetic smile. Now wasn't the time to tell her she'd been happy enough when I'd suggested there was no point the two of them getting soaked, so she may as well go straight to the guest room while her husband parked the car.

"You've checked Keith's definitely not there?"

"I've been out twice." As if to prove the point, another raindrop trickled from my fringe and rolled down my cheek. "Jason is getting the car to go out looking for him. I'm going back outside in case he drives past."

She gave me a small smile. "Thank you. I'm sorry if I'm over-reacting but he is terrible with directions."

"Don't worry, we'll find him." I patted her shoulder and left the room.

Back on the roadside, I stood under an umbrella buffeted by the wind, grimacing as cars passed, splatting me with grimy water that streamed down my bare legs. After cleaning this morning I'd thrown on a pair of shorts, expecting the weather to be like the Indian summer we'd been having since the start of September. Now dark clouds sat overhead spewing bucketfuls of rain. I pitied today's arrivals. It looked like this foul weather was settling in for a few days. Another car passed, spraying more water over my sodden shoes, so I edged back to the lip of the driveway, unable to go much further as I needed to see his car if it passed. I glanced across to the car park over the road. How could anyone get lost driving twenty yards? If he'd decided to go to the shops or something why hadn't he phoned his wife? Each time we'd tried to call him, his phone had rung off without being answered. Most odd. But one thing I'd learned in the past five months is that some people do the strangest things.

The dusk deepened, turning everything to grey hues, including the terrace opposite and most of the passing cars, which made it more difficult to spot Keith's blue Fiesta. The rain had become never-ending rods of water, crashing to the road which now resembled a river, flowing in thick channels on each side, bypassing choked drains. Water bubbled from a nearby manhole cover, while the streetlights and headlamps of passing cars barely cut through the gloom. I shivered and checked my watch. Eight thirty. He'd been gone over an hour. Behind me, the guesthouse door clanked shut and Margaret strode across the drive, sidestepping between the parked cars. She'd put her coat back on, a beige hoodless thing with long collars that were now pulled up to cover her ears. As she reached me, I lifted the umbrella to fit her in.

"He's still missing?"

I nodded. "I'll call Jason in a bit."

We fell silent, scanning the cars passing in either direction, up and down, up and down. Our heads rotating like the kids in the Green Cross Code advert, except we weren't going anywhere.

"That's him!" She pointed up the road.

What looked like a blue – it was impossible to tell – Fiesta headed down the road, fourth in a line of cars. How she knew, I had no idea, but she clapped her hands together in glee and ran towards the kerb, ignoring the spray pelting her legs. Lifting the umbrella aside so we could be seen, I was rewarded by jabs of rain stinging my face, cascading into my eyes and mouth. Margaret wasn't doing much better. Now blackened and soaked, her once silver curls plastered her forehead. Behind her glasses, droplets clung to her eyelashes. I couldn't leave her to stand on the roadside waving like a loon, so I joined her, alternating between waving to attract his attention and pointing towards Margaret. After all he was more likely to recognise his wife. The car slowed as it came towards us and a man stared open-mouthed, clearly baffled by the attention of two older women. Not only was it the wrong man but he was forty years too young.

Still Margaret waved, "Keith! Keith! Yoohoo!"

She needed better glasses. I touched her arm but as the man came alongside us she turned to me, shoulders drooping. "Oh! It's not him."

Embarrassed, I hid behind the umbrella as the car shot off. Fingers-crossed he was a tourist and not a local who would one day end up beside me in the queue at Co-op and remember me as the mad, waving woman.

I squeezed her arm. "He can't go far. This is Torringham, not some big city."

"You don't know him," she said. "He could be heading home for all I know."

"Did you have a bit of a to-do?" I didn't like to pry but some questions needed to be asked. It might explain why he'd disappeared for so long.

"No! We're not like that." She turned back to gaze at the traffic and sighed. "As I said, he's always been bad with directions."

"I'll give Jason a ring." I handed her the umbrella and headed inside.

After a dozen fruitless attempts at calling Jason – to be honest, I needed respite from the rain, so I kept trying even though I knew he must be driving – I headed back out. The sound of tyres on wet tarmac scarred the night air but the rain had eased and just a few drops smattered my face, one scoring a direct hit in my eye.

I couldn't see Margaret in the darkness, even aided by the glow of nearby street lamps and the headlights of passing cars cutting through the night. Had she disappeared too or gone back to her room while I phoned Jason? As I debated going back inside to check, I spotted a figure standing at the entrance to the car park.

"I've found him!" Margaret called and waved me over.

♦

Jason shook his head as he walked in and slumped onto the sofa. His fingers tapped the armrest; a signal to be left alone after a long and frustrating day. I'd wrapped a hand towel round my hair, but it wasn't tied securely so I had to keep my head upright while I slurped my tea.

He glanced over in irritation. "Most people drink tea, not suck it."

"I'm not most people."

"Don't I know it." He picked up the remote control and stabbed it towards the TV. "I found him at a petrol station in Kentingbridge. Can you believe it?"

"Kentingbridge? I thought his wife was joking when she said he had no sense of direction."

"That's not the best part," he said. "From what he told me, it seems he's been to Berrinton and followed the coast road before giving up and heading in the other direction."

"He must have done twenty miles. Why didn't he call?"

"He forgot he had a phone." Jason looked at my mug and at the empty space on the coffee table beside him. "Didn't you make me one?"

Thankfully, the outside bell tinkled – a definite saved by the bell moment – and I leapt up.

Mrs Morris stood in the hallway, holding an empty jug of milk. "It's been so miserable I stayed in all day. I came down a while back but you'd gone out. It's a long way down these stairs, you know." Her look suggested we'd been partying when she needed her cuppa. She had a thin, reedy voice and a lifetime of wrinkles, but when she smiled the years fell from her, as they did now when she added, "I'm as dry as my old bones."

When she'd arrived a few days before, she'd told me she'd come down for a break to get away from a house filled with memories of her Len, who'd died almost a year ago after a long illness. We'd chatted about him and how she missed being a 'we'. The longing for her beloved husband oozed from her. I hoped it would be sunny tomorrow, so she could get out, rather than being stuck inside all day with just a TV for company.

"You go back to your room and keep comfy. I'll bring you another jug right away." As she rested her hand on my arm in thanks, I added, "And more tea."

I'd flick the kettle on for Jason too. Behind me, Mrs Morris clutched the bannister as she hauled herself slowly up the stairs. On second thoughts, I'd take her milk and a few extra biscuits and stop for a chat. Jason could wait.

♦

We'd just finished cleaning the kitchen after another busy breakfast service, said goodbye to a lovely couple, and were trying to work out which guests had gone out, so we could service their rooms, when there was a tap on the breakfast room door. It squeaked open and Margaret's head poked through the gap.

"I'm leaving Keith in the room and going out for a walk."

"Have fun. Don't forget if you want your room cleaned, we'll need to get in by twelve," Jason said.

"We'll be out by then but you should know he's on his own."

"We won't disturb him," I said, as the door snapped shut behind her.

Without speaking, we both wandered over to the front window as, with a furrowed brow, she paused to gaze at her bedroom window before striding down the road. Behind her, Mrs Hollacombe rumbled along in her mobility scooter. This week's advert offered a free cup of tea with every meal at her son's café, aptly named Hollacombe's Café.

Puffs of cloud floated in a sky the colour of Keith's car, which sat across the road glinting in the sun. Impossible to believe that less than twelve hours ago I'd been drenched and cold. Thankfully, the weather forecasters had got it wrong again. Or I hoped they had. A sunny day made for happier guests. Not too hot, mind. Guests don't like hot rooms.

The front door clanged shut and the couple from room five headed over to their car. He'd arrived two days before and parked his Land Rover over the middle of the white line between two bays, saying our spaces were too tight, even though they were the same size as the average supermarket parking bay. When we'd insisted he either move into one space or move to the car park across the road, he'd plumped for the drive, which was a shame as if he'd moved we might not have had the previous night's palaver. Even Keith couldn't have got lost if he'd been given parking on the driveway.

The woman – I didn't know her name as they were too busy for pointless chit-chat – flagged the traffic to a standstill and stood in the middle of the road, waving her husband out. Unable to watch, I turned away.

"Their room's free now," Jason said. "Mrs Morris has also gone out."

"I'll do Mrs Morris's room first, in case she comes back. Fetch some towels for me."

♦

The bell dinged for the second time in seconds. Swiping my arm across my face to dampen the perspiration, I rushed from the guest room and down the stairs. Margaret stood in the hallway, hand hovering over the bell, ready for a hat-trick strike. She glared at me, eyes glistening, her cheeks blotchy.

In a querulous tone, she said, "I told you to look after him."

She strode towards me, giving me no option than to step back or be nose-to-nose with her. "Didn't I?"

Hands on hips, she stood demanding an answer. It took all my willpower to stop myself from pointing out we weren't a care home and whatever Keith had done was not our business – unless he'd damaged the room – but rather than inflame her further, I said, "We were cleaning. Does he need anything?"

"How do I know if he needs anything?" she spat.

My tongue must be an inch shorter for all the times I'd bitten it, but now it shrank to the back of my mouth fearful of being chewed off. One of us had lost the plot and I was sure it wasn't me.

"Look, I'm sorry but I don't know what you mean."

"For goodness' sake, how much clearer do I have to make myself? I need you to find him. He's gone!"

Chapter 26

THANKFULLY, WE'D CLEANED EVERY ROOM in the guesthouse, apart from Margaret's room and the one we were finishing when she'd interrupted us. My decision to service Mrs Morris's room first had been proved right, as it was just after eleven o'clock when she returned to tell us she was putting a few things away, having a quick cuppa and then she'd be out of our hair. An hour later we hadn't seen her leave, but we hadn't seen Keith either.

After I asked an unhappy Jason to finish the cleaning before he went shopping, I went back to Margaret who sat beside the window in the day room, hands entwined in her lap as if in prayer. She turned as I walked in.

"Have you found him?"

I shook my head. I hadn't even started looking. "He's definitely not in your room?"

"I'm not stupid, you know."

"And he hasn't popped to the shops?"

"Keith doesn't like shopping."

"You've tried his mobile."

She gave an exasperated hiss. "Of course, I have. It's in the room. Why aren't you helping me?"

I crossed over to the window and peered out to the car park opposite where Keith's Fiesta sat gleaming in the sun. It didn't make sense. Why was she so worried about her husband being gone for less than an hour? But this was a man who couldn't drive twenty yards without disappearing on a trek of the South Devon coastline and now he'd vanished while resting in his room. Then it struck me. It would explain everything.

"Margaret, does Keith have…"

She swivelled round, eyes glinting with anger as if she was

daring me to say the word. I swallowed, my cheeks burning.

"…dementia."

She leapt to her feet. "Of course not! How often do I have to tell you? He has trouble with directions."

I sighed. If he'd had dementia, we could have got help from the police. They'd be concerned about a man with dementia on his own in the middle of a strange town, especially with the harbour being so close.

"I'll get my trainers," I said.

"Isn't your husband going to help?"

"He needs to finish cleaning before he goes shopping. He's got to get to the butcher's before it closes."

"Sausages are more important than Keith?"

I didn't stop to answer. Putting it like that she was right. But we had twelve other guests tonight and the butcher had put the sausages by for us. Maybe, we should go to the supermarket later to get the rest of the bits after the new guests checked in, but we needed coffee sachets for the rooms and we'd run out of cereal packets too, which meant a trip to Booker which closed early on Saturdays. I shoved my feet into my trainers and pulled the laces tight. She insisted it wasn't dementia but he'd been only gone an hour, so why the panic? Anyhow, she'd gone out and left him, not us, so she wasn't getting both of us racing around the countryside. It would just be me.

Jason passed me in the hallway, clutching a tray loaded with cups and jugs.

"What are you doing?" he hissed.

I dragged him into the breakfast room and closed the door. "I've got to go out looking for Keith."

"No way!" he said. "We've got a million and one things to do today and babysitting isn't one of them."

I put my finger to my lips to shush him. Margaret might hear him.

"We've got no choice," I whispered. "I've told her you can't help."

"Too right," he said. "And neither can you. I thought you were going to catch up with some admin while I was shopping?"

He was right. After a flurry of bookings and bills, yet again I was behind with the paperwork. But what could I do? I had an angry wasp-like woman in the day room and Jason standing here, red-faced, in the breakfast room. Both furious that I wasn't doing enough to help.

"I'll sort it later," I muttered and shot out into the hallway, leaving the door to snap shut.

I handed Margaret a business card. "My mobile number's there. Make sure you phone me if he comes back."

As I strode from the room, she called out, "Don't you want me to come with you?"

I kept going.

◆

The harbour bustled with humans, dogs and gulls, which meant I spent as much time checking for tripwire dog leads as I did for Keith. I wished I'd brought my sunglasses as my hand was a poor substitute for a sun visor. Discounting the estate agents and restaurants, I'd stopped at the newsagents, the convenience stores, the ice cream parlour and three tea rooms. I headed into Hollacombe's Café, hoping the advertised offer of a free cup of tea might have attracted Keith.

"Have you seen a man, about seventy, with grey hair and glasses," I asked Gary.

He smirked and pointed out of the window to the milling crowds. Before he uttered a word, I knew what he was about to say.

It had been said at every place before.

"Just about describes every grockle out there, don't you think?"

"Tell me about it. If someone comes in who looks a bit lost and is called Keith, can you give us a ring?"

"Will do." He turned to a customer, who fitted Keith's description and laughed. "You're not this Keith, are you?"

Racing off along the promenade towards the beach, I slalomed past families with buckets of crabs, while dogs with wagging-tails circled each other as their owners chatted and blindly hogged the walkway. Couples sat on benches watching the boats churning past, their outstretched legs creating a further obstacle. Many looked like Keith but none were Keith. Or were they? Gasping, I slowed and plonked myself down on the sea wall. I'd seen him briefly last night and served them at breakfast this morning, but it had all been such a rush. Would I be able to spot him in a crowd? It seemed impossible he would be any place other than the shops or the beach, but what if he did have dementia and Margaret wasn't being honest for whatever reason. He could be anywhere. My chest heaved and my heart pounded. I'd run myself into the ground and not find him.

My flowery lounge pants caught my eye. Worse, I still wore my bleach-speckled top. Perfect choices for cleaning showers and making beds but never to be seen outside the guesthouse, especially when matched with trainers and pink socks. I'd been seen by just about every trader in central Torringham, except the other guesthouse owners who'd still be working. Which I should be. I checked my mobile. No calls, although I had full signal. He must still be missing.

Sighing, I stood up and headed towards the beach. The smell of brine and seaweed greeted me as I stood at the top of the steps, scanning for a grey-haired man amongst the holidaymakers dotting the beach. One man stood apart from the couples and families, but he bore more than a passing resemblance to Donald Trump in hair and skin colour. The only other solitary soul was a young woman who sat on top of a rock, her dark hair flapping in the wind. Unless Keith had infiltrated a family group, he wasn't here.

In the other direction, there were other smaller coves dotted along the coastline, but I couldn't believe Keith would trek up the steep Furzeton Hill to reach Summercombe Cove and beyond. As frustration overwhelmed me, I clenched my fists, my nails cutting into my palms. We had so much work to do at the guesthouse but instead I was out here on an impossible search. If Keith had driven the eight miles to Berrinton and then turned back on himself, somehow bypassing Torringham before Jason found him in Kentingbridge, he could be anywhere.

I'd keep an eye out as I headed back but I couldn't do much more. I sighed. I didn't look forward to Margaret's reaction when I got back without him.

♦

A tear-stained Margaret and teeth-gritting Jason met me in the hallway. She held out a shaking arm and collapsed into Jason's chest.

"You haven't found him!" she sobbed.

Jason patted her back. "Don't worry, Margaret. I'm sure he's fine."

"How do you know?" Her muffled voice sounded as if she was buried deep in Jason's chest. He'd have a sodden t-shirt when she dug herself out. "You don't know him."

Obviously, she wasn't telling us the whole story about Keith. "Perhaps we should call the police?"

Margaret nodded, although she kept her head entombed in Jason's top.

"We'll go into the day room and wait," Jason said.

I watched in amusement as Jason, unable to tear her away, shuffled her forward. As I went to find the phone, the front door opened and Mrs Morris stepped into the hallway, her handbag in one hand and a Co-op bag in the other. A pack of prepacked sandwiches jutted through the thin plastic. Salmon, no doubt. Something she insisted on every morning for breakfast. The waft of perfume filled the air and I chuckled. Her daily routine included a stop at Boots to spray herself with one of the tester bottles. I wondered what the staff made of her daily outings. Had they missed her yesterday?

"Racing about as usual?"

"Just another busy day." I felt mean brushing her off but I had no choice. "Excuse me, I have to make a call."

"She's not saying much but I'm sure there's an issue like dementia or something," I was telling the 101 call-handler when I heard a scream. *A woman's scream.* Mrs Morris!

"Hold on! I'll phone you back in a minute!" I cut off the call.

I raced into the hallway and up the stairs where I met Jason and Mrs Morris in the landing.

"There's a man in my room." Her shaking, crooked finger pointed towards the door.

"Give me your key," Jason said.

"It's on the latch," she said.

Jason shot her an odd look but said nothing. He pushed the door ajar and crept inside, turning back with a frown.

As the door brushed shut, a man's indignant voice echoed into the landing. "I'm trying to sleep!"

"This isn't your room." Jason's voice. A moment later, there was a thud. "Flaming bag! Who left that in the middle of the floor? Look Keith, you really need to go to your own room."

The door shot open and a red-faced Jason appeared. "Go and get Margaret. He's refusing to move."

I ushered Mrs Morris downstairs to the day room and sat her in the chair opposite Margaret, who was fanning her face with a magazine.

"We've found your husband," I told her. "Can you go upstairs as he won't get out of Mrs Morris's bed."

"What on earth is he doing there?" She shook her head as if it was my doing and strode off.

Clutching her chest, Mrs Morris waited until the stairs creaked before she turned to me. "He could have killed me. I've got a dicky heart."

I patted her shoulder. How could I have not locked her door after cleaning? We didn't need to put the door on the latch as we each had a set of keys.

"I'm really sorry. I don't know how he got into your room." I said. "I'm sure I locked it."

Her gaze fell to the floor and her cheeks flushed. "It's a mystery. No harm done though."

I laid my arm around her shoulders. She still trembled, although not as much as before. "Let me get you a cuppa and a biscuit. You can sit here while we sort out your room.

An hour later I sat in the lounge, waiting for the new arrivals. We were expecting two couples at three thirty and another set around five o'clock. We'd replaced Mrs Morris' bedding and tried to check on Margaret, but she'd shouted through the door to say she needed a bit of peace. I'd called the police back too and told them we'd found Keith.

Jason ducked through the doorway as he came into the lounge, carrying a tub of sausages in the crook of his arm and a small polythene bag stuffed with coffee sachets. Kim and Shona had come up trumps. I took the sachets from him, the OCD part of me dismayed to see they were a cheaper brand than ours and would look out of place on the refreshment trays. But they and the supermarket sausages would have to do, thanks to Margaret barricading the door to stop Jason from going shopping because 'she wouldn't have a sausage put before her darling Keith'.

I rechecked the payment amounts on the registration forms for the new arrivals. All correct. When Jason returned from the kitchen, I shut the laptop lid.

"What I don't understand is how Mrs Morris's room was unlocked."

"It's obvious. She all but told us she put it on the latch."

"But why would she do that?"

He shrugged but a moment later, he said, "Wasn't she the one who needed to be let back into her room the other day?"

Just two days before, Mrs Morris had locked herself out of her room after leaving her keys behind. Worried she would be bothering me, she'd sat patiently in the day room until I came past. I'd rather take a minute to open her door than three hours out of our day dealing with a missing man.

"I'll have a chat with her."

"No need. She'll bolt the door now," Jason said.

"He's definitely got dementia," I said. "But Margaret won't have it."

"She knows," he said. "Maybe she's worried we wouldn't have let him stay here."

"I wouldn't have minded if I'd known. At least none of this would have happened."

♦

The next morning, I heaved the last of the filled trays into the kitchen and sorted the plates, teapots and cutlery, ready for the next dishwasher load, placing the cafetières beside Jason, who was arm-deep in washing-up water. It was a lovely feeling to clear the breakfast room, although it just signified round one was coming to an end. Round two was guests checking out, although this was usually a short round as it comprised a key handover, bags carried out and goodbyes. Round three, on the other hand, involved cleaning the guest rooms which could take hours, round four was shopping and round five was guests checking in. Round six was a knock-out, when we fell into bed. Today, round two would signify a moment that couldn't come quick enough but also one I'd rather Jason endured than me.

As Jason put a dripping saucepan onto the draining board and delved back into the soapy water, the bell rang in the hallway. I had no choice but answer.

Tapping Jason's shoulder, I hissed, "You need to come out now."

"Margaret!" I kept my voice as light as possible. "You're off. Can Jason take your bags?"

She dropped her room keys into my hand. "No need. Keith has taken them."

Through the open front door, I spotted Keith by the open boot of his car, thankfully not lost, although he looked it as he stood wringing his driving cap as if it was a damp cloth.

"It's a shame you missed breakfast. Can I get you water for your journey?"

"My husband doesn't have dementia," she said. "Not that it's any of your business but it has been ruled out. We were hoping for a restful break while waiting on his results but that proved wishful thinking." She paused, her mouth contorting into a sneer. "I will thank you for your help yesterday, although it should be noted that it wouldn't have happened if you didn't leave your guest rooms open."

As she turned to go, I heaved a sigh of relief but then Jason strode into the hallway, slapping his hands together as if he was pleased with himself.

"All sorted? Anything I can fetch?"

The hand clapping was bad enough but when he used the same jovial tone as he did for happier guests, it felt like he'd walked into a funeral using his pub voice. Fancy a pint anyone? Drinks on me! Cringing, I prodded the back of his leg in warning, hoping Margaret didn't spot it.

"Keith's sorted the bags and I've got the keys, so they're off now," I said.

A moment ago, she'd been seconds away from leaving. Now she stood there, her lips pursed into a line as thin as red biro as she uncurled her fingers from the door handle.

She turned to Jason. "Quite how you get the reviews you do is beyond me. Not only did your wife not ensure we had enough tea and coffee in our room after we went out last night, but the bin in our room was full too."

And with that she pulled the door shut with a clang, leaving us in shocked silence.

"Well, if he hasn't got dementia, he must just like getting into strange beds."

Jason snorted. "I'd be desperate to get away from her too."

We walked into the day room to watch them leave. Keith hunched forward in the driving seat with his glasses and cap – a perfect Mr Magoo – inches from the windscreen, while in the passenger seat Margaret jabbed her finger up the road, pointing him the right way out of the car park.

"She's got her work cut out if she has to direct him back to Hampshire," Jason said.

"I can't believe she complained about the bin. It didn't get done because I stopped cleaning to help her. Then she wouldn't let me in the room."

When Jason chuckled, I punched his arm. "It's not funny. Bet we get a bad review."

And we did. Our worst ever.

Chapter 27

THE WOMAN STOOD ON THE DOORSTEP, her hair a vibrant auburn frizz apart from two inches of grey which sprung from her centre parting. Thick lines travelled from the corners of her mouth to the edges of her chin, giving her an unsatisfied air. She extended her hand and, with a firm grip, shook mine. Ouch. It wasn't the handshake of a human but a gorilla.

"Ava Opelt. And this is Louis."

Clenching and opening my hand to restore circulation, I turned to her companion. I had to tilt my head back to meet his eye. Great! The world's tallest man in our smallest guest room. Hadn't they seen the word 'small double' in the room name when they booked or was this another couple thinking I'd called it small for a joke. After two poor reviews in just over a week, I didn't fancy a third. First, we'd had Margaret with her abysmal rating, followed by a couple who gave us a low score three days ago for the small double room being small and the gulls noisy. A bit like holidaying in a vicarage and complaining about the church bells.

Now someone taller than the Harlem Globetrotters towered on my doorstep. As he ducked to get inside our front door, I wondered how he would manage to sleep in a standard-size double bed. For eight pounds more a night they could have had a kingsize one but I couldn't invite them to swap as it had sold yesterday.

"Can I help with your bags?" I glanced outside to see if they'd left them on the driveway.

"We'll get them later."

Their email had said they were coming by train and would be arriving around noon. While they appreciated this wasn't our check-in time, they had to put medicines in our fridge which must be kept cool. I'd agreed and asked them to let me know if they were going to be late.

It wasn't long before I regretted agreeing to their request. Last night I'd seen an advert for the M&S sale and wanted to grab a few cardigans and a pair of trousers, especially with the cooler September nights drawing in, so I'd asked Jason to wait for me. If we went to Berrinton, he could do the shopping in Sainsburys, while I shot next door to M&S.

At one o'clock I'd phoned the Opelts but left a message when it went through to answerphone. Half an hour later, I sent a text to ask their whereabouts but they didn't respond. Finally, at two o'clock Jason got to his feet saying I should just go but with the next check-in arriving at three thirty, I couldn't chance getting into traffic and being late. It was only after he disappeared, I realised I should have offered to do the shopping while he waited in. Unless, I wanted an evening drive out – which I didn't – my next opportunity to do an afternoon shop was four days away, after the busy weekend. I hoped there would be some cardigans left in my size.

As it was, Ava and Louis deigned to arrive at three thirty, bang on our standard check-in time. I kept my expression bland and a smile in place, as they traipsed into the hallway.

"What about your medicine?"

They gave me a blank look.

"You wanted to use our fridge."

"Oh!" Ava flicked her wrist as if swatting me away. "He's finished his course now."

As I took them up to their room, I made sure to say, "You've booked the small double room," as we went inside. They fell silent as they gazed around the space – or lack of space – taking in the double bed, the two bedside tables, the refreshment tray, TV, wardrobe and ensuite. No frills but a clean, budget room.

"Where will we sit?" Ava said.

"You've booked the small room. I sent an email with all the details on it."

Something about this couple set my teeth on edge and it wasn't just their thoughtlessness or lack of ability to read. I'd rather lose the money for their weekend stay than have unhappy guests.

"We're full but if you're not happy you are welcome to find more suitable accommodation."

She looked at me as if I'd gone mad. "Right, so where would we find that in Torringham at the weekend?"

"I don't know. But if the small room you booked is too small you could try Berrinton. I won't charge a cancellation fee."

Huffing, she threw her handbag on the bed. "Berrinton? This'll have to do."

I smiled. "Well, I'm sure you'll enjoy your stay."

"From what we'll see from the inside of a church."

As I closed the door, I puzzled over her comment but then I realised they must be going to a wedding or even a funeral. With Torringham being such a popular destination for retirees, we had quite a few bereaved guests who travelled miles to give their relatives a good send-off, one couple from Australia. But where were this couple's wedding or funeral clothes? Or any clothes for that matter. Perhaps they'd left them round someone's house.

It hurt my head to think about it, so I gave up and headed into the kitchen to make a cup of coffee. When Jason staggered in with the shopping bags ten minutes later, I gave him my nicest, most loving smile. He was just in time to check-in our guests once they'd uncurled themselves from their little room.

♦

Later that afternoon Kim knocked on the door. Unusually flushed, she pointed at a battered maroon 4x4 on their drive.

"I don't suppose you have any idea who that belongs to?"

Arms swinging, Shona stomped over. "Some idiot has parked on our drive. Can you believe it?"

I rolled my eyes. "I'm starting to believe anything nowadays. It's not one of our guests. Have you tried elsewhere?"

"We checked with our other neighbours but we've got at least a dozen more potentials." Kim nodded to the terraced cottages opposite. "Our guests have arrived with nowhere to park. We'll have to pay extra to put them across the road as all our permits are being used."

I shot off, returning with a parking permit. "One couple has come by train, so we don't need this for the next few nights."

Dismayed, Kim gazed at the car. "I hope it's gone by then."

"Or they'll be getting this!" Shona held up her fist.

While Kim went to show her guests to the car park across the road, I started knocking on the cottage doors with Shona. We agreed to start at each end and meet in the middle. With no answer from the first two cottages, I moved on to the third. The dog-shaped knocker creaked as I tapped it against the wooden door and flecks of paint drifted to the path. A noise came from inside. Someone calling out, probably to tell me they were coming. After waiting for an age, I knocked again. Then I cupped my hands against the dusty windows to peer through the yellowing nets. Nothing.

Wiping the grime from the sides of my hands, I stepped back to let Kim and her guests shuffle past, the man with a walking stick, while the woman had a pronounced hunchback I hadn't seen since my childhood when it was more common in elderly women. I could see why Shona had been so angry. If anyone needed to park on the driveway, these people did.

As I turned to go, I heard someone call out again; the cry reminded me of Mrs Morris's thin warble.

"Shona!" I waved her over. "Come here."

"You found them?"

I put my finger to my mouth. "Listen. Can you hear anything?"

This time I rapped the door twice, but we heard nothing other than cars zooming past. As Shona took a step back to check the upstairs windows, I gave it another try, hammering the poor metal dog onto the door. When Shona's eyes widened, I knew she'd heard the noise too. She dropped to her knees and called through the letterbox.

"Hello!" After a moment, she turned to me. "There's definitely someone inside. Sounds like 'help' but I thought this house was empty."

No point asking me. I could count the number of people I knew from these cottages on three fingers. The young couple who'd helped when that horrible man – James? – had tried barging his way into the guesthouse to find his estranged wife. And Moaning Mitch who we knew by sight after he'd had a blazing row with Shona in the street. When I'd asked her if she was okay, she'd rubbed her hands together and rebuffed me with, "It's just Moaning Mitch. He loves a good row, but he's picked the wrong person. So do I."

I didn't, so I made sure to keep away from him. And Shona too, if she ever went back to book club, which she told me she wouldn't as we were a load of 'boring old farts who couldn't handle a wind-up'. Apparently, that included me. If being a boring old fart meant I got to drink wine in peace and quiet, I would wear the label with pride.

She glared at me. "So?"

Had I missed something? Then I realised we had to decide what to do about this voice in an empty house. Would we call the police or an ambulance? Was it an emergency? Probably not.

"Have you got your phone on you? Mine is inside."

Shona dragged her phone from her pocket. "999?"

"I don't know. Try 101. Let them decide."

She dialled the number. I half-listened while she spoke to the operator, my attention taken by Ava and Louis who stepped from the guesthouse door. Louis cut across the drive towards Jetsam Cottage. Following him, Ava spotted me and grabbed his arm, pointing in the direction of the harbour. He shrugged her off, but she said something and they both looked my way. Not smiling, he lifted his hand in acknowledgement, before following her. As they walked off, they kept glancing back. Most odd.

Shona finished her call. "They're sending someone now. Can you stay here while I tell Kim?"

When Shona came back, I took the opportunity to shoot back to Flotsam to use the loo and tell Jason what I was doing. I found him in the lounge ironing the load of bedding I'd promised to do the day before.

"Thanks," I said.

"Someone had to do it."

"I would but Shona's got a problem with a car on her drive. Now someone's stuck in a house across the road, so the police are coming."

He put the iron down. "Do you want to say that in English this time?"

"Oh, ferme ta bouche!"

Before going back, I went into the kitchen to find something to eat. I had a feeling we would be outside a while. Swallowing the last of a hurriedly eaten sandwich, I headed back.

A police car sat outside the cottages, blue light flashing, while two policemen knelt by the front door peering through the letterbox. Fingers-crossed, whoever had been calling out was trapped in the house and it wasn't some weird joke or Shona and I were going to look very silly. A few doors up, a couple leant against their doorway watching, while a child gazed down from an open window.

One of the policemen spoke into his radio. I couldn't make out what he said but when I got closer, Shona whispered, "They're going to break in."

Somehow, I expected the policemen to smash down the front door – as featured on TV – but they headed into the alleyway that led to the back of the properties. Another police car drew up and a man and woman got out, following their colleagues down the alley.

A larger crowd had gathered, muttering to each other. I heard a woman asking several people around her what was happening but thankfully she didn't come over to Shona or me. I longed to move away, feeling nosey rather than needed. After ten minutes or more, the front door opened and the policewoman stepped out. Ignoring us, she glanced up the road.

"Did you speak to them?" I asked Shona.

"They just questioned me about what I'd heard." Shona craned her neck to look through the open doorway. "They obviously heard it themselves."

Soon we heard the faint sound of a siren and an ambulance came into view, heading at speed down the road. It overtook two cars and then veered across to pull up behind the police cars.

"Amazing how quick they are when the police call them," Shona muttered.

"Perhaps it was nearby."

After the paramedics wheeled a stretcher into the cottage, nothing seemed to happen for an age. Bored, I told Shona I needed to get back, but she insisted we might be needed. How, I had no idea. Finally, a policeman came out, followed by the paramedics who carried a young man on the stretcher through the narrow doorway. The lad grimaced in pain, his face pale, his forehead mottled with dried blood.

Thinking back to the faint cries I'd heard earlier, I said, "I thought it sounded like an older woman."

"So did I. Maybe he's gay."

I prodded her arm. "You can't say that!"

"*I* can!"

Deciding this led into territories I couldn't debate, I practised what I'd advised Jason to do and shut my mouth.

The ambulance doors slammed and one of the paramedics jumped into the driver's seat and turned on the ignition. They drove away without sirens.

"He must be okay," Shona said. "I'll find out."

She strolled over to one of the policemen who'd been first on the scene while I gazed around. A group of hardy onlookers milled by the cottages, while others moved away disinterested. I recognised a few faces but most seemed to be tourists, several from Jetsam Cottage. Thankfully, all our guests were out for the day.

In the distance I spotted Ava and Louis heading back. He carried two full holdalls, which must be the belongings they'd said they would collect later. For some reason she flung her hands in the air, stamped her feet like a child and spun round in the direction of town. As she stomped off, Louis paused where he stood. He seemed to be shouting but she threw her arm up again – I'm sure she gave him the V sign – and carried on. Bags knocking against his legs, he ran after her.

Shona came back grinning and rubbing her hands together.

"He-he! Have I been given an idea or what?"

I waited for her to say something, but she stood expectantly until I said, "Okay, what?"

"I asked that policeman about the car on my drive and he said there was nothing they could do. But…" She clapped her hands together and all but fizzed in delight. "He told me that the white line in front of our driveway is advisory. You can't park outside yours because of the double yellows but, apparently, the old owners would have put the white line down to stop people parking in front of our drive. But we can! I don't think he realised what he was telling me, but it's flipping brilliant!"

"So?" I shrugged, but then it dawned on me. "You're going to block that car in?"

She nodded. "They'll have to beg to move it. Then I'm going to pretend I've broken down." Her face darkened. "But I hope they don't wait too long to beg. Just a day or so if we can keep your parking permit until then."

"It's fine for a few days. What about your other guest's car though?"

"They don't use it while they're here. They've got bus passes and Marg hires a mobility scooter."

As she turned to go I remembered why Shona had gone over to speak to the policeman. "Did you find out about that man."

For a moment she gave me a blank look. "Oh him! Homeless, poor bloke. Broke in through the back window but fell, bust his legs and hurt his back. No phone, locked back door and too injured to climb out. Gotta go. Have a car to move."

♦

After tersely giving me their breakfast orders, Ava and Louis ate in silence. The atmosphere seeped throughout the subdued breakfast room and many of the guests left within minutes of clearing their plates. There was no respite in the kitchen with Jason in full-on grump mode after the yokes on a batch of eggs kept breaking. When the last couple left, I sighed with relief. Another breakfast over.

Moments after I shut the breakfast room door, it creaked open and Louis strolled in. Gone was yesterday's haughty demeanour, replaced by a sheepish look he carried well.

"I forgot to ask, please don't clean our room. We've got some things in there we don't want to get damaged."

"Will you need us to change anything in your room? More tea, the bin?"

"Nothing. There's no need for you to go in. We might even go back to bed before the church service, so please don't disturb us."

A red flag to a B&Ber is a guest who is desperate for you not to go in their room. On one occasion we'd found bedding covered in red wine, while on another, remnants of sick on the carpet. I'd pop in there later to check, no matter what.

Clearing his throat, he pointed to Shona's old Passat, currently utilised as a bollard to block her driveway but, noting the traffic queued behind it, an excellent chicane too. At least no one could moan about cars speeding past.

"I don't suppose you know whose vehicle that is?"

As soon as he spoke, the pieces I hadn't even been considering fell into place. He and Ava must have parked at Jetsam Cottage. But why hadn't they asked us for parking? Maybe they thought the train story and medicines would get them an earlier check-in or possibly – but unlikely – they had accidentally parked next door. But why say they'd come by train? Either way, I wasn't getting involved. He could face a furious Shona.

"I think it's something to do with the guesthouse next door. They'll be dealing with breakfast now but they're around all day." I placed the last of the cups onto the tray and moved away. As I neared the kitchen door, I found him staring out of the window, rubbing his chin.

The devil inside made me say, "I don't think it's for sale but you could ask."

With that I shot in to the kitchen to find Jason still washing up. He slammed a saucepan onto the draining board and upended the bowl of dishwater, refilling it in preparation for the cafetières. He'd been grumpy all week, making me feel as if I had to tiptoe around him. Maybe he should have married a ballerina. I stuffed the plates and cutlery into the dishwasher and shot off to make a start on the guestrooms.

Through the open front door, I heard a commotion outside. Shona's voice! From where I stood in the hallway, I could hear every word.

"Reasonable? You want me to be reasonable? You made our guests park over there because you *accidentally* parked here."

Low murmurs. Probably Louis trying to pacify her. Wrong move. Anyone who knew Shona would understand the futility of doing so. Like a volcano she needed to blow her top and only then could she calm down.

"Katie didn't tell you to park here. You're not only a liar but stupid too!"

Louis or Ava must have told Shona I'd given them permission to park there. What sort of people were they? It felt like I could hear just one side of a telephone conversation, so I went through to the day room to see more. Hands on hips, Shona glared at Louis, while he held out his palms in a conciliatory gesture.

"I don't fricking care!" Shona bellowed. "If you tell me one more time Katie had anything to do with this, I'll wait until next weekend to organise the mechanic."

At that moment, I loved Shona.

Jason came into the room. "What's going on?"

"Our guests are trying to tell Shona that I said they could park there."

Shona's voice cut through again. "Wedding? Do you want to make anything else up?"

"Their guests must love this." He peered out through the window. Then he groaned. "I hope ours have gone out."

Arms-folded, a smiling Kim leaned against the 4x4, still in the pink apron she wore each breakfast, her hair pulled back in a matching ribbon which sashayed in the breeze. Beside her Shona danced forward and backwards like a boxer. When Louis walked away, throwing his arms in the air in disgust, Ava took over. Her frizzy hair seemed wilder than ever, giving her the look of a cavewoman. Now I could hear both sides of the conversation.

"Move it!"

"No!"

Kim glanced in our direction. When she grinned and gave us a little wave, Jason and I shot back into the shadows. No doubt we'd be dragged into this, but I hoped it would be much later rather than sooner. If we went out there now, our guests would expect us to intercede on their behalf and I wasn't minded to help them.

"Monday!" Shona shouted. "That's the earliest I can do. And if you touch it, I'll give you this."

I could imagine what 'this' would involve.

"I'm going to get on," I said to Jason. "If Louis or Ava come in, I'm indisposed."

"You're not leaving me to deal with it. I'll just tell them to wait to speak to you."

"Good luck with that one. I'll be busy."

From the look on Jason's face, I had a feeling both of us would be finding urgent jobs outside the guesthouse later.

Chapter 28

THE BELL RANG FOR THE FOURTH TIME. I'd hoped Jason would get it but no such luck. Sighing, I stepped from my hiding place in room three's shower and headed downstairs. As expected, a flustered Ava and Louis waited in the hallway.

"Your neighbour…" Louis started but Ava butted in.

"That idiotic woman next door is blocking our car in."

It took a lot of effort not to smile. "Car? But you came by train."

"No," she spoke slowly, as if speaking to an infant. "We came by car."

I glanced at Louis but he wouldn't meet my eye, so I turned back to Ava. Pinched blotches stained her cheeks and her watery eyes had become a startling blue. I stayed silent. She could try all the games she liked, but I wouldn't play ball.

"So, are you going to help?"

"With what?"

Now she gave me the hands in the air treatment. "Getting her to move, stupid."

I'd had enough. We'd been at Flotsam Guesthouse nearly six months and in that time we'd had hundreds of wonderful, friendly, fun guests and less than a handful of difficult people but she got a gold star for being the rudest. (Except for James, who'd tried barging in, but he hadn't been a guest. And those lads who'd not paid for their taxi fare, but lovely Ozzie's fearsome snarl had been a great help there). But Ava and Louis were liars to boot.

"Okay. Give me your keys."

She rifled through her handbag, dragging out a wad of keys crammed onto several looped keyrings, which included the Flotsam Guesthouse keys I'd seen her clipping on the day before. After asking them to give me a moment, I wandered off to find Jason, while detaching our keys from the set. I found him in the laundry room, which meant he had good reason not to have heard the bell, unless he'd escaped there after they'd started dinging it.

"I'm going to ask them to leave. Can you come and back me up?"

I didn't need to explain more. He nodded, stuffed the last of the towels into the dryer, and followed me out. With a tummy buzzing with butterflies, I clenched my fists to stop my hands shaking. Shona might love it but I hated confrontation. As I reached them, I took a deep breath.

"We're refunding your money for tonight. And Jason will bring your belongings down."

"What?" Ava screeched.

"This is our guesthouse. We don't want guests who lie about us, call us 'stupid' or create scenes with our neighbours."

Ava's lip curled. "Don't be so melodramatic. We're asking a reasonable request."

Jason stepped in. "Why did you park next door?"

While Louis examined a print of Torringham harbour, Ava carried on digging, "We thought it was your drive."

I found myself butting in. "But you needed an early check-in because you came by train and your medicine had to be kept chilled." From the corner of my eye, I spotted Louis sidling towards the day room. "Isn't that correct, Louis?"

"Excuse me? Oh yes. I mean, no." As he pulled a handkerchief from his trouser pocket to dab his forehead, one of the guestroom coffee sachets fell to the floor. "We had a change of plan."

"Can't we just stay? It's my cousin's wedding," Ava pleaded. "We need our car to get there."

For some reason, she started crying. I mouthed 'Help!' to Jason but he shrugged. He had no idea either. If she thought tears would change our minds, she'd got it wrong. Six months ago, I might have crumbled at her crocodile tears but, to use Shona's words, no longer was I so green I believed everything. Jason and I turned to Louis who hovered just inside the day room. His fingers nipped his jacket sleeve as he glanced from Ava to us.

When her sobs became howls, an exasperated Jason said, "For goodness' sake! Give her your hanky."

As Louis stepped forward, the coffee sachet crunched beneath his feet. Something disturbed me about it. I mean, taking a coffee sachet wasn't that big a deal but… I couldn't connect the dots from the coffee sachet to Louis, to the lies about bringing a car and then to Ava wailing about not being allowed to stay. But I knew beyond doubt I needed to see their room.

Clutching my stomach, I turned to Jason. "Won't be a moment. I've got to use the loo. We'll sort this when I get back."

He gave me the 'you are not leaving me with them' look but I shot off. At the top of the stairs I glanced down to check no one was following me and headed to their room, where I slid the key carefully into the lock. The door brushed over the carpet. Louis hadn't been wrong when he'd said they had a lot of things. A stack of boxes sat on top of the bedside table. Mobile phones! The hotchpotch of stuff on the bed included half a dozen boxes of perfume and aftershave, all with labels, as did the clothing which came from one of the posh shops by the marina. When I left, I turned the key so the door didn't click shut and alert them downstairs.

It must be stolen. That would explain why they did an about-turn yesterday when they saw the police cars outside the cottages. If I called the police from the lounge, our thieving guests might overhear.

Back downstairs, I kept my voice breezy. "Sorry about that. Needs must. I've been thinking. If you can give me a minute, I'll speak to Shona and see if she'll move her car."

Stunned by my apparent about-face, Jason threw me a furious look, but I rushed out hoping the Opelts wouldn't guess I'd been in their room. At Jetsam Cottage, I rang the bell and hammered on the door until it was thrown open by a furious Shona, who must have assumed Ava was back again. Spotting me, her anger changed to confusion.

"Katie?"

I put my finger over my mouth. Shush. Then I spoke loud enough for Ava and Louis to hear me, "Please can you move your car?"

"What?" Shona's chin jutted like a bulldog.

"Shush!" I hissed. "Look, can you call the police for me?"

"Wha…" Without explanation, she grabbed my arm to drag me inside.

Before she did, I needed to reassure Ava and Louis that I was dealing with the car, so I shouted, "We'll help you push your car if you give me the keys. Our guests need to get out."

Assuming I was hurt or upset in some way, Shona tried to make me sit down in her breakfast room, but I refused. "I'm fine, honest."

When Kim appeared wiping her soapy hands on a tea towel, I told them about the mobile phones, perfume and clothing I'd found in the guest room. When they remarked that all the items could have been bought, I could see their point.

"Plus," Kim said. "Louis may not have wanted you to go into their room as he thought you had cleaners who might steal something."

Plausible. But I had a strong feeling there was more to it.

"Please call the police and explain that Ava and Louis will be leaving shortly. They'll be taking all their stuff with them. If they think it's worth pursuing, they'll come."

"I'm not moving my car though," was Shona's parting shot.

◆

With the appearance of several police cars, the previous day's onlookers had moved to the front of Flotsam Guesthouse, where they milled aimlessly until something interesting happened, such as a third police car turning up. Yesterday's loud woman also appeared, asking everyone what was going on, until through them all trundled Mrs Hollacombe tooting madly and refusing to pull onto the road.

Shona and Kim had taken up residence in our day room, even though they – like us – had guestrooms to clean.

"It's not every day we get front row seats," Shona laughed, while Jason stood morose in the corner after hearing that we might lose money on the room which had almost certainly been paid for with a stolen credit card, as had most of the goods in their room.

"They shafted us for breakfast too." I heard him mutter to Kim who patted his arm.

"It could be worse," she said. "It was just a full English, not fillet steak."

"Have you seen the size of our bacon? Costs a fortune."

Two of our guests broke through the swarm of people. As they pottered up the drive, I rushed out to greet them and explain that they wouldn't be able to get into their room just yet. Not with several burly police blocking the landing while they catalogued the haul in the room or, at least, that's what I assumed they were doing upstairs. After they'd taken Ava and Louis away, I hadn't been given an update.

Margaret and Reg smiled as I told them about the couple. Margaret tapped her husband's arm. "I said there was something odd about them, didn't I!"

She waited until he nodded, then turned to me. "Now, don't you worry dearie. We won't be needing our room cleaned today, you've got enough on your plate." She winked. "Just make sure you tell us all the gossip tomorrow."

When I explained that it meant they couldn't get into their room yet, Reg whispered to Margaret. "But the toilet."

At times like this, we could have done with a ground-floor loo, but that was one of the many things on our wish list. I could ask the police if our guests could access their room for a few minutes, but I didn't like the idea of this frail couple trying to squeeze past the people upstairs or stepping over the boxes on the landing. Instead, I went inside to beg a favour from Shona and Kim. Without much prompting, Shona volunteered to take Reg and Margaret to use the loo at hers.

"You might as well send all your guests over. It's got a bit boring here anyhow." She paused by the door. "Just make sure the police get that dump of a car off our drive."

Chapter 29

UNCLE BERT SAT ON OUR SETTEE, one leg strung over the other, nursing his cup of tea. He'd lost more weight, so his jowls – sadly a family trait I'd inherited – hung like lobes from his jawline, his cheeks sagged and it seemed as if I could see the skeletal orbs beneath his hollow eyes. How was it possible that he looked worse than the last time I'd seen him? Worry gnawed at me, but I deflected it. When I'd called and spoken with Doreen a week ago, she'd sounded chirpy and had been talking about going on a holiday. Not the voice of someone who worried about their husband's health.

He listened and nodded as I talked about what had been going on since his last visit, giving the odd chuckle but mostly he frowned and muttered under his breath.

"I can't believe it. Why did they park next door? Surely it brought more attention to them."

"We think they knew we'd have to take their registration details if they parked with us. It goes on our forms. And the car park requires reg numbers too. I reckon they told us they came by train, so if the police approached us when they noticed about the stolen card being used, we wouldn't know their car's details."

"But why next door?"

I shrugged. "Either they thought it was a guesthouse and their car wouldn't be noticed or maybe they only meant to park for a while, perhaps to get their things out until they took the car to a side street or something. When they came out after checking in, they looked as though they were heading over to their car but then they saw me and went off towards town. And then, like I said, when they came back with those bags, Shona and I were outside with the police because of that homeless man being hurt."

"It's all go around here." Bert shook his head. "Torringham used to be such a quiet place."

I giggled. "What? In the olden days."

He became solemn. "I don't feel old. What with having Callum late, I made sure I did all the things younger blokes do. But…" He trailed off. "Where's your Jason?"

I tried not to snarl but it came out as a huff. "Out. Again."

For once, he wasn't with Mike, but he'd taken a drive to Berrinton as he needed a pair of trousers, which he could have picked up when he went to Sainsburys the other day. I'd wanted to go too but one of us had to wait for a check-in and the laundry delivery. Apparently, his need for a second pair of lightweight trousers he could wear when cooking breakfasts outweighed my wish for a couple of cardigans. After he'd spread his legs to show me his white pants bulging through the split seam in his crotch, I'd agreed. No point scaring – or scarring – the guests.

"Are you both alright, love?" When I glanced at him in surprise, he flushed and looked away. "I don't mean to pry."

He put his cup on the coffee table and leaned forward, elbows on his knees. I caught the familiar scent of Lynx.

"It's just that…" He looked down, his attention taken by one of his fingernails and paused to pick at it. "Well, you know."

I fell silent, unable to respond. Yes, I did know. But how did I explain to my uncle that in just six months we'd become business associates rather than husband and wife.

When we moved into Flotsam Guesthouse, we'd been full of hope for the future. We had a strong marriage. We loved each other. We could do this. But we hadn't thought that our jobs gave us at most two days a week together and the occasional holiday. Being forced to live and work together 24/7 in a demanding, unrelenting job had buckled our marriage and I simply didn't know if we could put it back on track. Did we even want to? I no longer knew how I felt about it and I certainly couldn't answer for Jason. We'd have to speak to each other in more than monosyllables for that.

But then I remembered Jason, legs apart, showing me his 'bits' escaping from his trousers and I smiled. He may have been doing it to gain the advantage, but it proved we were still more than business acquaintances.

"Look, love." Bert squirmed in his seat. "I came over as I have something to tell you both."

The front door thudded shut and footsteps clomped across the hallway but the stairs didn't creak. Not a guest. Moments later the lounge door opened and Jason ducked in clutching an M&S carrier bag. His face brightened and, extending his arm, he headed over to Bert.

"How are you? Long time, no see."

"Good, good." Bert shook Jason's hand. When he released it, he settled into the back of the settee and scratched his chin. "Well, okay, not so good but sort yourself out and we'll have a chat."

Jason darted a questioning look in my direction but all I could do was shrug my shoulders. No point asking me. Hurriedly, he kicked his shoes off, planting the toe of one against the heel of the other, rather than untying his laces, and plumped down next to me.

"That sounds worrying."

Bert gave us a watery smile. "It is a bit. I've just been told I've got kidney cancer."

I gasped. Poor Uncle Bert, poor Callum and not forgetting Doreen – a lovely lady and perfect for Bert – who I'd met just the once, but I talked to her each time I phoned. How would they be dealing with the shock?

And he was my last link to Mum. My only living relative on that side of the family and the only person with her eyes. Sometimes I found myself lost in his smile, watching his eyes crinkle as he laughed, and remembering Mum. Emily had Jason's eyes, while I had my dad's.

The last time he'd come I'd had a feeling he was poorly, but I'd discounted it and got on with running the B&B, bickering with Jason and missing Emily. Remembering how scared and upset I'd been when Emily had been injured in the car accident only made me feel worse for Doreen and Callum. Life was fragile. Family was precious. I ached to see Emily again. Thank goodness it was just two weeks until we closed for a few days at the start of October to see Emily and Lucy. I'd give my darling daughter a cuddle and tell her how much I loved her. I wouldn't give her a lecture about the car accident either, although I knew Jason would. But she wouldn't mind it coming from him.

My thoughts turned back to Bert. His cap sat on the arm of the settee. It had been five months since I'd first met him down here. I'd hoped for years more to get to know each other but the ground had shifted and uncertainty lay ahead. I had to know more but I couldn't think how to phrase it. How do you say, 'Are you going to live or die?'.

A lump filled my throat, threatening to choke me, making it impossible to talk and not cry.

Thank goodness Jason said something.

"Bloody hell! I'm really sorry to hear that. What did they say?"

Bert's lips parted but no words came out. He steepled his fingers, then pressed his hands together as if in prayer.

Finally, he took a deep breath. "I'm having surgery to remove my kidney next week. We'll see how it goes from there. I'm a lucky man with a wonderful wife, an amazing son and…" He paused to give me a small smile. "I've just found you again. Let's hope I stay lucky."

He stopped a few minutes longer but deflected questions about his diagnosis. With a grunt he stood up, stooping to pick up his cap. His eyes welled as he gazed from Jason to me.

"You're both lovely people. I've always taken care to think well of Doreen, even the few times we don't agree. Marriage isn't just about how you act with each other. It's up here." He jabbed his head. "Being respectful in thoughts too. Seeing and doing the best by one another. If you put each other first, the rest follows."

He stammered to a halt. I'd never known Bert to give such a long speech before. Neither had he by the look of it.

Sniffing, he dabbed his palm to his eye and shook his head. "Blooming cissy," he muttered to himself.

Embarrassed, he patted Jason's shoulder, gave my arm a squeeze and shuffled out the door. I didn't want him to go, not without saying something. I ran after him and gave him a hug and kissed his cheek. He nodded. I didn't need to speak. He knew.

When the door closed behind Bert, I stood for a moment in shock before heading back to the lounge, where I found Jason with his head in his hands, sitting on the settee. As I crumpled beside him and sobbed, he drew me close. I could feel the warmth of his body, hear his heartbeat. I'd forgotten its steady rhythm. How long had it been since we'd sat close together, let alone touched each other? He drew back and gazed into my eyes. As I tried to look away, he tipped my chin upwards with his finger and leaned forward, his lips brushing my forehead.

"Your uncle's right. We need to look after each other better. I do love you, you know."

♦

Two weeks later Jason hefted the suitcases in the car and for the first time since April we closed the door to an empty Flotsam Guesthouse. We'd had two days without guests in mid-May but since then we'd worked one hundred and thirty-three days without a single day off, waking every morning to make breakfasts, cleaning rooms, washing, ironing, emptying and refilling the dishwasher three to four times a day, working through to the evening many days, all the time smiling and making sure everyone had a lovely stay. And it had taken its toll. We needed a few days to recharge, see our beautiful daughters and to simply spend time relaxing together.

And to reflect on how we'd follow Bert's advice to make our future at Flotsam Guesthouse happier, not just benefitting us but also our guests.

From the passenger seat, Jason smiled at me and patted my leg. "Let's go!"

He left his hand there, warming my thigh. I liked it.

In three days, we'd be back to a full house, including two returning couples, both from earlier in the year. It would be lovely to see them again.

Chapter 30

MY BREATH FOGGED THE AIR as I stepped from the warmth of the guesthouse to push another bundle of underlay into the crammed boot of our car. I headed back inside, slapping my hands together to clear the dust and grit, where I met Jason in the hallway. He slotted the phone into the holder.

"I've just agreed to a one-night booking next Wednesday. A tiddler as he's single occupancy but we are pretty quiet." He smiled. "It's a direct booking at least."

I shrugged. "It's your week for ironing, so I don't mind."

His face fell but then he grinned. "You're enjoying this job swap lark."

"Always good to see a man scrubbing a loo."

Laughing, we pulled the guesthouse door shut and climbed into the car, ready for our next 'dump' run. With the weekdays being quiet in November, we'd closed for a few days while we painted the breakfast room and had a new carpet laid in one of the guestrooms. That would leave us with one final guestroom to decorate in a couple of weeks and then all the guestrooms would have been carpeted and given a fresh coat of paint. There was still plenty to do, not least the exterior of the building which had been postponed until April, then there was the roof, most of the ensuites, the kitchen, our bedroom. If I thought about it too much I'd panic, but the list of work was diminishing as we nibbled at jobs.

"So what room have you put this one-night stay in?"

"He was happy with the small double."

"Aren't we decorating that one next?"

"We don't need to start until Friday."

A tack from one of the gripper rods stashed behind the seat snagged my hair and I yanked it free. I couldn't wait to finish that room. Even if we had further improvement work to do, it meant I would no longer worry about a guest's reaction when I took them into a clean but tired-looking room.

"Unusual surname," Jason said. He rolled the name on his tongue. "Towoshco."

"I knew someone with that name. Aleksander Tolloczko. He was a salesman at the company I worked for. Before I went to the residential centre."

Jason slapped the steering wheel. "That's his name!"

♦

After the journey to the dump, followed by a trip to the shops, I forgot about Aleksander until the following Monday when I checked the diary. His overnight booking sat short and stubby on the online calendar, in comparison to the longer stripes for the three and four-night bookings above and below him.

I clicked on his booking. If it was the same Aleksander, he must have moved. The one I knew had lived in Hatfield, whereas this one lived in Frome. Intrigued by the idea that someone from my distant past could have chosen to stay at Flotsam Guesthouse, I typed his name into Google. Sure enough, I found my Aleksander still working in Welwyn Garden City, which made it unlikely he'd moved to Somerset. But there was another one! As I clicked through to LinkedIn, my hand shot to my mouth. I grabbed the laptop and rushed through to the kitchen, where I found Jason bending over the sink peeling potatoes for our dinner.

"You won't believe it!" I jabbed the screen. "Look at this."

Squinting, he gazed at the laptop. "Aleksander Tow... Hotel Inspector."

I grinned at him. "Can you believe it?" Then I gasped. "Oh no! He's in the small room."

Jason rinsed his hands under the tap and wiped them dry. He pulled the laptop towards him to examine it. "I didn't think you were signing us up for the ratings scheme until we'd finished all the rooms."

"I didn't expect them to come so soon. Sod's Law he's booked the only room we haven't renovated."

"Can't you ring them and ask them to wait a few weeks?"

"And say what? I've stalked Aleksander and discovered he's a hotel inspector, so please can he come when our guesthouse is in perfect order."

Jason shrugged. "In three weeks, it would be."

I gave him an apologetic hug. He'd showered after we'd finished cleaning the rooms and the aroma of his favourite aftershave clung to him, masking the starchy smell of peeled potatoes. I shouldn't have got carried away and sent off the application to join the ratings scheme, but I'd been desperate to see stars sooner rather than later. I knew how many I wanted too. Count the fingers on one hand, minus the thumb. My haste would be our downfall. We'd worked so hard to make Flotsam Guesthouse as good as possible for our guests, yet our only hope for a good rating would be residing in our one unrenovated room.

"We'll move him," I said. "If he'd come in three weeks it would have been finished. And anyhow we wouldn't get the signage for our rating until then, so it's not cheating. We'll tell him we had no choice as the room is down for maintenance."

♦

With three hours to go before his arrival, I had more than enough time to do the necessary work. Jason shook his head as I stomped past with the mastic gun. I'd refused his help, certain that relining the bottom of the shower with fresh mastic couldn't be too difficult.

With the old mastic scraped away, it was just a case of not squeezing the gun too hard to ensure the mastic oozed out in a perfect line like a toothpaste advert. Then I wet my finger and ran it round the bottom of the tiles, removing the excess mastic. Pleased with my efforts I stepped back as Jason came into the ensuite and peered over my shoulder.

"Not bad," he said.

"Well, we can say in all truth that the ensuite in this room is unusable, so we've had to move him."

Chuckling, Jason wandered off shaking his head, leaving me to admire my work and savour the pungent smell.

♦

The hotel inspector stood at the door, wearing a pristine white shirt, tie and dark trousers with a vertical crease that would make a tailor proud. His shoes had been polished into a black mirror upon which our hanging basket reflected in the toe cap. He swept his hand along his forehead to clear a channel between his fringe and his glasses. I took in his serious eyes tempered by an easy smile, his dark hair not yet greying, his unlined face. And I felt old.

It wasn't that long since Mrs Morris had been telling me at breakfast one morning how she'd asked a policeman for directions and could have sworn he was a schoolboy in costume. One of the other guests had leaned across their breakfast table to hiss, 'Maybe he was a strippergram?' and made her blush.

The hotel inspector returned my smile and held out his hand, "Aleksander Tolloczko but please call me Alex."

I shook his hand and stepped back to let Jason undertake the introductions. As he carried the hotel inspector's bag upstairs, we slowed as we came to the room originally booked. I'd purposefully left the door open.

"You would have been in this one, but we've upgraded your room as we had work to do in the ensuite."

"I can smell it. Shower issue?"

"Something like that." I blushed. While I didn't mind being devious for a good cause, I wouldn't lie. "But I'm sure you'll be very happy with the room we've allocated you instead."

An hour later, the bell in the hallway tinkled. Jason heaved himself from the sofa and ducked out of the lounge, leaving me to finish my email response to a booking enquiry. In his rush he didn't close the lounge door, which meant the quiet murmurs of the hotel inspector filtered through, followed by Jason's jovial voice. "It's not a problem."

The stairs creaked and I assumed the hotel inspector had gone back to his room but then Bill's deep voice boomed. "Ironing service, eh? I've got a few bits. Would you mind?"

I sat upright, straining to work out what could be happening. Who was running an ironing service? Maybe the laundrette had posted a deal through the door. We got a lot of flyers from local businesses. I was doing a final read-through of my email when Jason came into the lounge clutching a striped shirt on a hanger. Not one of his. He spotted my raised eyebrows.

"That hotel inspector wanted to use the iron, but we've got a mark on the ironing board cover."

"And?" I shrugged in confusion. "It's a small scorch mark. He won't downgrade us on that."

Jason scratched his chin. "Well, I've offered now."

When the bell rang, he hooked the hanger over a painting of Torringham harbour in Victorian times and shot out. Noting it was my turn to deal with guests, I watched in surprise as he disappeared. Why the rush? The door clicked shut, muffling but not concealing Bill's loud voice.

"I wish I'd known about this. I was just telling Paul."

Jason kept his voice low, so I couldn't make out what he said. I pressed send on the email and opened the tab for Facebook, ready to relax for the evening, when the door snapped open and Jason came through carrying what seemed to be a dozen hangers with assorted shirts and tops. He didn't meet my eye as he draped the items over the sofa arm, but he must have felt my gaze burning into his back as he said, "I know. You don't need to say anything."

I didn't utter a word while he set up the ironing board and switched on the iron. The hotel inspector's shirt was clearly expensive. It didn't need much other than a whizz of the iron to press its barely crumpled appearance, while the batch of clothes on the sofa seemed to have been tossed into a suitcase and crushed by the weight of a hundred other pieces. Hadn't Bill arrived with the world's heaviest suitcase? And he'd just been talking to Jason too. These must be his. But what were his clothes doing in our lounge?

I pointed to the pile and opened my mouth. "Are they…?".

"Yes." Jason cut me short. "And in a minute Paul will be down with his ironing too."

Bill and Paul had arrived together, but I hadn't spotted Paul and his wife sitting in the back of the car when we'd answered the door. While Jason had taken Bill round to the car boot to fetch the bags, I'd gone to fetch the registration form, returning as Bill stepped inside. I'd smiled and welcomed his wife, not noticing he'd swapped his shirt for a striped jumper. It was only when the real Bill came to the door a moment later, that I stepped back in surprise. Identical in all but clothing, Bill and Paul were our first twins. Luckily, Bill had a love of chunky jewellery, so we could tell them apart.

Jason replaced the hotel inspector's shirt on the hanger and turned to pick up the first of Bill's clothing. As he shook a shirt and hooked it over the ironing board, I burst out laughing. "How? I mean we've done the odd item in the past but not this many. Why not just give them the ironing board?"

"He heard me telling the hotel inspector that I'd iron his shirt. After that, I couldn't say no, could I? I did put a limit on it. Six each."

I sifted through Bill's clothing. "There's eleven pieces here. Are we ironing their clothes for when they get home?"

"I forgot to specify six each couple." From the hallway came the sound of a bell tinkling. Jason groaned and put the iron down. "That'll be Paul."

He came back a minute later clutching one of the small milk bottles we used in the minifridges. "The hotel inspector. He's run out."

When the bell dinged again, I took the bottle from him and pushed him out the door. "I'll sort this. If that's Paul don't give him any ideas about ordering a float's worth of milk too."

♦

The next morning, Jason and I were up ten minutes earlier than usual, even though we had half the number of guests. While Jason ran through everything, I checked the items on the buffet, fearful that I'd forget something obvious such as the orange juice. Back in the kitchen, I made a start on chopping the butter into dishes, while Jason brought through two loaves from the store cupboard.

"We've run out of bagels."

I picked up the packet of muffins and counted six. We had enough of those to cover breakfast, thank goodness. "Can you wipe them off the specials board?"

Bill's loud voice and the clatter of chairs came from the breakfast room. I gave my hands a quick wash and rushed out to greet them, passing Jason as he returned with a damp cloth.

The service went well. The hotel inspector – or Alex, but that seemed a bit informal – didn't come down until we'd served all three couples, which meant I could focus on asking him the right questions, while keeping an eye on the other guests. While they were as important as him – after all they were paying for their stay – they'd been here several days now and knew the drill. From the back of the room, Bill waved a teapot, so I hurried over to fetch it before he called out. On my way back, I took the bowl from Alex. He wore the shirt Jason had ironed the previous evening.

"We've also got specials if you would like something different. Have a look at the board. I'll come back to take your order in a few minutes."

He smiled and picked up the menu.

Teapot replenished, I placed it next to Bill, who wiped a smear of egg yolk from his lips and thanked me. Then, pad in hand, I headed over to Alex. What would a hotel inspector order? Hopefully, nothing like as much as our *Four in a Bed* couple did a few months ago.

He smiled at me. "What are your specials?"

I turned to point at the framed blackboard, only to find the word 'Specials' in chalk-white capitals, with the little asterisks I'd drawn on either side, and nothing below. Everything had been wiped clean. I glanced from the board to the hotel inspector and back to the board. What on earth?

"Erm," I stuttered. "It should read Eggs Benedict or there's Salmon with either scrambled eggs or cream cheese on muffin. Usually we offer bagels, which may explain why there's nothing on the board."

His smile faltered as he shot me a puzzled look.

"That didn't make sense." I'd started to gabble but I couldn't help it. My nerves were mounting as I imagined the coveted four stars twinkling, then fading. "I asked Jason to take the bagels off the specials and it seems he wiped everything off. Except they're still there, if you see what I mean. Pretend it's invisible ink."

I flushed. What sort of waitress would tell a hotel inspector to imagine invisible ink? I could picture Jason's face if he could hear this, although he had caused the problem in the first place by not listening.

The hotel inspector laughed. "Salmon with scrambled eggs sounds delicious but I'll try your full English. Just one slice of bacon and no fried bread, please."

When I took the order out to Jason, I slapped it onto the counter and hissed, "You wiped everything! I've just made myself look like a right idiot."

He grinned. "No help needed there, darling. I only did as you asked."

"I told you to wipe off the bagels. Not everything."

I stuck my tongue out at him, not in the way I may have done several months before, but with a smile. There was no point pursuing it. I had no evidence to back up what I'd said. Instead, I headed back into the breakfast room to check on our other guests.

After clearing his plate, the hotel inspector dabbed his mouth with the napkin and pushed his chair from the table. His heels clipped against the laminate floor as he strode from the breakfast room, returning downstairs ten minutes later with his suede case to say goodbye and hand over his keys. When Jason reached for the door handle and Alex stepped forward to leave, my heart stopped. Surely, he couldn't be just a normal guy who shared a name with a hotel inspector and my old work colleague. What were the odds on that happening? But then he reached into the inside of his jacket pocket and presented me with his business card.

I gasped in shock. (I had to. It would be odd if I didn't).

"I'm your hotel inspector," he said.

♦

A few days later Shona and Kim popped round. Shona slapped her thigh and burst into fits of laughter, while Kim shook her head, but a smile played at the corners of her mouth. She studied the sheets the hotel inspector had left with us, her elegant fingers flicking between the pages. Before they'd left for their recent holiday, she'd had her fingernails painted at the local nail bar and they glittered under the lamp light. It might only be four thirty but November shrouded the window in darkness. Inside we basked in the warmth of our new ornamental fire, which cast a flickering glow that danced in her eyes. Her cheeks were radiant. An unneeded bonus after their relaxing fortnight in St Lucia.

As Jason settled the tray on the coffee table and handed out the mugs, Kim turned to him. "So what part did you play in this?"

Wide eyed, he planted his hand on his chest. "Honestly. Very little."

"Apart from wiping our specials. Luckily, the hotel inspector said I dealt with it in a humorous way."

After two guests checked out, the hotel inspector had visited all the guest rooms bar the two being occupied by Bill and Paul, even the small double room, which we'd explained would be decorated and re-carpeted soon. He'd asked questions about the work to be undertaken, but it hadn't proved an issue as we'd done so much in the other rooms. Our breakfast was top notch and he could only offer a few suggestions on improvements, bar the specials board featuring a few items. I'd flushed with embarrassment at that, but mostly with pleasure.

Our hard work had paid off. We were worthy of four stars. We'd have got them even if we hadn't known the hotel inspector was coming but I was glad we'd found out. It had made the process a bit less stressful. I grinned to myself. Except for the ironing. Jason wouldn't be offering to do that in future, although he might not have a choice. As Paul and Bill had left, they'd promised to be back. No doubt with suitcases full of ironing.

"I'm so proud of you." Even though she wore a thick jumper, Shona snuggled into the cushions. She was the only person I knew who could spend two weeks in thirty-degree heat and come back as pale as she'd left. "You've learned a lot from me this year."

Kim picked a bit of fluff from the knee of her jeans and deposited it on the tray. Then she turned and gave Shona a hard stare. "What, being devious, scheming and wily?"

Shona rubbed her hands together and all but cackled. "All of those and more. I would never have thought of the mastic. Actually, if you're any good at doing it, give me a hand. We've got a few showers that need sorting out."

I laughed. "As long as you don't leave me to it, while you sit downstairs having a cup of tea."

She grinned. "Moi?" Then she winked at Jason. "She's definitely got more nous about her. I bet she's got the measure of you too. I notice you're out together more now. Less pubbing it with Mike."

Jason stiffened and caught my eye. I shrugged. I hadn't said a word.

"While Katie's new improved nous has been seen on more than one occasion." He air-fingered quotes around 'nous' and I made a note to look it up later. It sounded positive. "But for the other changes, we have to thank Bert."

He gave me a warm smile, which I returned. When we were out having a romantic meal later that evening – which I had no intention of telling Shona, Mike or anyone about it – we'd raise a glass to Bert and wish him good health in his recovery. I couldn't wait to see him back to his usual self again.

Chapter 31

BRACING MYSELF AGAINST THE COLD BLAST as we opened the door, I tightened my scarf and pulled my woolly hat over my ears. Emily gambolled outside, calling Lucy to join her. Strange how the children – even as adults – got excited about the idea of seeing Torringham on a stormy day, while I looked forward to tonight's promised meal and glass of wine by a crackling fire at Shadwell House Hotel.

Jason took my gloved hand in his and, head down, we walked into the wind, relieved to reach the sheltered area by the shops. The gusts picked up slightly by the harbour but, shielded by the hillside bowl, the breeze did little more than skim the water, so the moored boats bobbed up and down. The pinks, blues and yellows of the cottages rising in tiers from the harbour were muted by the mist, but winter didn't dampen Torringham's charm. In a few hours the Christmas lights would twinkle along the harbour to be mirrored in the sea.

The tourist boutiques and ice cream parlours may have closed for the winter but, with Torringham's thriving fishing industry and large resident population, the food shops and pubs stayed open throughout the year. With Christmas over and New Year a few days away, businesses were making the most of the feast on offer to get them through the famine months until the season started to pick up again in April.

Not everyone packing the pubs and restaurants lived here. While we'd closed for the whole of Christmas to spend time with Lucy and Emily, many of our other B&B friends had stayed open, welcoming people visiting relatives or those who simply wanted to get away. We'd thought about staying open – we could do with the money to renovate the guesthouse – but we needed family time more. Anyhow, Emily and Lucy had proved themselves handy with the paintbrushes this morning, leaving Jason to get on with renovating room two's ensuite.

Ahead, Emily whooped and pointed to spray crashing over the breakwater wall. Ducking low, we pushed through the shuddering wind. A faint tinkle rose in the air, dipping as the gale howled. It grew to a jangle, which seemed to come from all around, not just the trawlers opposite but the marina. As we moved closer, the noise heightened as ropes and wires chinked against the masts, the yachts making their own choir of windchimes while, beyond in the outer harbour, tall masts swayed like pendulums.

Rain splattered my eyes and I gasped as a gust hit me head on. Whose idea was this? While huge tankers had taken shelter in the bay and anyone with an ounce of sense was tucked up in front of the TV with the heating on, we'd decided to go for a walk. Hard to believe that not more than a few months ago this promenade had teemed with holidaymakers eating ice creams or strolling along with their dogs, while parents stood by crabbing buckets laughing as their children dangled lines over the harbour wall. We passed the lifeboat, thankfully moored, and headed onwards.

Jason called to the girls cautioning them to keep away from the sea but the waves crashing over the breakwater offered enough warning.

In silence, we stood well back by the car park, fighting to stand our ground against the buffeting wind, in awe of the foam-capped grey sea which thundered into the rocks and flicked spray high into the air. Pebbles rattled, dragged out by the sea, until another wave pounded them back onto the beach again. I gasped as a huge roller smashed into the breakwater, burying it beneath a wall of water at least twenty feet high.

"Whoaa!" the girls shouted. "We got that one on video!"

I gazed out to the tankers bobbing in the bay. If something their size had to shelter from the storm, what chance did the trawlers have? I was glad to have the cosy B&B to go back to. My vision had become a blur of raindrops, so I turned and pointed back to the harbour.

"Let's go to the pub."

No one outvoted me.

♦

In the hallway, Emily and Lucy teetered on stilettos, their necks strung with silver tinsel which flickered pink beneath their flashing bauble earrings as they posed for photos. Jason turned to show me the camera screen and I smiled. That one would make the family album.

"How do we look?" they chorused.

"Fab!"

I squeezed Lucy's arm. Last time we'd gone to a party at Shona and Kim's she'd had her own hurt and issues to deal with. I hoped she'd found peace and the New Year would bring her happiness. Her cheeks glowed as she smiled at me.

"You look lovely too," she said.

With Jason bringing up the rear, we headed into the melee of Jetsam Cottage. I still couldn't believe that Shona and Kim had chosen to have a party on New Year's Eve, especially with Kim's family descending en masse. According to Shona they had high standards when it came to food, with Kim's aunt – I didn't know if she was the infamous one who'd left behind her sex toy – insisting on a Caribbean touch to New Year's dinner.

"She's not jerking my turkey," Shona had grumbled.

Kim had rolled her eyes. "If she wants to cook, just be thankful."

For the past week Shona had moaned about eating nothing but turkey: curry, stew and sandwiches and now they were having turkey again for New Year, while our meal would be a huge beef joint. Uncle Bert would be joining us with Doreen and Callum, his first trip to ours since his operation, although we'd visited him at his home several times.

Raymond, from Waves B&B, greeted us by the Christmas tree. When I spotted a twig of mistletoe hanging from an upper bough, I steered Emily and Lucy in the direction of the kitchen, where I found Kim standing by a worktop filled with an array of bottles. As she bent to kiss my cheek, I caught the smell of perfume. Not her usual one. She gave Lucy and Emily a warm hug and took them off to Shona, who had been put in charge of the cocktails.

After an hour chatting to Laura, Mike and Josie, I spotted Maggie and Jeff, minus their dog Ozzie, standing in the lounge by the fireplace and wandered over.

"I could have done with Ozzie the other day." I went to tell them about our thieving guests, but Maggie pointed out that Shona had beaten me to it, along with the story about the homeless man and even how I'd abandoned her at the book club.

"Our Shona pretends to have a thick skin," Maggie said. "But it's no thicker than a wafer."

We glanced over to Shona who stood just inside the kitchen, balancing a pint of beer on her head. When I spotted Emily attempting to do the same thing with a glass of wine, I excused myself.

"Mum, look!" As she spoke, the glass toppled. She caught it but not before it splashed herself and me with sweet rosé.

As I reeled off a tree-worth of kitchen roll to wipe us and the tiled floor, Shona grinned. "I would help but I have a pint on my head."

But moments later, when someone turned up the music and 'I wish it could be Christmas everyday' boomed into the room, she tore the glass from her head, slammed it onto the counter and shouted, "Let's dance," dragging Lucy and Emily into the lounge.

Kim wandered over. Eye lids heavy, movements unsteady, her Prosecco sloshed in her flute like yesterday's stormy sea.

Slurring, she said, "I've had a bit to drink. Just this much though." She held her finger and thumb a centimetre apart. "I'm trying to find the lights. Have you seen them?"

"Lights?"

She waved me away. "You know! The disco lights."

When I shrugged, she staggered off. A moment later she came back and jabbed a crimson-nailed finger at me. "Someone hid them in the cupboard but I found them. Give me a hand."

She led me out to the hallway where we – or in reality me, as she kept stumbling backwards – extracted a long box from the understairs cupboard. She ripped open the lid and dragged the cumbersome lights from the box, leaving me to put it back while she lurched away.

Back in the lounge, I was surprised to find Jason and Mike dad-dancing in the middle of the floor with the girls. Behind them stood Kim, who had managed to put the two sets of lights on either side of the room. She kicked off her shoes and, plug in hand, bounced onto the settee to dangle, bum in air, over its back.

The lights flashed for a second – success! – followed by huge bang and yelps of fear. Mine included. Heart thumping, I clamped my hand to my chest, straining to see into the darkness. What on earth had she done?

A hush fell over the room, until Shona shouted, "Don't panic! It's just the fuse. Anyone got a light?"

A flicking sound and Lucy's face lit up. Shona stumbled past, followed by Lucy who cupped her hand round the small flame of her lighter. It meant she must be smoking still but I vowed not to say anything.

Jason came over and hugged me. "It's all go here." He pulled away. I could just make out him brushing his hand on his trousers. "How come your arm's sticky?"

He moved to the other side to cuddle me while we stood in the dark, warmed by each other's bodies.

"Don't worry, I'm alive everyone," Kim called, her voice thick with alcohol. "Just in case any of you wondered. You there, auntie? Help me up."

As Jason chuckled, I heard what could only be Shona's voice. Who else would shout, "For frick's sake!" in a roomful of Kim's family?

This time closer. "You won't believe it!" As Lucy's guiding light appeared behind her, she said, "The fuse box won't turn back on. Someone call the electricity board."

A few people groaned, while others muttered in agitation or anticipation. After telling me he wouldn't be long, Jason disappeared.

The tinny sound of music rang out as Emily held up her mobile phone, joined by Lucy who'd activated the torch on her phone – why hadn't she used it earlier instead of the lighter? – and waggled it around like a strobe light. As a few others joined in, their lit-up faces strangely disembodied, I realised it was bright enough to find the wine glass I'd abandoned. At times like this only wine would do.

Jason reappeared. "Western Power has been called. They'll be a few hours though."

"Their batteries won't last that long." I nodded to the phones.

Shona grabbed my shoulder, her hot breath pummelling my ear. "I've an idea! I've looked outside. You've got power, we've got drink."

Without further explanation, she jumped onto the settee and cupped her hands round her mouth to bellow, "Party at Flotsam! Everyone grab a bottle or two! Let's conga!"

"Yes!" Lucy's voice, followed by Emily's, "Party at ours!"

Aghast, Jason looked at me. For a moment we stood in shock until we both shrugged. Kim and Shona had done so much for us and opened their house more than once. We should do this. I smiled at him.

"Why not? There's enough of us to clear up tomorrow morning. Will you take the lead?"

He threw the keys to Shona, who fumbled and dropped them. "You can be the head snake. Just don't make an asp of yourself."

A one-armed conga made it to Flotsam, each person clutching a bottle or glass. As we made it into the hallway, Lucy and Emily rushed off to turn on the music, while Jason and I welcomed friends and strangers into our home. Following her aunties, who gamely lifted their colourful dresses to join in the conga dancing, Kim brought up the rear waving an empty bottle of Prosecco. I gave her a hug. Bless her! Tonight she'd have fun, tomorrow would no doubt bring a hangover. She gave me a slobbery kiss on the cheek.

As I wiped it dry with my sleeve, she said, "I'm so glad you both moved here."

Jason drew me into his arms and cuddled me. We were too. With friends and family like these, I couldn't wait to see what the next year would bring.

About Bedlam & Breakfast

While Bedlam & Breakfast is fictional, I am a guesthouse owner. Thankfully, we have been blessed with lots of amazing and kind-hearted guests, who are nothing like some of the characters featured in this novel. Many of our guests return on a regular basis and I look forward to seeing them. While unusual events occur in a guesthouse – as they do anywhere – most of the stories featured in Bedlam & Breakfast are imagined or taken from snippets I've heard in passing.

The same applies to the B&B owners featured. Many guesthouse owners undertake work when they move into a property and our current B&B was not an exception. While, thankfully, our previous owners were nothing like Jim and Maureen, this also means we don't get to live next door to the fabulous Shona and Kim. But we do have many lovely and kind B&B friends. B&Bers are a fabulous bunch.

Torringham is loosely based on Brixham, a seaside town in South Devon famed for its fishing industry. All the people and businesses featured are fictional, but if you do visit Brixham you will find some of the scenery familiar, including the beautiful harbour bowl. When I wrote about Shadwell Point, I pictured the stunning Berry Head, although many other locations are fictional. Brixham is a wonderful town and Devon is a gorgeous place to visit.

A plea! If you do stay in a hotel or B&B, please **book direct**. B&B owners are couples and families trying to get by, so please fund a small local business rather than giving a substantial percentage of their fee to a global corporate giant, as happens when booking through a third-party. You'll often get better rates by booking direct too.